DEVOTED FRIENDS

BOOK TWO

SAHAR ABDULAZIZ

SHAGGY DOG PRODUCTIONS, LLC

ISBN: 978-1-950625-04-8

DEDICATION

Devoted Friends is dedicated
to all the quirky, honest, unpredictable, loveable, sincere, KIND,
trustworthy people in the world.
YOU are the real rock stars...
—the heroes and sheroes.
Never change.
Trust me—the Universe needs you.

DEDICATION

Devoted Friends is dedicated
to all the quirky, honest, unpredictable, loveable, sincere, KIND,
trustworthy people in the world.
YOU are the real rock stars...
—the heroes and sheroes.
Never change.
Trust me—the Universe needs you.

"Sometimes the bravest and most important thing you can
do is just show up."
—Brené Brown

CHAPTER 1

Irwin Abernathy

"HIGHER," coaxed Harper, her head of long dark tendrils tilted back. "Nope. You still gotta go higher." She stood on her tippy toes pointing one of her many ring clad fingers in the direction where Irwin had failed to aim. "Okay, okay. *Stop*." She let out a deep sigh. "That's good. Now keep it steady."

Arms stretched high and wide, Irwin held up the cord, struggling to maintain his balance on the rickety old stepladder, but miscalculated. "Whoa!" he yelped, gripping the sides for dear life, his legs wobbling. "Sheesh, I almost fell that time."

"Be careful," admonished Harper, doing her best to steady the stepladder.

Irwin hung his head and scowled.

How do I get dragged into these things?

The corner of Harper's mouth quirked up. "Whenever you're ready, Evel Knievel."

Knobby knees knocking, Irwin again stretched his arms to raise the string of white lights higher.

Harper clapped. "Steady, steady...don't move! That's perfect!" She pivoted backward, bent over, and peered up to inspect. "Hmm, you're gonna need to move it a smidgen more to the left."

"So much for perfect," he griped, his eyebrows squeezed together into a frown.

For as far as the eye could see, busy shoppers filed along Main Street briskly skirting in and out of stores. Some strolled, taking their time, while others window shopped on a mission. A few bustled to and fro, gripping paper cups filled with hot chocolate, tea or coffee for dear life. Perhaps something a wee bit stronger. Others, apparently bushed from a day of dragging large packages along bustling streets, tottered about, their holiday spirit dampened by fatigue. Fortunately, the town had already cleared the roads from the heavy snow that had fallen the evening before; however, the current intermittent flurries flitting and swooping about lent a festive air, piquing passersby's' curiosity, especially the children. By dusk, the streets would again quiet down, alight with the glow bursting from garland decorated streetlamps, one after the other. Most of the many storefronts on Main Street proudly featured magazine perfect window displays, all except for *Abernathy and Crane*, the town's lone bookshop.

Irwin shifted his feet into position. Then stretched his

arms to shift the string of lights as instructed. "Remind me again, why we need to do this?"

"Because, Irwin, lights add a bit of festive excitement and holiday cheer. They spruce a place up, making it feel more inviting for potential customers."

Irwin cautiously shifted his foot on the wobbly rung. "Correct me if I'm wrong, but aren't our customers coming here to buy books?"

"Yes," Harper sighed again. "But ask yourself this—what sets us—*Abernathy & Crane*, apart from all the other stores in this area?"

"Books."

"—and energy."

"Well," Irwin snorted, "if they're coming here to look for energy, they are flat out of luck. I'm exhausted."

"Not you—*the shop*!" Harper shot Irwin a dirty look, then threaded her way past the stepladder toward the other side. "Hmm...I think you need to still pull your side up more on the left."

Irwin pulled.

"No," she corrected. "Your other left."

Irwin released the string of lights, letting them clatter into a messy pile on the floor.

"Aw!" Harper stomped her foot. "Don't be like that. You can't quit now." She gathered the fallen white lights, checking for damage.

Gripping the handle, Irwin took two tentative steps down, landing firmly on the floor with a thump. "I most certainly can."

"But why? We're almost done, and look around. Everything's so pretty and inviting." As usual, Harper had been the driving force behind getting the bookshop ready for the holiday season. She had even researched which ornaments would lend an inclusive and celebratory feel for Christmas, Hanukkah, as well as Ramadan, which for the first time in over a decade, had fallen close together.

Irwin, hands clamped on his waist, studied the length of the store. From every corner, something either twinkled, flickered, or glowed. And while he hated to admit it, and never would aloud, Harper's flair for the dramatic had turned the bookshop into something quite...*welcoming*. The semi-permanent frown on Irwin's face softened, leaving behind a teeny tiny crack in his characteristically grouchy demeanor.

Harper noticed and took her shot. "Come on, Mr. Grumpy," she nudged. "Only a few more minutes. I promise. Girls Scout's Honor."

"Like they would have ever let you join."

"Minor details. Now climb back up. Come on. Get a move on."

Irwin stretched his shoulders and cranked his neck. First right, then left. Then half-heartedly repositioned the stool.

This impertinent girl will be the death of me yet. Undeniably, Irwin sought to please Harper by being a good sport, but all the holiday fanfare had left him stiff and achy in practically every joint and muscle he owned.

"Stop fooling around, Irwin," prodded Harper again, nudging him in the back. "Where's your holiday spirit, anyway?"

"I left it on the floor."

Harper pitched her head back and groaned. "You promised."

"That you did, Irwin," shouted Cornelia in agreement from her armchair a few feet away, pointing her walking cane like a scepter, and almost toppling over an entire

4

bookshelf. "I heard you, and heck, even I remember." Cornelia winked, never missing the opportunity to drop a bit of gallows humor at the expense of her early dementia symptoms, although most of the time, she missed the amusing mark entirely.

Irwin shot Cornelia his infamous *'give me a break glare'* before glumly meeting Harper's hopeful- *'stop complaining and get up on the ladder stare.'* "Fine, fine," he grumbled, and proceeded to climb up again. "Let's get this over with."

From the back of the store, a basement door banged open.

"Here's the last box of lights," puffed Harper's father, arms full. If a task required anything to do with lifting and carrying, Darren was the man. "I gotta tell you, for lights, this damn thing's heavy." He lowered the cardboard box gently onto the floor.

Irwin slapped the wall with his palm. "I'm sorry, but what did he mean by *the last box*?" complained Irwin. "I distinctly recall you saying we're done."

"We are." Harper shoved the box off to the side and out of the way. "For now. This box is for the outside of the store, but we can tackle that after lunch."

"Oh, goody." Irwin's head drooped in mock defeat.

Darren laughed and clapped Irwin on the shoulder.

"Oh sure," griped Irwin, staring heavenward. "Laugh all you want. You're not the one up here risking life and limb."

Darren gripped the ladder. "Maybe so, but I find it safer to smile in the presence of the Crane women than complain."

"Don't be so sure." Irwin clapped his hands to get Harper's attention. "Ah, excuse me, Captain Bligh? Are the lights where you want them or not? Answer now or forever hold your peace because frankly, I can no longer feel my lower extremities."

"Yes, they're fine," she replied without glancing up, perched on the floor leaning on her knees, rummaging through the box.

"I counted three, maybe four more boxes of decorations downstairs," added Darren. "Where do you want me to put 'em?"

"I know exactly where you can put them," drolled Irwin.

Ignoring Irwin, Harper continued to sift through the contents of one of the boxes. "Give me a minute, Dad. I'm going to want to go downstairs with you." She dangled a sorry, torn cardboard elf in the air. "*Ewww.* Did you actually put this up, Irwin?" She *tsked.* "This must have terrified children."

Irwin shrugged, seeing *no* issue.

Harper wrinkled her nose and sniffed. "*Uck*...everything in here smells like mildew!" She lifted another questionable ornament in the air and dangled it, unsurprised when the handle popped off. "Yeah, ah, listen...most of this stuff is seriously worn out and dated." She tossed the dustier items off to the side.

"I call it vintage," snarled Irwin.

"I call it hideous," Harper retorted. "Gross," she grumbled repeatedly, wiping the dust and grime off her hands onto her jeans. "I'm going to go downstairs to see for myself exactly what's left. Okay, Irwin, can you climb back down without killing yourself?"

"Why?"

"Because we're done for now."

"Hallelujah." Irwin tapped the tip of his shoe against the tread in search for the last rung before stepping down, grateful for this most welcomed, albeit temporary reprieve.

Meanwhile next door...

"SAME TIME NEXT WEEK, THEN?" questioned Stanley Hatcher, his face half hidden under a wool cap and scarf with the rest of him bundled into a winter coat looking like a cast-off from the 'Nanook of the North.' Stanley worked at the dry cleaners six doors down from Alastair's antique shop. The men had known one another for years having served on the town council together. While not necessarily always seeing eye-to-eye on every issue, as of late, the two men had come to a mutual understanding— or at least they had agreed to somewhat of an *arrangement*.

"So, there's still the issue of time," sniffled Stanley, through his stuffed, bulbous red nose.

"Time. Always time." Alastair handed Stanley a tissue and checked his watch. "Well, what you've proposed is suitable—*for now*. I accept your terms but do remember, I expect to see you next Wednesday. Promptly at eleven and not a minute later."

"Works for me."

Alastair turned around in search of pen and paper from beneath the shelf behind the register. Without missing a beat, Stanley whipped around and poured a powdery substance into Alastair's decanter, pocketing the tiny plastic baggy in one fell swoop.

"Here's my private number." Alastair handed Stanley a card. "Message me before you come."

"Will do."

"Don't test me, Stanley," warned Alastair, brows knitted. "I'm not a man to be hoodwinked."

"Cross my heart and hope to die," mocked Stanley, before sluggishly strolling off, his wet rubber snow boots leaving a damp trail behind him.

"Oh, for heaven's sake." Alastair scurried out from behind his desk and seized Stanley by the elbow, practically perp-walking him out the front door.

"Wednesday, then," repeated Stanley, waving.

"Yes, yes, fine." Alastair poked his head out the front door for any sign of Beatrice. Disheartened, he allowed the door to close.

My lord! I thought that moron would never leave.

Bursting with nervous energy, Alastair paced the length of his stuffy store, somewhat impervious to the beads of sweat forming above his upper lip and brow. Even his neck had begun to dampen. He rubbed his stiff jaw with the damp palm of one hand, startled to find the start of a new patch of stubble sprouting from beneath his chin. He stopped for a peek, glaring into one of the store's overelaborate hanging mirrors to confirm his suspicions.

"Focus." Alastair dabbed his clammy face with a hanky kept in his jacket. Realizing how dry his mouth felt, he reached for the decanter but stopped.

I could use something stronger than water.

Alastair reached behind the register for the hip flask he kept filled with alcohol —brandy, to be exact. He unscrewed the top and took a long, hard swig. Then another. And then one more for good measure.

Why am I so thirsty?

Still parched, Alastair indulged in one last greedy gulp.

Ah... much better.

One of the store's many grandfather clocks chimed.

She should be here soon...

Beatrice hadn't sounded any too pleased on the phone the evening before. Screeching and yelling into his ear, and not letting him get a single word in edgewise. Now, as he waited, he wondered how she'd react when he proposed his terms. Knowing Beatrice, he anticipated the worst.

If she'd only give me a chance to explain...

Part of Alastair's grand scheme consisted of proving to Beatrice how this was all one big misunderstanding. A mere silly ruse to get her here. He wanted a chance to tell her face-to-face how much he had missed her, and how his every thought and dreams revolved around nothing else but her. Maybe then, her heart would soften toward him once given the opportunity to realize the lengths to which he'd go to bring her closer to him. Then again, this was Beatrice Aston, and holding a grudge was one of her most appealing traits. Alastair patted his coat pocket, checking for the folded newspaper clipping, satisfied to find it still safely tucked inside, exactly where he had left it.

And what a juicy discovery too!

While it had never occurred to Alastair to actually go through with his threat, it certainly wasn't past him to wag his titillating find in Beatrice's face to see which way the wind blew.

On second thought, flashing this paper around could easily backfire on me. I'll take it out only if I have to. Hopefully, it won't have to come to that.

BANG, BANG, BANG.

What in the blazes!

Alastair covered his ears.

BANG, BANG, BANG

Bloody noise...

Damn bookstore.

He'd hardly slept the night before. Indigestion perhaps? Anxiety, most likely. Perspiration poured from every pore on his clammy body. He removed his hanky from his coat pocket and again dabbed above his bushy brow at a newly formed pool of sweat. He raised his wrists and sniffed both his shirt sleeves, wanting to ensure that the scent from the last three earlier applications of his expensively lavish cologne still lingered.

Ah, just enough.

After all, the plan wasn't to overpower Beatrice. Just woo her.

At five-feet-three, Alastair could easily be described as a short, doughy man. Typically, dapper in dress and exacting in personal grooming, he wouldn't dare get caught outside in anything less than his Sunday best, excluding today. Today, he chalked up his slothfulness to nerves. Unlike Abernathy, the dodgy, lanky knob head from next door, who dressed most of the time like a homeless man hiding in a trench coat.

Why does he insist on wearing that ridiculous hunter's cap of his with the droopy flaps all the time—even during the summer? He looks like something straight out of an episode of 'Alaska People.'

Alastair never missed an opportunity to curse the day Irwin Abernathy—of all people—purchased the building next to his. Up until then, Main Street had been more serene. Predictable. Classier. *Less bizarre*. But no. Not anymore, and never again. Not since Abernathy and his cast of crazies moved in. Nowadays, it had been one prickly annoyance after the next, most notably when Abernathy's wayward cat slunk over to park his furball arse on Alastair's furniture.

Growing annoyed, Alastair twisted his stubby fingers,

confused as to how that irascible old man next door didn't seem to give a single hoot about how his uninvited, four-legged monster wound up daily in his store, encroached on his treasured sofa. Worse, Alastair couldn't manage to make the trespassing pest leave. After much haranguing, Abernathy would eventually meander his way over demanding Alastair return his cat—*as if I have ever had any intention on God's green earth of keeping the mangy animal.*

Lately, though, it had been Abernathy's ditzy friend, Cornelia Parish—the alleged locally celebrated mystery writer, who would waddle over to Alastair's to retrieve the furry runt. Alastair hated when she'd start chattering away...as if he cared one fig about anything that nutter had to say. The old woman's tall tales and abhorrent jokes, if one could call them that, left a lot to be desired. But at the end of the day, it remained and would forever be Abernathy that Alastair detested the most. He had loathed the man ever since he began working at the library years ago and liked him even less now that he had taken up residence next door.

Professing to run a bookshop. Preposterous...more like an insane asylum for wayward humans.

And yet, much to Alastair's dismay, Abernathy's bookshop stayed full. Day in and day out. The townspeople couldn't get enough of that place. For the life of him, Alastair could not fathom how anybody in their right mind could be swayed by that petulant old sod's act.

Terribly discouraging.

Fed up with trying to reason with Abernathy about the noise and dubious foot traffic, Alastair launched a full-blown complaint campaign. He began his line of attack by first writing countless letters to Abernathy, marking the start of an official paper trail. Then, when that tactic failed to garner any constructive response, Alastair penned his long length of grievances in triplicate, all the way up to the mayor's office. Eventually, he filed numerous complaints with the borough, township, and local newspaper, eager for somebody—*anybody*—to put an end to this madness, but nothing worked. In fact, Abernathy, in his usual cheeky fashion, blew him and whoever else off.

Simply intolerable. The man's nothing but a Neanderthal.

But for now, Abernathy and his annoying antics would have to wait. Battling an abundance of nervous energy, Alastair darted aimlessly about his store in search of something to do, periodically stopping to pat his brow or mop the perspiration accumulating on the back of his neck. On one of his passes, he noticed a picture frame hanging slightly crooked on the wall near the front of his store by the window.

"Hmm, that's not quite straight." He fussed and repositioned it. "Much better," he said, just in time to catch a pair of unkempt-looking college students passing his store. "More bookshop bums," he muttered, incensed how *those types* never once stopped to appreciate the tasteful holiday décor displayed in his window.

All sorts paraded in and out of that dodgy bookshop—and at all hours of the day and night. Old, young, rich, poor...people of every complexion and faith. Hordes of weirdos. Some with unnaturally colorful hair, while others sported tattoos galore, their faces punctured with multiple rings gracing noses, lips, and pinching eyebrows. Alastair often compared these meandering misfits to those found on display in the *Ripley's Believe It or Not Museum*. Nothing at all like his select clientele. People with a refined and cultured demeanor and deep wallets.

While waiting, Alastair stared out the store window,

and couldn't help but notice three Muslim women entering Abernathy's bookshop. They were cackling on about something or another. He watched as one of them lingered behind to hold the door open for an older couple exiting. The man had his hands full schlepping two heavy shopping bags, while the woman walking ahead of him, presumably his wife, tottered without a care, pointing in every which direction except at Alastair's shop.

Unbelievable.

While Alastair openly and with a passion despised Abernathy, he blamed the constant stream of unsuitable human spectacles next door mostly on that young Harper Crane girl Abernathy had working for him. Her desire to promote 'inclusiveness' —no matter how socially abhorrent, really got under his skin. Alastair made every effort to give that girl a piece of his mind. Much like earlier today...

"Gibberish," he snarled, punctuating each syllable with a squirt from his glass cleaner.

"How can you even say that?" said Harper, while the two were stuck outside cleaning their store windows. "Man...you totally need to loosen up and get with the times, Mr. Brooke. I mean, seriously, you've got to know by now, the clout that supports classism is slowly disappearing."

"Nonsense, young lady." Alastair used the term *lady* loosely, unable to peel his eyes away from her multiple piercings. "You are quite mistaken. The world as we know it, will never be devoid of rank and class," he haughtily informed her. "It is the way of the world, despite whatever you and your throng of slapdash minions profess otherwise." Alastair plunged his pointer finger high in the air before roaring loud and clear, "History has and will most certainly continue to uphold this indispensable standard."

"Standard?" Harper clamped down on her bottom lip as if finding it difficult to suppress her scorn. "Sorry, Mr. Brooke, but you're the one who's terribly mistaken. My generation of 'slapdash minions' aren't going for it. Not anymore. We're sick and tired of the bigotry, sexism, racism—and the entitlement mentality. Not to mention the way your generation continues to destroy the planet and pander to war mongers."

Alastair's smile vanished. "Is that so?"

"It sure as shit is."

"Well, young lady, we shall see, won't we?" Alastair slipped an envelope out from his coat pocket and handed it to Harper. "Please deliver this missive to your Mr. Abernathy."

"Another complaint?"

"Another directive. As the paperwork clearly indicates, that horrid noise being discharged from your establishment must cease and desist immediately. It's driving away my customers, and I simply won't have it."

"Noise?" Harper asked, somewhat confused. "What noise?" Harper glowered. "Oh. You must mean the music." With a jerky sweep of her hand, she snatched the envelope out of Alastair's hand. "You know something, Mr. Brooke? Irwin's right about you."

"Oh?" Alastair raised a single, thick brow. "And what does our illustrious Mr. Abernathy have to say on the matter?"

"Only that you are the most wretched, miserable, little —"

"Harper!" shouted her mother from next door, and just in the nick of time. "You have a phone call." Arms locked across her chest, Olivia shot Harper the evil eye. "It sounds urgent," she cautioned, donning her best fake, toothy sneer.

Harper, fist clenched tight, managing to crumple the envelope. Somehow, though, she held her tongue long enough to take her leave, but not before staring long and hard into Alastair's bemused face.

"You have a lovely day, Miss Crane," taunted Alastair at the young woman stomping away. "And make sure to extend to your Mr. Abernathy my sincerest and most wretched, miserable regards."

Fuming, Harper burst into the bookshop, ready to vent, but stopped when she found her mother busy assisting a customer. She instead went to answer the phone but found it still on its base—obviously her mother's ruse to keep the peace. Without missing a beat, she stomped her way through the aisles until she found Irwin off to the side. "Here," she said, thrusting Alastair's latest correspondence at him.

"Charming," Irwin ripped the envelope in two without reading it and tossed it in the nearest can.

"He's a prick," snarled Harper way too loudly.

"Shush," Irwin reprimanded, pointing at Olivia, whose own volume suddenly elevated three octaves to overcompensate for Harper's less than pleasant vernacular.

"If you're shopping for gifts, this is our local authors' table," Olivia explained, over enthusiastically. "We carry a wonderful selection of books. Everything from cozy murder mysteries to fantasy, romance, thrillers...and steampunk. I think they're calling those alternate histories or something now. Oh, and over there," she pointed to another small table, "We have vampires."

The woman selected a glossy covered book, *The Case of*

the Slain Soprano. "Love the cover. I don't know what it is, but there's something incredibly sexy about red high heels." She flipped it over to read the blurb. "Oh. Now, this does sound intriguing." Her eyes scanned the front jacket. "And I know just the somebody who would love a cozy murder mystery mixed with elements of music and theater."

Bones, the bookstore's anti-social feline mascot, yawned. He couldn't be bothered with the customers, so instead, he stretched his furry body under Cornelia's over-stuffed chair situated at the far side of a little reading nook Harper had designed against Irwin's predictable vocal consternation.

"A nook?" he had complained. "Why not drag a couch in here while you're at it? Or perhaps a chaise lounge?" grunted Irwin in protest. "Next thing you'll be installing is a massage table or a coin-operated vibrating bed."

Harper rolled her eyes. "Just you wait and see, Sir Grumpy. People will love it. Gravitate to it because it's fun. Trust me, nooks make folks want to grab a book and stay for hours."

"And we want that?" asked Irwin, evidently appalled by the thought of unnecessary prolonged human interaction.

"Yes, Negative Nancy. That's precisely what we want. Stay, sit, read, buy," she explained, for over the hundredth time.

Bones licked his paws—ostensibly wearied by the machinations of his human companions. However, as of late, the naughty cat had been driving everyone bonkers, caught on too many occasions darting out of the book shop, and making a beeline straight into Alastair Brooke's dreaded *Antique Shop & Collectibles.* Much to the proprietor's dismay, Bones had claimed squatter's rights on Alastair's prized and allegedly quite valuable antique sofa—presumably a gift which the irascible little man swore came straight from Windsor Castle and the Queen Mother herself. Irwin, however, highly doubted the veracity of that claim or anything else the pompous weasel had to say. Nevertheless, Irwin, under direct threat from Olivia, kept most of his razor-sharp, barbed retorts to himself.

"Here. You might also like this one." Olivia handed her enthralled customer *Tressa's Treasures, from the King's Jewel Series.* "This is a wonderful fantasy, written by another one of our talented local authors."

The woman fondled the book, pretending to swoon before gripping it possessively to her bosom. "Now, how about romance? Something funny."

Olivia pointed to the K. Jensen series.

"Gosh, Olivia, you're making it awfully hard to decide," she purred, admiring the gorgeous covers. "Hmm, what about that one over there?" she asked, pointing directly to another book on display.

"Ah! That one's called, *Secrets That Find Us.* Another great read."

"Mystery?"

"Uh, no. Not a mystery," Olivia shook her head. "But there's definitely a lot of intrigue. I'd categorize it more as a psychological thriller slash suspense."

"Oh?" The woman flipped the book over, her eyes moving quickly over the back copy. "I love a good thriller. Have you read it?"

"I did. Loved it. Tons of twists and turns. Goose bump approved. The author had me turning pages late into the night. I also read two of her other books. Real nail-biters."

"Really?" The woman grabbed all three. "I have to tell you, I never realized we had so many authors in our area."

"We do, and our boss—Wave, Irwin," shouted Olivia. Irwin, trying to make himself scarce, barely moved a muscle and offered a less than limp half-wave. "That's Irwin, the owner. He's partial to local authors, hence the table."

The woman leaned into Olivia and lowered her voice. "He sure doesn't look too happy."

"Who?" Olivia glanced at Irwin, skulking. "Him? Oh no. That's the way he always looks. Trust me, inside that droll, cynical interior is a thrilled, happy, happy man."

The woman shrugged. "If you say so," she stacked two more books in her arms, grabbing a few more on her way toward the register. "I think I've done enough damage for today," she announced, ready to check out.

With Olivia busy behind the register, and Harper and Darren in the basement accessing what decorations they had left to hang, and Irwin somewhere in the backroom doing whatever Irwin does, not one person was paying attention to Cornelia, or the fact that Bones had crept up to the front of the store.

For most of the morning, Cornelia had remained perfectly content to stay seated, occasionally humming to the music being piped through the store's amplifiers. Another one of Harper's bright ideas.

Olivia bagged the woman's purchase, slipped in a bookmark and a few chocolates, and handed her the receipt. "I hope whoever is lucky enough to get these books really enjoys them," she said. Olivia gave the woman the store's business card. "These are our hours if you want or need anything else. Happy Holidays!"

The store's phone rang right after the woman accepted the card.

"Hello? *Abernathy & Crane*. Olivia speaking. How can I help you?"

From behind the desk, Olivia mouthed a 'thank you' to the departing woman, whose arms were full. Using her shoulder, she shoved the front door open. As if on cue, Bones, apparently lying in wait, darted full speed straight out the door. Olivia, her back still half-turned, never noticed the cat's great escape or the fact that Cornelia, busy fumbling with her cane, came barreling out the door in hot feline pursuit.

"You wicked kitty!" muttered Cornelia rather loudly. "How many times do we have to go through the same thing? I swear, one of these days, Alastair's going to kill you."

CHAPTER 2

Irwin

OLIVIA CLEARED a large enough spot at the front register to make room for a bowl of assorted chocolates, a tall glass jar packed with candy canes, and a blue and white bowl jam-packed with dreidels and chocolate Gelt. For those fasting during the month of Ramadan, Olivia had filled a wicker basket crammed with lovely ink pens, each stenciled with a 'Ramadan Karim' greeting on the side.

"Covered all your bases I see." Irwin leaned in to pluck a chocolate. "What about the atheists?"

"Don't be absurd." Olivia snatched the chocolate back out of Irwin's hand. "Atheists eat chocolate too," she huffed, guarding the dish with her shoulder. "By the way, Christopher phoned."

Irwin's ears perked up. They hadn't seen Christopher since he left for his next semester at college, and more than overdue for a visit.

"He said to expect him late tonight."

"Why so late?"

"Well, he's actually finished with class but decided to get a few last-minute things done before heading this way. I told him to take his time and drive safe." Olivia fussed with the candy canes. "We don't need him rushing and getting into an accident."

"Good advice." Irwin snatched another chocolate, jamming it into his pants pocket before Olivia could get her claws on it.

Harper dropped a huge box of books on the floor in front of the counter. "Who got into an accident?" she asked, out of breath.

"Nobody," explained Olivia. "You caught me relaying to Irwin what I told Christopher when he called a few minutes ago." Olivia peeked over at her daughter, squelching a knowing grin. For the past year, she and Darren had suspected Harper of having a massive crush on their former boarder and friend, but so far, they weren't entirely sure if the feelings were mutual.

"Let me speak to him, Liv, man to man," urged Darren one evening while Harper attended class. "He's coming in a few days for winter break, right?"

Olivia nodded. "For about three weeks."

"There you go."

Olivia tilted her head and cringed. "I still don't think it's a good idea. I mean, what if Christopher doesn't feel the same way about Harper? Then what?"

"Then I'll let Chris know he needs to tread cautiously. Make him aware of how Harper feels so he doesn't do anything stupid—even by mistake, to hurt her." Darren smiled. He extended his hand to hold Olivia, but just as quickly yanked it away. "All I'm saying is this. When he comes, I'll take him for a walk and talk. She never has to know, and that'll be that."

Olivia shrugged, fiddling with the button on her blouse.

"I know how men think, Liv."

"I don't know." Olivia hugged herself. "You know Harper. She's not a child anymore, and she won't take kindly to us interfering in her love life."

"—Which is why, as her father, I will handle it, on the Q-T," he said undeterred. "Besides, like I said, Harper never has to know." Darren smiled, this time reaching out to gently hold Olivia's arm. "Trust me."

Not entirely convinced, Olivia returned the smile with a frown. "Okay. If you say so, but heed my warning, daddy dearest, you had better hope Harper never finds out."

HARPER'S CHEEKS could turn an instant rosy pink at the mere mention of Christopher's name.

Confused, Irwin shot Olivia a concerned look, but she merely shrugged and turned away, pretending to organize her desk.

"Why do you look flushed in the face?" Irwin asked Harper. "Do you need some water?"

Olivia turned to stifle a giggle.

"I'm fine," insisted Harper, tersely. "The box was heavy is all."

"Of course, it was," agreed her mother wholeheartedly.

Olivia leaned over the desk and pinched Irwin as soon as Harper glanced away.

"*Ouch*," he yelped, gripping his arm. "What the heck was that for?"

Harper scowled first at her mother, then back at Irwin. "Okay, you two, what's up?"

"Don't look at me, ask Mata Hari over there," complained Irwin, massaging his upper arm.

"Nothing's up," shrugged Olivia, her expression registering pure innocence. "Unless of course, you're referring to Irwin absconding with all the chocolates meant for our customers."

Irwin frowned. "I protest. I merely took one single chocolate. Hardly a crime spree," he objected.

Harper laughed. "Well, if you think he's bad, wait until Cornelia gets a load of them. I can almost guarantee the entire bowl will be empty before the night's—" Harper stopped talking. She craned her neck, peering around the shop. "Uh, speaking of which, where is Cornelia?"

Irwin, busy chomping on a second pinched chocolate, stopped mid-chew.

Olivia's eyes grew large and filled with dread. "Oh, no!" She sprang to the front of her desk. "I saw her here a minute ago with Bones." Olivia ran to the chair, bent over, but found no cat. "Darn it! He's missing too!"

The basement door kicked open. "The last box," announced Darren, struggling to carry the monstrosity to the front of the store. He dropped his box next to Harper's. "Good thing, too, 'cause my back's killing me." As Darren clapped away the dust left on his hands, he glanced around, noticing sheer panic spread across everyone's face. "Oh, no, what's wrong now?"

"Cornelia's missing again," Olivia shrieked. "And so is

Bones." Olivia tended not to deal with stress well, going from a scale of one to a hundred in seconds, especially whenever Cornelia pulled one of her disappearing acts. The last time it happened, they found her sitting across the street in the donut shop, flirting with an elderly gentleman. As Irwin approached the table, he had overheard Cornelia asking the man, "Do my buns still look as appetizing as the one your lips are currently fastened to?" — drawing raucous laughter from both staff and high-fives from those sitting close.

Irwin rubbed his weary eyes. Lifting his chin to the ceiling, he counted to three before exhaling a deep, resolute breath. "I'll go."

"Me, too," Darren nodded. "You two stay here in case she comes back."

"Wait, what about the phone?" asked Harper. Since the last disappearing act, they had decided as a group to have a unique necklace made for Cornelia. More like a GPS locator device designed as a heart, but in actuality, it contained a small electronic tag inside. Fortunately for everyone, Cornelia, so far, had never taken it off.

"Here you go," Olivia said from behind the register, handing Harper Cornelia's cell phone. "I keep it tucked safely behind the desk in the bottom drawer."

Without pause, Harper's nimble young fingers flew over the phone's screen and within seconds, she announced. "Got her. She's next door...again."

Irwin's head dropped, and his shoulders wilted. "Of course, she is," he grumbled. "Let's go," he told Darren, already trailing close behind.

Cornelia

"BONES! BONES!" Cornelia continued to yell, but by the time she returned to the front of the store, she had completely forgotten why she had come inside in the first place. Puzzled, and becoming increasingly disorientated, she rushed out the store, confused as to what to do next.

Too afraid to move in any particular direction, and forgetting the bookshop was adjacent to the antique shop, Cornelia stood on the sidewalk, wrapped in an over-sized sweater, leaning on her cane—scared silly. To calm her nerves, she began to hum an old tune, something she did whenever her memory failed her. Thankfully, she didn't have many refrains to get through before being rescued.

"There she is," pointed Darren from behind Irwin. "Oh, man, is she crying?"

"Singing. "The Toreador Song" from *Carmen*. It's one of her favorite operas," he grumbled. "Cornelia! Over here!" he waved, approaching her slowly. "Cornelia, it's me. Irwin."

At first, Cornelia gave a noncommittal wave, but once she recognized Irwin, she cracked a petrified smile, quickly covering her mouth, ashamed.

"We were worried about you," said Darren, sandwiching himself in the middle of the pair.

Cornelia stared long and hard at Darren, then to Irwin for help.

"Darren," Irwin reminded her.

Cornelia nodded gratefully.

"Are you okay?" asked Irwin.

"I'm not sure." Cornelia gave a half-shrug. "Shouldn't I be?" Her small frame shivered under her bulky sweater.

"Why'd you leave the store without telling anyone?" asked Darren.

"I...I don't actually remember why," she answered somewhat sheepishly.

Irwin noticed the corner of Cornelia's eyes quickly fill with tears. "Now, now, old bird," he said soothingly. "No need for any of that. We're here now, and you're safe." Irwin held Cornelia's trembling hand gently in his.

Unfortunately, Cornelia's dementia episodes were happening more frequently and lasting longer, becoming one of Irwin's growing concerns. He feared that one day she would get seriously hurt if left to wander about unsupervised.

"Everything's fine now," he assured her again.

Cornelia sniffled. "I hate this, Irwin," she said, squeezing his fingers. "The not remembering stuff. Turning up in places and not knowing how the hell I got there."

"I know," said Irwin, stroking her back. "Were you looking for Bones?"

Cornelia snapped her fingers. "That's it! Looking for Bones. That naughty boy got out again and I...I—" her scrambled thoughts trailed off once more.

"And you went looking to bring that scoundrel back to the bookshop," prompted Irwin, something he often did to help Cornelia fill in the missing gaps.

"Exactly, but, where is he? Did I find him?" Cornelia peered under her coat. "Nope. He's not in there."

"Alastair's probably holding him hostage," said Darren, only half-joking.

Irwin shot Darren the death glare. "Why don't you run into Alastair's and find out while I wait here with Cornelia," prompted Irwin. The last thing he wanted was to deal with that pompous imbecile again.

"Sure thing." Darren headed straight into the antique store, but it hadn't taken long before Irwin and Cornelia heard Darren shouting. "Get over here, you rascal."

"Cornelia, you didn't happen to go inside Alastair's, did you?"

"I think I did." She frowned. "Hmm, maybe, I did. I could have." She shrugged. "I don't remember."

Already late afternoon, the temperature was dropping into the low double-digits rapidly. Coatless, Irwin shivered. "Are you cold?"

Cornelia teeth chattered. "A tad."

"Come on. I'm taking you back to the shop. We'll wait for Darren and Bones where it's warm." As the pair started to walk, they heard a deep, pained groaning coming from the direction of the antique shop.

"Irwin—stop!"

Irwin turned.

Darren barreled out of the store, frantically waving his hands. "Wait!" he called, virtually gasping for breath. "Don't go anywhere."

"What the blazes is the issue now?"

"Ah, Irwin," Darren stammered. "We, um, we got a problem," he sputtered, choosing his words carefully in front of Cornelia.

Irwin's brow creased. "Is this a big problem or a small problem?" he asked, eyes darting from Darren's trembling body to Alastair's store.

"Category five," panted Darren, bent over, and squeezing the blood out of his knees.

"If that son of a bitch did anything to hurt my cat—" roared Irwin, marching towards the antique store, dragging Cornelia behind him.

Darren flapped a hand and jumped in front of Irwin to

block his way in. "Bones-is-fine," he said, spitting out each word through quick gulps of breath.

"Then what's the damn problem?" shouted Irwin, clearly annoyed. "Better yet, watch Cornelia. I'll handle Alastair."

Darren used his body this time to block the door. "You can't go in there."

"And why not?"

Darren's eye's widened. "Trust me. You don't want to go in there."

Irwin, his lips pressed tight together, had all but lost his patience. "Enough of the histrionics," he snapped. "What's the issue, and where is my rotten cat?"

Darren, struggling to remain standing, leaned in closer. He clasped Irwin's shoulder for support while simultaneously tugging him down to whisper into his ear. "Alastair's dead."

Irwin stumbled back. "He's what?"

"He said Alastair's dead," repeated Cornelia flatly, her grey eyes gazing blankly, seemingly unaffected by the news.

"Dead?" repeated Irwin. "Like, dead-dead?"

"Is there any other kind?" sputtered Darren.

"Come to think of it," interjected Cornelia, casually leaning on her cane. "I remember somebody lying on the floor."

Both men stared down at Cornelia.

"What?" she asked the ogling pair, not registering their disbelief. "Oh, for heaven's sake. Let's not all start pretending we're upset. Alastair wasn't a very nice man, and you both know it," she stated matter of fact.

Darren's mouth dropped wide open. Irwin's face drained of color. Neither man looked able to respond.

"You ask her, Irwin," nudged Darren.

"Yes, fine," Irwin huffed, clearly exasperated. "Cornelia?" he said gently. "Do you remember going inside?"

"In where?"

"Alastair's," repeated both men.

"Nope. Can't remember. Why? Is it important?"

Both men groaned.

Irwin gripped Darren by the arm, leaned in and murmured. "You're absolutely sure he's dead, right?"

"Oh, I'm positive," groaned Darren, making a show of cranking his head to the side, his tongue hanging out of the side of his mouth as if being strangled.

Irwin blanched. "He was strangled?"

Darren shrugged, baffled. "I don't think so."

Irwin gnashed his teeth. "Idiot."

Cornelia clapped, appearing to have the time of her life. "This reminds me one of my mysteries—*The Case of The Strangulated Sailor*."

"You wrote that?" asked Darren, impressed. "I've been meaning to read that one."

"*Darren!*" Irwin hollered, shoving him hard in the shoulder.

"Maybe Alastair had a heart attack," interjected Cornelia. "Lord knows that silly man's blood pressure must have been through the roof."

Irwin and Cornelia waited for Darren to say something, but instead, he stared at the sidewalk, refusing to lift his gaze. "Oh...I don't think it was his heart either," he mumbled. "No, sir. Not his heart," he kept muttering, head swooshing back and forth as he ran a slightly shaky hand through his close-cropped hair.

"How can you be so sure?" Irwin probed. Both men exchanged a long stare, then glimpsed at Cornelia, waiting for her to say something equally as bizarre, but remarkably, she remained quiet, eerily unfazed.

"Cornelia!" Harper and Olivia bolted out of the bookshop, screaming. They ran over and hugged her tight.

"You scared us," panted Olivia, out of breath. "Where were you?"

"Alastair's dead," said Cornelia. "Right, Darren?"

Olivia blanched. "I'm sorry, what did she say?"

Harper turned to face her father for an answer. "Explain."

"Tell 'em, Darren," coaxed Cornelia.

"Yes, Darren. Tell us," snarled Olivia.

"What Cornelia said...Alastair's dead. Like on the floor not breathing, dead."

"Oh-my-God!" shrieked Olivia.

"Strangled," added Cornelia.

"Strangled!" Olivia shrieked.

"No!" Irwin motioned for everyone to disregard what Cornelia said.

Olivia, close to hyperventilating, screeched, "What happened? Did he have a heart attack?"

"Not exactly," said Darren.

"Irwin—" implored Harper. "What the hell's going on? Wait—you didn't do anything *crazy*, did you?"

"Don't you dare look at me," snapped Irwin, highly offended.

Everyone's eyes spun toward Darren.

"Oh, Darren! How could you?" Olivia thumped him square in the shoulder.

"*Ouch*," shouted Darren. "Stop that. I didn't do anything. Tell 'em, Irwin. I found him like that."

"Like what?" Harper locked arms with Cornelia, her big brown eyes wide and reproachful.

Darren cringed. He looked to Irwin, who merely shrugged. "Like with his head cracked in two."

Everyone gasped.

Darren flinched. "Trust me, it's pretty gruesome in there."

Everyone appeared upset—except for Cornelia. In slow motion, they all turned wordlessly toward her.

Cornelia recoiled. "Oh no, you don't," she barked in full form. "You're not pinning this caper on me. Don't get me wrong, I thought Alastair was a first-class asswipe. Still, do, but I didn't dislike him enough to murder him."

Everyone exhaled.

"At least, not that I can remember," she added, before cracking up.

Irwin groaned again.

"Bones!" Harper shrieked, her eyes watery. "Oh my God, is he also?"

"Relax. The cat's fine," said Darren. "He's lounging out on Alastair's sofa."

"What do you mean *lounging out*?" Harper pinched her father's arm. "You left him there?"

"*Ouch!*" Darren squeezed his arm, stepping further out of harm's way. "First, your mother, now you? I swear—"

"I can't believe you, Dad."

"What?"

"You left poor Bones with a dead guy?"

"How could you!" Olivia stared furiously at Darren. "The poor thing must be so scared."

"Whadda, you mean *how*?" Darren moved a bit further away, nursing his forearm. "Excuse me, ladies, if I didn't have the stomach to climb over a dead body to retrieve him."

The group quieted down, only somewhat assuaged.

"Well, somebody's gonna need to call the police," announced Harper, shivering. "I mean, that would be the right thing to do."

The group murmured in agreement.

"Don't forget about Bones," added Harper.

"I'll get him," offered Cornelia.

"No!" shouted everyone.

Olivia placed a protective arm around Cornelia's shoulder. "Don't worry, Bones will be fine until the police arrive. Irwin, I'm taking Cornelia inside with me to call. Harper, you come as well."

"Maybe I should stay here with Dad and Irwin."

Darren gripped his daughter's shoulders and spun Harper gently in the direction of her mother. "Not this time, kiddo. Go with your mother."

"But maybe I should—"

"No, Harper. Your father is correct. Back to the bookshop, all of you," ordered Irwin. "We'll be in soon," he told them, not entirely convinced.

The two men waited on the sidewalk, freezing but neither one willing to voice aloud what they both were thinking. Eventually, Darren broke the silence first.

"Do you think she did it?" he asked.

"Who? Cornelia? How? You're the one who said it looked like a bloodbath in there. Did you see any blood on her?" Irwin peered over his shoulder to make sure the three women were inside safely.

"Ah...true. You're right," Darren nodded, relieved. "But what about the statue?"

Irwin's head jerked back. "Statue? What statue? You never mentioned anything about a statue."

"I didn't?" Darren shrugged sheepishly. "It was this naked mermaid thingy with blood caked all over it."

Irwin cocked his head and gripped his waist. "Would you care to elaborate?"

"Ah, well, sure, I guess." Darren lowered his voice. "When I looked down at, *err*, the body, there was this ugly mermaid lookin' statue saturated with half of Alastair's brains on it. I assumed at the time it was what was used to knock him into la-la land."

Irwin rubbed his arms to keep warm. "If that's so, the police will check it for fingerprints. I seriously doubt Cornelia possesses the strength or wherewithal to clobber a grown man hard enough to kill him, even if she wanted to."

Darren slapped his hands. "Damn it!" he cursed, shaking his head.

"What do you mean, *damn it*? What is the *damn it* all about?" demanded Irwin.

"Well, when I first noticed Alastair lying on the floor, I went to check to see if he was still breathing..."

Irwin's nostrils flared. "Go on."

"Well, I kinda..."

"Say it! All of it!"

"I might have moved the statue slightly out of the way."

"You did what!" shouted Irwin, his hands squeezing his head in utter disbelief.

"I wasn't thinking."

"No, kidding, Sherlock!" Irwin suppressed a growl. "Moved it—moved it how? Where'd you put it?"

This time Darren gripped the side of his head. "I don't know," he shrieked. "I mean, all I saw was blood and him lying on the ground with his head all open and stuff oozing out, and I guess I panicked."

Irwin glared at Darren, unblinking. "Tell me you

kicked it out of the way and didn't use your hands to pick it up."

Loud sirens alerted the squabbling duo to the two police cars swerving in front of the building. Within seconds, four police officers rushed out from their vehicles, weapons were drawn. The man apparently in charge spoke first.

"Where is he?" barked the officer.

Darren and Irwin pointed at the shop in unison. Three policemen entered the building, weapons drawn. The one in charge stayed outside with Irwin and Darren.

"Who found the body?" asked Detective Moore.

"Me," said Darren, side-eyeing Irwin. "I'm the one who found him."

Moore's eyes narrowed to slits. "Hold up. Why do you two guys look so familiar?" he asked, scowling at Darren trying to place him. "I swear, I know you two."

"All clear," yelled one officer, his head peeking out the shop door.

"Gibson, stay with these two while I go inside," ordered Moore.

"Yes, sir," replied Gibson, his posture stiff and erect.

"And don't let either one of them out of your sight," Moore added, unable to stop staring. "Especially this one," he pointed a finger directly at Darren. "It'll come to me," he muttered. "I never forget a face."

And neither did the anxious pair of eyes gawking out the glass window from a safe distance across the street, carefully accessing every move made.

CHAPTER 3

Alastair Brooke

ALASTAIR CHECKED THE TIME.

Again.

His eyes grew heavy, his limbs weighty. "Whoa," he moaned, gripping the corner of the desk. "That's odd." He greedily swallowed a few large gulps of water straight from his decanter. "Uck, disgusting," he bellowed, gagging on the strange taste. "What the bloody hell?"

Pupils dilated, he tried in vain to focus ahead of him, but strangely, everything looked blurred. As Alastair loosened his shirt collar, an eerie sensation of becoming detached overtook him. Lightheaded and breathing heavily, he leaned against the counter, head bowing forward, overcome with waves of dizziness. A bead of sticky sweat slid down the back of his shirt collar and onto his already clammy palms as he struggled to massage the stiffness out of his thick neck. Heart pulsing rapidly as if about to split in two, Alastair scanned the desk for his water, disappointed to find the decanter less than half-full. Grabbing it anyway, he swallowed the rest in two voracious large gulps, ignoring the gross taste, but as he guzzled, he felt his chest constrict, making it harder to inhale.

It's only anxiety, he assured himself. It had happened before, causing chest pains and shortness of breath. He rested against the wall, willing his body to relax.

Breathe.

Attempting to regain his equilibrium, Alastair inhaled slowly, then exhaled. He did this until the room stopped spinning. In, out. In, out. His stomach clenched, while another, different kind of panic spread—this one sharper than the last.

Strange...

Moments later, the discomfort resided. The dizziness from before—all but gone. He used what little time left to straighten his crinkled, damp attire.

In need of emotional reassurance, Alastair slipped the folded newspaper clipping from his coat pocket for a quick peek. His eyes rested on the aged, but surprisingly still quite vivid image of a youthful, voracious Beatrice Aston. Since its discovery, he had indulged in making a mental note of every delicate nuance and tantalizing curvature of her face and body but couldn't get enough.

She'd been considerably younger then, and provocatively svelte. Her youthful face, less angular. *Awfully pretty*, Alastair decided, holding the black and white faded image as close to his face as possible. He admired how Beatrice's curly hair had once framed an exquisitely heart-shaped face. And while considerably thinner then, Alastair preferred his women of today with a bit of extra padding. After all, who in their right mind would want to snuggle up next to a bag of bones when one could just as easily wrap their hungry thighs around an invitingly ample caboose?

Head slightly clearer, Alastair made one last check of his reflection in one of the antique hanging mirrors displayed auspiciously by the store's entrance. A truly hideous piece. A gold trimmed number scooped up for mere peanuts at a local estate sale. Alastair hoped the revolting monstrosity would fetch him a nice sum come auction time, unless, of course, it sold sooner to one of his more pretentious, affluent customers.

The noise from next door abruptly stopped.

Ah.

Alastair's shoulders relaxed.

Much better.

Then the music started — *The rock and roll—as it were*.

"Bloody hell," barked Alastair, thoroughly miffed, and fed-up with his obstinate neighbor, Abernathy, who blatantly continued to ignore his numerous appeals for common civility. "That's not music!"

Being somewhat of a self-anointed classical music connoisseur, Alastair boasted about his unparalleled ability to interpret musical acumen. But alas, music wasn't his only expertise. He'd even, on occasion, made use of his refined palette and an exceptional sense of smell to cultivate a proper wine cellar in his home, replete with rows of expensive aged bottles acquired from his many trips abroad. After a long day at the shop dealing with mind-numbing, stupid people, Alastair liked to indulge in a glass or two, something to dull his nerves. Much like the sparkling beauty chilling in his fridge in the back store-room. A judiciously selected celebratory champagne in anticipation of Beatrice's visit. However, after much delib-eration, Alastair decided that he might have jumped the gun a tad regarding today's projected outcome. To combat the negative jitters, he resumed his foolhardy pretense of dusting. Scurrying around the store in one direction to the next. He wanted to stop, knew he needed to stop, but couldn't. Too much rode on Beatrice's answer for him to lay back and play it cool.

At the front of the store, Alastair stole a peek through the display window, proud of how beautiful Main Street looked decorated with variously sized wreaths and uniformed holiday lights, each tastefully hung from antique, cast iron black street poles. As a long-standing and respected, reigning member of the town council, it had been one of Alastair's annual responsibilities to infuse as much culture and tradition as he could into what he considered 'a backward piece of earth' —appalled to no end over some of the ghastlier designs suggested by a few of the town's 'less sophisticated' council members.

Utterly dreadful, to say the least.

Alastair shivered. Despite dipping, frigid winter temperatures, the afternoon skies shone bright. However, in the Pocono Mountains, that could change in an instant. Without exaggeration, the region was known to experi-ence all four seasons—sometimes in a single afternoon. Biding his time, Alastair stepped outside for a much-needed breath of fresh air. However, much to his dismay, he found his nemesis, Irwin Abernathy, perched on a wobbly stepladder hanging a wretched ornament onto his shoddy, bookshop window.

"*Ahem*," Alastair coughed, pretending to clear his

throat. "I say, good afternoon," he yelled over the blasted music assaulting his eardrums.

Irwin never glanced his way.

"I say, good afternoon!" shouted Alastair, face scrunched and flushed.

Irwin offered Alastair an irked, somewhat sharp side-nod.

"Nice weather we have today." Alastair clasped his hands impatiently, waiting for a reply. "I, *err*, wish to discuss something vitally important with you when you have a free moment."

Irwin fidgeted with the ornament with total disregard for Alastair, who continued to stand below him, fuming.

"I assume you received my last note via that, um, Harper person?" Alastair stated, practically stomping his foot.

Irwin's pupils flared, as he purposely took his sweet time securing the decoration into place. "I did."

"Well, then?" Alastair shuffled his feet.

Irwin tilted his head, then readjusted the decoration. "Well, then, what?"

"Well then, what? Oh, for heaven's sake..." Alastair had had enough. "Am I safe to assume, by the sheer volume of that incessant noise blaring from your establishment, that you have decided not to heed my warnings?" roared Alastair, coming off a tad irrational, even for his tastes.

Irwin scowled. "If you mean, did I disregard it? Why then, yes, Brooke. That would be a safe assumption. Go with that."

Alastair's temper flared. "Ignoring my appeal is a poor decision, Abernathy."

"Is that a threat, Brooke?"

"I'd call it a stern warning, sir."

Irwin chuckled.

"I fail to see what you find so amusing."

Stone-faced, Irwin twisted his body so he could fully stare down at Alastair's pasty face. "What I find amusing, is you, Brooke. You and all your little sanctimonious, trivial, and utterly meaningless grievances."

"Well, I never—"

"I'm sure." Irwin descended from his stepladder like a pro. "However, do me a favor anyway, and find someone else to dump your useless tirade of officiousness on because frankly, I couldn't be less interested."

Alastair cleared his throat, ready to interject. He had a finger raised high in protest when Darren appeared, his arms wrapped around yet another box of holiday paraphernalia, and nudged the shop's door open with a shoulder. "Hey," he nodded to Alastair. To Irwin, "Harper said she wants these put up, too, and not to be sloppy about it."

"What does she mean, sloppy? Who's sloppy?" asked Irwin, miffed. "Hand me that one."

"What in blazes are those?" demanded Alastair, staring inside the box, his mouth agape.

"What? This?" asked Darren. "It's called a star and a crescent."

"And what, pray tell, do you plan to do with it?" snapped Alastair, scowling.

Irwin snatched the ornament from Darren. "We plan on hanging it up."

Alastair's mouth twisted. "That much is obvious, you idiot. My question, is why?"

"For Ramadan."

"Ramadan?" Alastair's nostril flared, unable to comprehend what he just heard.

Darren handed Irwin the next decoration. "Yeah. We

42

figured that since Ramadan falls close to the other holi-days this year, it would be kinda cool to incorporate every-body's celebration."

"Tape," barked Irwin, snapping his fingers.

Darren handed Irwin the roll of tape.

Alastair stood stone-faced. "I don't see why any of this is necessary."

"Well, Brooke," replied Irwin, "Here's the thing. We—and I am referring to everybody here at *Abernathy & Crane*—believe everyone has a right to feel appreciated, including our Muslim neighbors. This," Irwin said as if speaking to a third grader, "is called a menorah, a symbol of Hanukkah. We've decided to display it for our Jewish neighbors. And this over here?" he said, pointing to the ornament in Darren's hands. "is called a Christmas—"

"Don't be daft," snorted Alastair, pressing his chest with his balled-up fist. "I know what that is. My question is why! Why do you feel compelled to clutter the exterior of your shop with this—this rubbish! Certainly, even you and your band of nitwits realize, especially in lieu of the tasteful decor explicitly selected by the council for outside display, that these—" Alastair struggled to find the right word, "other embellishments simply do not belong."

Irwin's face grew taut as he clunked back down onto the sidewalk. "Listen carefully, Brooke, because I am only going to say this once. Go away. Slink back into your store and take your bigoted, xenophobic, closed mind with you. And while you're at it, refrain from sending me any more of your vile, injudicious not*es*. This might come as a shocker, but nobody, and I do mean *no-bo-dy* gives a damn what you think."

Alastair lifted a stubby finger, prepared to interject, but Irwin beat him to it with his finger already in Alastair's face. "And while you're at it, stop with all the idiotic commentaries. I swear, you're like some earth-vexing, hairy wart on the back of society's ass."

"Who do you think you're speaking to?" thundered Alastair, causing more than a few passing heads to turn and gather round.

Darren stepped up to face Alastair next. "Ah, Mr. Brooke, I suggest you listen to Mr. Abernathy before I do something drastic, like permanently dismembering those useless lobes from both sides of your misshapen, round dome."

A few people in the crowd gasped. Irwin tapped Darren hard on the shoulder. "Shut up, please."

Alastair puffed out his chest. "You don't scare me, hooligan," he snapped, eyes wide and fuming. "I've got a good mind to summon the police."

"You do that," taunted Darren, undeterred. "Summon away."

Alastair, hating to be the brunt of anyone's joke snapped back. "I'll have the pair of you thrown into the pokey."

"The pokey?" Irwin scratched the side of his head. "Did he just say the pokey?"

"Oh, no!" Darren fake trembled. "Anything but the pokey."

"That's it." Alastair reached into his pocket in search of his phone. "Damn it," he muttered after soon realizing that in his haste for fresh air he had left it inside. Infuriated, he marched off in the direction of his store. "Sod off, Abernathy! You, too, ruffian."

Darren stepped ahead of Alastair, blocking his way. "Not before I cut that tongue out of your flabby mouth and feed it to the bears," he hissed.

Beyond fuming, Alastair stomped past Darren, but couldn't resist pointing back at Irwin. "You'll be hearing from my solicitor."

"Mmhm," said Irwin, rocking back and forth on his heels, thumbs hooked into the loop of his pants. "I reckon I will, partner, but until then, giddyup."

Darren cracked up laughing and went to high-five Irwin, but Irwin, slightly appalled by the gesture, merely shook his head in an emphatic, 'No.'

"Mark my words, Abernathy, this won't be the last time you'll be hearing from me on this matter," threatened Alastair still yelling. "I guarantee it!"

Darren pitched towards Alastair, but this time Irwin forcibly tugged him back.

"Threaten us again, Brooke, and I'll wring an apology out of you," shouted Darren. "In red, if you get my drift." Darren rubbed his calloused hands together to show he meant business.

Eyes ablaze, Alastair stomped the rest of the way over to his store. Once there, he flung the shop door open, slamming it firmly closed behind him, but not before hurling one more insult. "Idiots!"

Irwin

PALMS FACED FORWARD, Irwin addressed the crowd. "Okay folks. Nothing more to see here." The crowd reluctantly began to disperse.

"What a jerk." Darren clamped his hands to his waist. "Hooligan...the pokey...ruffian? Who the hell talks like that?" Darren mocked. "You know, we had a lot of guys like Mr. Brooke back in the joint. All big talk and theater until you stepped to them."

"Yes," nodded Irwin, barely half listening. "One can only imagine." Irwin dragged the folded stepladder back inside the store. "However, in the future, I'd appreciate it if you would please refrain from threatening our exasperating Mr. Brooke with bodily harm or dismemberment. It really does unnecessarily complicate matters."

"Sure thing, Mr. A.," Darren flipped Irwin the thumbs up. "You got it."

Alastair

IF BEATRICE WASN'T ALREADY on her way, Alastair would have indeed phoned the police on Abernathy and that idiot friend of his as threatened. Instead, he reached behind the counter for a fresh dab of cologne.

This is ridiculous, he told himself, removing the newspaper clipping from his pocket. *I won't need this thing.*

While busy wondering where to hide it, he heard the front doorbell clang when opened, causing his heart to jolt. *Beatrice.* Unsure of what to do next, he swatted at Bones, rooted on Alastair's prized sofa. "Move out of the way, you revolting animal," he hissed. However, Bones refused to budge, and instead, hissed back, clawing Alastair's hand as he attempted to slip the folded paper beneath the sofa cushion for temporary safekeeping.

"*Ouch!* You rotten mongrel."

"*Hiss*," replied Bones, teeth bared, ready for round two.

Alastair barely had the chance to take another swipe at

Bones before Beatrice stormed into the shop, hoofing it straight for him. Alastair cringed and took steps back.

Oh, no.

"How *dare* you!" she roared, flailing her arms in his direction.

"Now wait a minute, Beatrice," protested Alastair, his palms raised in mock surrender. "Let me explain—"

Beatrice swung her handbag over her shoulder. "Oh, I think you've explained yourself plenty. What the hell is wrong with you?"

Alastair winced.

"The antique business not paying off enough?" Beatrice stepped closer. "Had to set up a side hustle blackmailing now?"

"Blackmail?" contested Alastair, visibly offended. "I would never do such a thing to you—" he exclaimed, his words escaping through sputtered clipped, sporadic breaths. "I-I can explain—"

"What kind of person does this?" Beatrice's nostrils flared, while the veins on her forehead pulsed and protruded. "I'll tell you what kind—a smarmy, no-good, unscrupulous one!"

Overheated, and feeling a bit woozy, Alastair reached out his hand, grabbing for Beatrice's shoulder for support, but got forcibly slapped away.

"Don't you dare touch me," she snarled. "Maybe I should start digging around in your past—see what filth I can find lurking in your creepy closet. Then I'll spread your business across town and embarrass you. Let's see how you'd like it!"

"Beatrice..." Alastair gripped his chest.

"Don't you, Beatrice me, Alastair Brooke. I don't take

kindly to being threatened. Now give me that damn paper if you know what's good for you."

Breathing heavy, Alastair rubbed his damp brow with the back of his sleeve. "There's no need. The paper is safely tucked away. In fact, I can do one better. I'll destroy it, and we can start over...forget this entire debacle ever happened. Shall we?"

"Forget the entire thing?" Beatrice repeated hysterically. "Forget the entire thing...like, why in the *hell* should I trust you?"

"But you can trust me, Beatrice. I swear." Alastair wiped his sweaty face with his other sleeve. "Is it hot in here?"

Beatrice scrunched up her nose, pretending to sniff. "Smells like the stench of your immorality oozing out of your pores. It's what happens when a creep like you lacks a moral compass."

"You have to believe me. I never meant for any of this to happen."

"Like *hell*, you didn't."

"I mean it."

Beatrice sneered. "Oh, really? Then why all the cloak and dagger stuff?"

"Oh, Beatrice," Alastair blushed. "Can't you see? I have been trying to speak with you for months, but whenever I phone, you either won't pick up or return any of my messages," he wheezed. "I've been going clear out of my head trying to think up ways to see you."

Beatrice's eyes grew wide in disbelief. "So, you decided to resort to blackmail?"

"Well, no. Not exactly." Alastair attempted to catch his breath before continuing. "When I found the newspaper clipping inside the armoire—the one you dropped off last week, well, I believed it was..."

"Was what? Spit it out."

"Don't laugh."

"Count on it."

Alastair sighed. "A sign."

Beatrice cringed. "A sign?"

"Yes. Well, perhaps more akin to fate, if you will."

"Fate," Beatrice mocked. "Did you just have the audacity to say fate?"

"Yes. It was as if fate had given me one more chance to express to you my undying love. I wanted to prove to you once and for all how happy I could make you if only you would give me another chance."

Beatrice snorted. "Are you completely deranged?" She covered her mouth with her white-gloved hand. "I never heard of anything so—so pathetic in my life."

Alastair bristled.

Arms crossed, Beatrice unwaveringly shook her head. "You're nothing but a petty, narrowminded piece of work, you know that?"

"Now, see here," Alastair stiffened. "There's no reason to be unpleasant."

"Let you tell it." Beatrice stepped close enough for Alastair to feel her hot breath. "Give me the paper," she snarled, shoving his shoulder with her palm. "I mean it, Alastair. Give it to me."

Alastair swayed. He clutched his throat, gasping for air. Leaning back as far as he could, he wound up knocking over the carafe of water, causing it to crash to the floor. "Oh, no," he mumbled at the mess.

Beatrice, who had Alastair by a good three inches, moved closer. "Forget that. Hand over the paper."

"Let's," he wheezed, "calm down and talk this out."

"Talk? There's nothing left in this life we need to talk about. Why can't you get that through your thick, bald skull?" Beatrice huffed. "We dated. What? Twice, maybe? It didn't work out. End of story."

"It could have," Alastair grunted.

"Perhaps—if you weren't such a dreary, tedious little man—but you are who you are, and frankly, Alastair, I'll never be that desperate. Now give me the damn paper!"

Short of breath or not, Alastair stood his ground. "No. Never."

"Fine. Have it your way." Beatrice began digging into her handbag. "I see how this is going to go. How much do you want for it? I have a bit of savings left in my..."

"I don't want your money."

Beatrice stopped searching in her bag, looking puzzled. "Then what the *hell* do you want?"

Puffing out his pudgy chest, Alastair lifted his bulky frame, attempting to stand as straight as possible. "Beatrice Aston," he squawked, "will you marry me?"

"Marry you?" Beatrice gasped. "Marry you!"

"Yes. Marry me."

Beatrice, balancing someplace between shock and outright indignation facepalmed herself. "You have got to be kidding me."

"Why? Is that so terrible?"

"Positively revolting."

"I see," murmured Alastair stiffly. From the sofa, Bones nestled his furry head onto his outstretched paws for the remainder of the show.

"Well then, let me make myself clear," Alastair puffed. "Unless you agree to become my bride, I'll do everything within my power to expose you. Why, I'll even hand-deliver copies of your less than demure past to everyone you know—including your current place of employment."

Beatrice snarled. "You wouldn't dare."

"Indeed, I would. I'll sprinkle them around town like confetti if forced to."

"How could you?" Beatrice took a small step forward.

"I'd rather not." Alastair shrugged, "but the decision is entirely yours."

Beatrice lost it and shoved Alastair as hard as she could in his chest. "Give me the paper," she roared.

"*Ouch*, and no! Not until you agree to my terms."

"I will *never* agree to marry you."

"Are you certain about that?" taunted Alastair.

"You have no right to do this!"

"Perhaps, but my terms remain."

"Never!" Beatrice stomped her foot. "I'd rather be tarred and feathered and raked over the proverbial coals before sharing either your name or bed."

"So be it," he sighed, gravely wounded. His pudgy legs woozily turned sideways.

In a fit of unbridled anger, Beatrice twirled on her heels to leave, then stopped. On impulse, she snatched the nearest thing within her reach; a hideous pewter statue of a naked mermaid. Raising the figure high above her head, she aimed for Alastair's head but managed only to slightly clip his slumped shoulder.

"*Uh, oh*," he groaned, weaving to and fro before finally collapsing forward, his head striking a sharp protruding corner of a nearby dresser before crashing backward, smashing against the floor. Blood spurted everywhere.

"Oh, my God," Beatrice screamed out, petrified, rocking back and forth. "Ewww." She stared at the hideous mermaid clutched in her fist and tossed it, intending to chuck it to the ground. But instead, she flicked her wrist mid-toss, causing the damn ugly thing to plop on Alastair's neck. "Ahhh—" she sputtered, nearly retching.

What do I do? What do I do?

Mouth clasped with her gloved hand, Beatrice leaned over Alastair's body, lightly patting his jacket and pants pockets in search for the paper.

"Ewww...ewww," she squealed, never having touched, no less been this close to a dead body before.

Hysterical and incapable of making sense out of what just happened, Beatrice spun in every direction, desperate to find the paper. "Nothing," she groaned, coming up empty-handed. "Where could it be?"

Bones flicked his tail and purred loudly, clawing at the sofa cushion.

"*Ich!*" she screeched, startled. "You scared me half to death, cat!"

A wall clock chimed, and almost immediately, the rest of the other timepieces throughout the shop followed suit. With time quickly slipping away, and no immediate idea where to look, Beatrice gave up her search, anxious to hightail it out of the store and escape undetected. She rushed to the front, ready to pull the door open when an unwelcome blast from the past pushed her way in from the opposite direction, practically toppling Beatrice down.

"Oh, my goodness!" cried Cornelia, startled.

In shock, and unable to respond, Beatrice sprang aside, pressing her back firmly against the doorframe as if willing herself invisible.

"Oh? It's only you, Beatrice. Silly me. I didn't mean to mow you over like that," said Cornelia. "I'm looking for my naughty cat. You didn't happen to see him, did you?"

CHAPTER 4

Darren Crane

DARREN WAITED in the back of the cramped seat of the police car, shifting his weight on the smooth, vinyl seat. He squirmed, desperate to find a comfortable position, but found it challenging to manage with both arms cuffed behind his back. The unfortunate lack of leg space forced him to sit low, lean forward, and bend his head down. He remembered reading somewhere that police cars were specially designed to psychologically subdue people. The powers that be wanted to make it harder for anyone to gain momentum should they decide to lose their minds and launch an assault. Since he no longer felt the lower portion of his extremities, he had to agree.

Darren twisted his neck, barely able to see out of the

reinforced rear windows covered with an intimidating wire mesh, all too reminiscent of prison buses. However, he had little difficulty observing the utter chaos transpiring outside the bullet-proof window. First, with Irwin playing the role of the despondent peacemaker, then Harper and Cornelia competing for chatterbox of the year, and finally, Olivia, her face bright red from arguing, waving her arms bombastically in Detective Moore's face.

"This is the stupidest thing I've ever heard," Olivia exclaimed, huffing and puffing. "You can't go around arresting people for finding dead bodies!"

"Your husband's on parole, ma'am. And we can do exactly that."

"Olivia, please—" Irwin reached out to touch her shoulder, but she jerked away.

"No, Irwin. This is ridiculous. There's a real killer on the loose, and this idiot is wasting everyone's time harassing *innocent* people." Olivia made sure to shout the word *innocent*.

Darren groaned.

She's gonna get me the chair.

"Ma'am, I'm not going to tell you again," reprimanded Detective Moore. "Please step back and away from the police car."

Olivia recoiled her arm, positioning her index finger from the tip—back.

Oh, no—Darren cringed.

Olivia inched closer.

Don't do it, Liv—

Closer...

Ah, shit—

Closer...

"I didn't want to get old anyway," Darren muttered under his breath.

"Ahem." Irwin swooped in, thrusting his body to block the looming pinch attack in the nick of time.

Darren exhaled.

"Listen, Detective, we can vouch for Darren's whereabouts. Case in point, we spent the entire blasted day hanging up puerile holiday decorations together," grumbled Irwin. "Look for yourself. The shop is practically North Pole Central."

"I don't know," said Cornelia nudging Harper. "I think it looks nice."

"So, do I," agreed Harper. "Irwin's just salty because I made him throw out a bunch of questionable decorations from the turn of the century and hang a few lights."

"I am not *salty*—whatever the hell that means," retorted Irwin. "I am trying to explain that Darren couldn't have done this because he was busy with all of us."

"That's fine. You can tell that to one of the officers when he takes all of your statements," explained Detective Moore, turning around.

"The old, guilty until proved innocent, ploy?" muttered Cornelia under her breath. "Officer, is that a real gun?" she asked, reaching out to touch it.

Irwin snatched her hand away.

Harper circled around Irwin and Cornelia to face the detective. "My dad didn't do this," she declared, foot tapping and ready to fight.

"Of course, he didn't," Cornelia wholeheartedly agreed, squirming her way to the front. "This is obviously the work of a serial killer."

That shut everybody the heck up.

"A what?" asked Irwin.

"A serial killer," Cornelia repeated. "Like in, *The Murder at Sweeney Run.*"

Detective Moore flipped a page in his notepad. "I don't think I'm familiar with that case," he said, appearing somewhat perplexed. He lifted his pen, ready to jot notes.

"Because it's not a case, officer," snarled Irwin. "It's one of her confounded, blasted murder mysteries!"

This time the entire group, including the Detective, chorused a groan. Except of course for Cornelia, staring into space, deep in deliberation.

Inside the police car, Darren bounced his head against the plexiglass window. "No-no-no-no-no...Make it stop... Better yet, kill me and get it over with."

Irwin noticed Darren throwing his body upon the altar of doom and tapped the glass. "Hey, motormouth—" *Tap-tap.* "You alright in there?" he asked, bending down, face mashed against the glass.

Darren glanced up and scowled.

Irwin raised a brow and smirked back before joining Olivia busy making her case with Moore. Cornelia, however, took advantage of the distraction to tiptoe over to the police car.

"*Pssst,*" she whispered to Darren, her small frame crouched low enough to peer directly through the glass. Cornelia cupped her cheeks and mouthed, "As-soon-as-he-opens-the-door, make-a-run-for-it."

Darren frantically shook his head no, but Cornelia failed to notice or didn't care.

"Hey, Copper!" she shrieked at the top of her lungs. "I think your prisoner's ready to puke in your nice clean car!" Cornelia hopped from foot-to-foot, waving her arms wildly. She turned her head long enough to give Darren the—go ahead and *RUN* wink.

"What?" Detective Moore rushed past Irwin and yanked the car door open.

"Run, Darren!" Cornelia screamed at the top of her lungs. "I'll cut him off at the pass!"

Darren didn't dare move a single muscle. He didn't even dare breathe.

"That's it!" roared Moore. "You, you, you, and especially you," he pointed explicitly down at Cornelia. "Leave immediately before I have you all arrested."

"Darn it," Cornelia mumbled. "Foiled again."

Before Detective Moore replied, Harper stepped in, tossing a protective arm around Cornelia's shoulder. "Come on, Cornelia, let's wait over there," she said, soothingly.

Apparently impervious to Moore's threats, Darren watched Olivia cross her arms, refusing to budge.

Irwin, equally as obstinate, arched his back defiantly and took a step closer to Olivia. The two stood, pressed shoulder-to-shoulder.

Biting his bottom lip, Detective Moore looked ready to blow a fuse, but instead rubbed his forehead.

Inside the car, Darren held his breath. He recalled the last time he and Moore met head-on years ago. Not the best of first meetings. At the time, Darren had just been released from prison, and he and Harper had a major falling out. The detective, then a street cop, had been called in to keep the peace. Since then, a lot had changed, but apparently not Moore's memory.

"Now, I remember you," Moore blurted out.

Oh no.

"You're those people from the library from a couple of years ago."

Olivia, lips pursed, turned a disquieting shade of embarrassed, flushed red.

Moore chuckled. "The one with the kid who locked herself in the woman's restroom." He glanced at Harper. "That was you, right?"

"That's it. I'm screwed," mumbled Darren, banging his head against the plexiglass again. "Throw away the key."

"And you're the librarian, right?" Moore directed his question to Irwin.

Irwin, about to reply, was handed a temporary reprieve when two additional police cars drove up to the antique store, one parking directly behind the other. A few uniformed officers already working the scene approached the newcomers and the group got busy swapping notes.

Moore, grinning like a Cheshire cat, clasped his hands in triumph. "The name didn't ring a bell at first," he said, "but like I told you, I never forget a face."

"Yes, well," Irwin blanched. "As you have said. Now, Detective, as Mrs. Crane and I have already explained in excruciating detail, Mr. Crane is a victim of an unfortunate and untimely circumstance. He merely lifted the statue to move it out of the way so he—being the good citizen that he is—could check for any life signs emanating from our now dearly departed, Alastair Brooke. All perfectly reasonable, wouldn't you agree?"

Moore shook his head. "I'm bringing him in for further questioning."

Darren bolted straight up. "What?" he yelped, mistakenly banging his head on the inside roof of the vehicle. "No. Listen, you—you don't have to do that," he screamed, bouncing irascibly in his seat. "Ask me anything you want right now. Go ahead. I've got nothin' to hide."

Wide-eyed and furious, Irwin snarled at Darren and

pressed a finger across his own lips. "Shut up, Darren," he hissed. "Keep your mouth closed and don't utter another single, solitary word."

"But—"

"Darren!" Irwin warned, this time clamping his entire hand over his own mouth, before coolly turning around toward the detective. "Mr. Crane wishes to remain silent until he's had the opportunity to consult with an attorney."

With one hand on the car roof, Moore bent down to face Darren. "Is that right, Mr. Crane? Are you invoking your privilege against self-incrimination?"

"My what?"

"He is," answered Irwin.

"Are you?"

"Yeah, I guess," Darren shrugged. "I mean, yes. Yes, I am."

"So, to be clear," said Moore, tempering his voice. "You are now refusing to speak?"

"You're damn right," Darren said while exchanging a succession of rapid head shakes and killer glares with Irwin.

"And that's well within your rights, sir," agreed Moore. "Officer Gibson! Read our Mr. Crane here his Miranda rights."

"Wait, what?" shouted Darren, head turning side to side, confused.

Gibson leaned over, one arm gripping the car door. "You have the right to remain silent," said Gibson.

"*Irwin*," snarled Darren through clenched teeth.

"Anything you say will be used against you in a court of law."

"I can't believe this."

"You have the right to an attorney. If you cannot afford one, one will be appointed to you by the court. With these rights in mind, are you still willing to talk with me about the charges against you?"

Irwin waited until Gibson finished before adding his two cents. "Keep your mouth shut," he whispered to Darren. "The police are going to try to question you, hoping you'll inadvertently give them enough information to support a charge against you."

"But I didn't do anything!" protested Darren.

"I know that, and you know that you imbecile," hissed Irwin, "but this is what they do, even if they don't believe they have enough evidence to hold you."

"What about a warrant?" whined Darren, hunched forward. "Don't they need a warrant?"

Irwin rolled his eyes. "Yes, well, they no longer need one now, thanks in large part to your already admitting to the entire police force that *you-moved-the-damn-statue*. Brilliant, by the way."

Darren glared at Irwin, sufficiently reprimanded, his lips sealed tightly shut.

"He's not a suspect you—you...," snapped Olivia. "*Ugh*, he found the body. Found, as in F-O-U-N-D," she yelled, seething.

Annoyed, Officer Gibson stepped towards Olivia, but Harper blocked his way.

"Don't even think about it."

Irwin quickly shimmied between the officer and the two women in an attempt to diffuse the situation. "Officer," he practically yelped. "Are we able to follow you to the police station?"

Officer Gibson glared at Harper but spoke directly to Irwin only. "There's nothing any of you can do by coming to the police station right now. My suggestion, call a lawyer."

Darren heard it all and slunk lower in his seat, his head pressed against the backseat, his eyes closed. "Yup. I'm screwed," he muttered. "Off to the hoosegow I go."

"This is ridiculous," groaned Olivia, peering over Irwin's shoulder, her index finger pointing at Gibson. "Do something," she insisted, tugging Irwin's sleeve.

"What can I do? As long as they've got probable cause to believe a crime has been committed, and Darren might be the guy who committed it, they can arrest him."

"Mr. Abernathy's correct," added Gibson. "Sir," he said to Darren. "Did you understand your rights?"

Darren glared at Irwin.

Irwin, brow furrowed into a scowl, merely glowered back.

Gibson waited for Darren's answer, ignoring Olivia's hostile glares.

"Darren—for the love of my sanity, zip your lip," insisted Irwin.

"Yeah, I got that part, Irwin," muttered Darren. "No," he said to Gibson. "I got nothin' more to say."

"Good enough." Gibson reached for the door handle, ready to shut the door.

"Wait," yelled Darren, before the door slammed closed. "Irwin, get me a lawyer!"

Irwin's head throbbed. "That's probably the smartest thing he's said all afternoon."

SOON AFTER, the police cleared a path to allow the autopsy technicians to roll Alastair's bagged body out on a gurney and placed it in the van. A few local reporters huddled together behind the crime scene tape took the lull in excitement to taunt and probe Moore with a battery of questions as he walked past. Despite being scared shitless, Darren appreciated the detective's ability to take command of a crime scene.

"Is it true you've apprehended the killer?" yelled one burly reporter called Hank, all of five feet tall, slightly balding, and somewhat thick around the middle. Due to his notorious propensity for telling lecherous jokes, he had been dubbed in some circles as, 'Hank the Skank.' "How about giving us a suspect's name?" he added.

Moore kept walking.

"How long has the victim been dead?" hollered another reporter, shouldering their way forward.

"What's the name of the victim?" shouted another.

"Who found the body?" bellowed Hank, easily drowning out practically everyone else.

Moore, refusing to take the bait, informed his men to have the media moved even further back and walked away.

"Ah, come on already. We're tryin' to do our jobs, too," complained Hank. "I gotta family to feed."

Moore ignored Hank's pleas, and instead gave the flamboyant reporter one last pageantry wave before stepping inside the building. At any other time, Darren would have laughed.

"Darren!" shouted Olivia, tapping the window. "Don't give up hope. We're going to get you out."

"Olivia, stop," said Irwin.

"Do you hear me, Darren?" she cried, waving her arms. "We won't give up on you."

"Come on, Olivia," coaxed Irwin gently. "We need to go."

"I'll get you the best lawyer money can buy," she swore.

This time Irwin refused to take no for an answer and tugged her back. "Let's go before Moore arrests you as well."

"Let him try," she bit back.

"Mom, *please*," Harper pleaded with one hand still gripping Cornelia while the other tugged her mother's sweater. "This isn't helping."

Olivia huffed and puffed but finally conceded, but not before blowing Darren a kiss.

Sure. Now she loves me...

Darren rapidly blinked away the tears welling in his eyes.

Harper sniffled and smeared her face dry with the back of her flannel sleeve.

Darren turned his head in the opposite direction, unable to bear seeing his daughter fall apart.

Damn it.

Eyes clamped shut, Darren pressed on his stomach to suppress the burn surging in his gut.

I did it again.

Right back, where I started...

Head bowed in disgust, Darren did the only thing left to do.

Uh, Dear God. It's me. Darren E. Crane. Look, I know it's been a while since you and I last talked, but as you can tell, I'm in some mega-trouble over here, and I could seriously use your help. First off, for the record, this time, I'm happy to report, I'm one-hundred percent innocent. I didn't do it.

Darren steadied his breath, wishing he could use his arms to wipe his face with his sleeve.

Look at me—what a schmuck, right? Like, how am I telling you—God—what you already know?

His head shook, *sorry*.

Glancing up, he caught from the corner of his eye Irwin tenderly guiding a sobbing Olivia, an irate Cornelia, and a forlorn Harper back into the bookshop. Darren squeezed his eyes tight again and bowed his head.

I have been doing everything I promised you I would, and then some. No more drugs, no more drinking. Hell, I even gave up cigarettes. He stopped to clear the phlegm lodged in his throat.

Please—you gotta help me out here, God. These people, he paused to catch his breath. *They got the wrong guy this time. I'm begging you, God. Don't let them send me back to prison— away from my family. I—I can't go through that again. I can't lose them.*

GETTING LOCKED up and sent to prison for six years had been Darren's fault, although, for years, he tried blaming everybody but himself. At the time, he adamantly refused to take responsibility for his actions or acknowledge how his drug habit had led him to make a host of poor choices, subsequently hurting the people he loved the most, especially Olivia and Harper.

But Moore wasn't the only one who held a less than affable opinion of Darren Crane from years ago. Because of Harper, Irwin and Darren had crossed paths on numerous occasions. At the time, Darren had gone out of his way to scare Irwin away, but Irwin, being the stubborn curmudgeon that he was and still is, had refused to be intimidated by the newly released convict.

"Mr. Crane," Irwin had said, waiting in the halfway house's hallway.

"Ah man, not you again," Darren grumbled upon realizing who was waiting for him. "What's with you coming here? You know, this could be construed as a form of stalking."

Irwin stood facing Darren, refusing to swap banalities. "Have you thought about what we discussed at our last meeting?" he asked, his voice resolute.

"Yeah." Darren locked eyes on Irwin. "I gave it some consideration."

"And? Irwin's stare remained fixed on Darren's sullen face. "What have you decided?"

Darren leaned back on the wall, his arms crossed over his puffed chest. "Before I say anything, I need to know why you're doing this. What's in it for you?"

Impervious to taunts, Irwin stepped closer, eyes locked ominously onto Darren's.

"Mr. Crane, I am not here to debate my motivations. As I explained to you before, if you intend on being a positive influence in Harper's life, then you are welcome. And I will do everything in my power to help make that happen. However, should you decide to leave, I will not stop you, but either way, you decide. Harper has the right to know where you stand."

"Yeah. I'm not an idiot. That part I get, but you haven't exactly told me what's in it for you? What's with all the super protective stuff towards *my kid?*"

"Fair enough." Irwin clasped his hands in front of his body. His shoulders remained stiff. "I have never had children of my own, but I've seen what happens when they've been neglected and abandoned. I've watched promising young lives dissolve under the angst of believing they are unwanted. I've witnessed families torn apart and forever impaired because of one person's self-centeredness. Mr.

Crane, Harper is smart, talented. She has succeeded in becoming an exceptionally good person despite the less than affable hand she's been dealt. I, for one, will not sit idly by and watch you unravel your daughter's questionable stability more than you have already." Irwin narrowed his eyes. "Be in her life, Mr. Crane. She needs and wants a father, despite her current protests. But if you can't and decide to disappear, then do it now before you cause further irreparable damage and heartbreak."

SOMETHING ABOUT THAT CONVERSATION, which took place over a lifetime ago, had snapped Darren to his senses. Since then, Darren had kept to his word, working hard to be the kind of father Harper could be proud of and rely on. Darren struggled to sit up as straight as possible, determined to put on a brave front.

I gotta stay strong.

With too much at stake to indulge in self-serving stupidity, Darren remained committed to not giving into temptation. Things were different now. He had people in his corner who loved him. His family and friends counted on him...believed in him.

I'm not giving up.

Not this time.

Gibson yanked open the door, entered the vehicle, and grabbed his monitor. "This is 1421 to County."

"Okay, 1421."

"I have a suspect in custody, and I'm transporting him to the Lanker County Jail. My starting mileage is 17201. Please place me on a six-minute timer."

Darren closed his eyes and sighed. "Here we go again."

CHAPTER 5

Beatrice Aston

BEATRICE ASTON'S WORLD HAD, in a matter of moments, turned upside down and inside out. Worse, after what she had done, there was no going back. No returning to a life of predictability. Nor would there be any way of avoiding the consequences from events never foreseen, promising to shadow her forever. Beatrice couldn't stop trembling, recalling how Cornelia had pranced around the shop, once less than two feet away from Alastair's bloody dead body.

"Bones?" Cornelia had shouted. "Come here, you naughty cat." Cornelia peeked under a table. "Nope. Not in here."

Beatrice had gasped, scared to death Cornelia would glance down. Thankfully, she took off in the opposite direction, her attention focused on an ornate, antique armoire.

"Are you in here, Bones?" Cornelia muttered, trying to pry it open. "My word," she mumbled out of breath, trying to force the latch to give. "Humongous. Would ya look at the size of this, Beatrice. An entire damn body could fit in this big boy. Come out, come out, wherever you are," crooned Cornelia, peering under benches and tapping tables, as well as other sizable pieces of furniture with her cane. "Okay. That's it," snapped Cornelia, pushing a soft, loose, white, wispy curl away from her face. "I'm serious this time, Bones. Come out right now before you get the both of us into a heap of trouble."

Shaking, Beatrice nudged the door open, mindful not to make the bell attached to the handle tinkle. As soon as Cornelia set off toward the right of the store, Beatrice hightailed it out, too petrified to turn around.

After fleeing from the antique store and unsure what to do, Beatrice, in shock, scrambled across the street. Something, maybe the familiar warmth and camaraderie of the neighborhood donut shop, drew her inside. Once seated, she watched and waited, *but for what?* She had no idea, but her body refused to budge—not until she spotted a man from across the street being handcuffed.

What the hell is going on?

Beatrice fought the urge to stare until joined by the rest of the patrons, all vying for space at the front window.

"What happened?" inquired one woman to nobody in particular. She pointed her straw at Irwin, currently seen arguing across the street with the police.

"I think that's the guy from the bookshop," said her friend. "The one who never talks except to say something sarcastic."

"Huh. I thought he looked familiar. Isn't he a librarian?"

"Was. He bought the book shop a few years ago."

"Look! An ambulance. Somebody's been hurt," informed a man craning his neck and practically leaning on top of Beatrice.

Now Kirk, the owner of the donut shop, ambled over to join the growing fracas. "Holy shit, that's a body bag they're wheeling out."

Kirk's wife, Gladys, whipped around the counter, drying her hands on her apron. "Oh, my Lord, it is. But would ya get a load of Cornelia," she said as Cornelia hobbled over to one of the officers, tapped him on the shoulder, and began jabbing him in the ribs with her cane.

"Whoa," moaned a couple of the gawking customers in unison. Beatrice stared, mouth agape, utterly dumb-founded and incapable of fully grasping what the heck was going on.

Meanwhile, a younger woman with a head full of long wild hair could be seen tugging on another older screaming woman's arm, apparently trying to get her away from the police car, while Irwin—who Beatrice recognized from past township business—managed to swipe the cane from Cornelia's grip, pulling it so hard that it recoiled, popping work boot girl in the butt. The entire spectacle would have been utterly hilarious if Beatrice hadn't wanted to die right there in her chair.

In silence, everyone in the donut shop watched the man being lowered into the police car. Beatrice, overcome with guilt, almost ran outside to set things right. "No, stop! It wasn't him, it was me!" she wanted to scream, but the fear of the unknown kept her fastened in her seat, motionless. Silent.

Cornelia.

Living in a small town, everybody knew everybody else's business—*or thought they did.* It hadn't taken long before Beatrice caught wind through the neighborhood grapevine that Cornelia, suffering from the early onset of dementia, had begun to show signs of losing her memory. Rumor had it that Irwin and his staff had to inform customers regularly to ignore Cornelia whenever she started behaving strangely. Beatrice sighed. Besides the fact Cornelia's loss of memory weighed in her favor, it was still sad that the older woman had to go through it. Losing memories, even the bad ones, were a terrible consequence of an already debilitating disease. Nevertheless, Beatrice, unable to quiet the panic doing summersaults in her gut, recognized the poor woman's dementia couldn't be counted on to keep her identity protected.

Who knows what that crazy old woman will say next—and to who?

Once the police cars left, Beatrice took off for home in a frightened daze, her chest tightening and burning with every anxious step, dreading the thought of being left alone with nothing but dark deliberations and fear for company. Yet, her legs couldn't get her home fast enough.

Beatrice zigzagged and swerved, instinctively taking back roads never before traversed. Eyes twitching, she glanced repeatedly over her shoulder, scared to death of being followed. Marred by shock, she dashed down side streets and through creepy vacant alleyways, only stopping long enough to catch her breath. Once home, Beatrice scrambled up the four steps, key pressed in her fist, hands quivering uncontrollably as she attempted to unlock the front door.

Beatrice owned a quaint, two-family house, located less

than six minutes from where she had been on Main Street—ten if she took her time. But today, the trip home twisted inside her like a maze...

The building had been purchased a few years back. She paid the rest of the outstanding mortgage by renting out the other side to a retired teacher. A pleasant enough lady with a steady pension and four shifty cats.

Nevertheless, having a tenant to offset the debt afforded Beatrice the luxury of renovating the house. Thus far, she had spent a pretty penny turning the old but lovely home into an oasis, upgrading everything from new windows to a new roof. She planned to eventually occupy both sides, but for now, her salary alone wasn't enough to turn that aspiration into a reality, and she certainly wasn't going to do what she did last time when money was tight.

Beatrice preferred her surroundings relatively unadorned and straightforward. A blank slate sporting spotless, white walls. Most of the rooms contained either bleached or light wooden furniture, high-gloss wood floorings covered with the occasional throw rug, also in muted colors, as well as an impressive collection of house plants and unscented candles, all arranged to give the place an airy, but sophisticated appeal.

While leaving most of her walls undecorated, Beatrice did make an exception upstairs along the ascending side of the hallway where she hung a series of black-framed black & white photos filled with impersonal art-deco. Beatrice's functional kitchen followed suit: bright, white, and hardly used, spotless appliances. Nothing adorned the countertops except for a large, ceramic white vase filled with over a dozen fresh, blemish-free, white, long-stemmed roses. The living room housed a single couch, one comfortable side chair, a simple coffee table, two rather tall, well-fed green plants, a small brick working fireplace, and a book-shelf filled to capacity. Beatrice kept her laptop off to the side in a little nook on a small desk, allowing her to work from home whenever necessary.

The moderately-sized bedroom accommodated a single, cast-iron king-sized bed, a tall white dresser, a single side table with a small lamp, and yet another stack of books. Every thread of clothing hung precisely forward on matching white hangers or stacked neatly away in cubbies. A blond, unadorned wood hope chest, a parting gift from her mother on the day Beatrice turned eighteen, remained lodged prominently at the foot of her bed. To Beatrice, the chest had symbolized independence and the start of a promising new life.

In a large wicker basket in the far corner of the bedroom, she kept an impressive collection of throw blan-kets, all knitted by none other than Beatrice herself. A skill she acquired as a child from her grandmother—the single person in her entire family who *got her*.

Typically, a solitary personality, Beatrice not only main-tained her home in pristine order but over time, had created a fortress—a way to seclude her private life from the messiness and disarray of the invasive world. Until recently, that is, when against her better judgment, she had compromised her safety by allowing that annoying little man, Alastair Brooke, an infinitesimal peek into her private domain. A decision she since regretted. Now, in less than a blink of an eye and a wave of a metal-mermaid, none of this mattered any longer.

Still, in shock, Beatrice moved around the house in a manic trance.

Everything has to go, she told herself repeatedly, although, at this point, she wasn't entirely sure where to ditch the evidence since her garbage had already been collected for the week.

She trashed her blood-tainted gloves first, tossing them into a garbage bag, along with her coat and everything else she'd worn—socks and shoes included—*just in case*.

After stripping down to her birthday suit, she knotted the garbage bag tightly closed and headed for the shower. There she stood under a stream of hot water, scrubbing every inch of her body until raw, all the while keeping an ear open for either an approaching police siren or an angry banging at her front door—much in the same way she'd seen play out a hundred times on TV cop shows.

Lost in a gazillion thoughts, Beatrice didn't emerge from the shower until over an hour later, uncontaminated and dirt-free. Her skin pink and puckered like a drenched prune.

With exhaustion threatening to overtake her, she wrapped herself in a cotton bath towel and headed to her bed, desperate to rest, but her mind wouldn't shut off, nor ward off the parade of intrusive thoughts refusing to allow her to surrender to sleep. Wired and overanxious, her brain raced through an endless barrage of possibilities while visions of imminent arrest topped the list.

Determined not to be seen dragged naked through the streets and driven to a police station by a throng of imaginary cop cars currently speeding across town any minute on their way to lock her up, Beatrice swiftly changed into a pair of sweatpants and an old, large tee-shirt—something comfortable for the ride. Fighting exhaustion, she managed to gather her damp hair out of her face, pulling it into a messy bun on the top of her head. Once dressed, she painstakingly tore through every drawer and closet searching for anything that might possibly link her to Alastair, outside of their business relationship.

Phone!

Her stomach constricted.

I'd almost forgotten.

Beatrice snatched her cell phone and proceeded to delete all calls and messages exchanged with Alastair over the past few months. She did this despite knowing it would do little to protect her should the police subpoena the phone company for her records.

Overly paranoid, Beatrice slowly peeled the curtain back in her bedroom, half expecting to see a horde of police lying in wait, and ready to storm her home. She pictured tomorrow's headlines—'Murderess Captured.' She hoped they wouldn't plaster some ugly mug shot photo of her across the front page of the paper—or worse—use the old one taken of her the last time she'd gotten into a legal kerfuffle.

For now, though, the block remained quiet...undisturbed. Beatrice squeezed her eyes closed, and released the edge of the curtain, allowing it to flutter shut.

"Oh God, what have I done," she wept, crumpling to her knees, sobbing inconsolably into her folded, trembling hands. "What have I done?"

Beatrice awoke sometime during the middle of the night, still sprawled out on her bedroom floor and drenched in sweat. Frazzled, she sat up too fast. "*Ouch*," she groaned, gripping her tender arms. She tried to stand, only to realize her entire body ached and plopped back down. The pounding behind her eyes from crying hurt even more. Eager for the warmth and comfort of her bed, Beatrice shifted her weight onto her knees and crawled the remainder of the way over to the bed.

"One," she groaned. "Two...three!" She flung herself on top of the bed, flopping down on the starched white sheets face first.

"Now roll." In one big, sloppy movement, she twisted and rolled far enough to land beneath the luxuriously soft, inviting, white cotton covers. Staring at the ceiling, she imagined an itchy, institutionalized, gray wool blanket draped across her body.

WITH THE MORNING came filtered rays of bright light shining straight into Beatrice's bedroom. Usually, that would have been enough motivation, but not even the glare from penetrating sunshine managed to rouse her. It wasn't until moments later when her phone alarm blared did she bolt straight up and finally jolt awake. With an extended sore arm, she swiped at the button, missing the first three times.

"Damn it, damn it, damn it," she muttered, her face still under the blanket. In a huff, she reached out again and turned off the annoying alarm, snuggling under the covers for a few more minutes—only to be jarred when her cell phone rang. She glared with blurry eyes at the screen.

The job—

She checked the time. "Shit. I'm late," and let the call go to voice mail.

Do the condemned still go to work or do they stay home, using what precious time they had left to pack all their personal effects, she wondered miserably.

Beatrice glanced around the room. She kept everything considered personal in that hope chest. The rest of her stuff, while essential, could be replaced.

But what about my life?

At fifty-two, she considered herself reasonably young. Indeed, nowhere ready to die behind prison walls, becoming some strapping, tattooed chick's girlfriend, and fated to be buried six feet down in some prison potter's field.

Who'll come to visit me?

Beatrice sniffled...

Her mother had passed years ago, and her father, while presumably still alive, had left them both decades earlier. Painfully aware of how much her former coworkers disliked her, she assumed they would probably be the first to celebrate her demise.

Beatrice sighed.

They think I don't know what they call me behind my back.

Beatrice the Ball Breaker...

Beatrice Sticky Fingers...

Beatrice from the Block... (Beatrice didn't quite get the inference to that one.)

Beatrice...the Prying Bitch.

But of all the names she'd been crowned, *Beatrice the Bandit* was the worst. This was the thoughtless nickname bestowed upon her during an excruciatingly and embarrassing period in her life when she had lost all common sense and given into embezzlement to pad her pocket and pay her bills. Getting caught had been nothing short of humiliating.

Beatrice, who liked nice things more than she should have.

Leading up to that disgraceful debacle, Beatrice had been considered by her supervisors as one of their most dependable and trustworthy employees...one of their top accountants known for accuracy and meticulousness. Under her attentive, eagle eye, every penny that came in and out of the company would be scrupulously accounted for. After working for the same company for a mere three years, she had been granted full custody of the company's funds—monies that she would eventually appropriate to support an extravagant lifestyle her meager weekly paychecks failed to cover.

In the beginning, Beatrice had convinced herself that she was merely 'borrowing' the funds, making sure to only skim off a tiny bit at a time. A little bit here, a little bit there to ward off the possibility of suspicion. Then, as soon as payday rolled around, she'd return what she *borrowed* in full, and for a time, her system worked perfectly with no one the wiser.

'Borrowing' funds, as Beatrice called it, had become increasingly too tempting for a young woman whose hunger for a more comfortable life outweighed the risk. It hadn't helped that the company's lax accounting methods and inadequate supervision made committing larceny ridiculously easy.

Soon enough, Beatrice began absconding with sizable chunks of money under the misguided presumption that somehow the company underpaid her and owed her at least this bit of extra. *Besides*, she told herself, *they made money hand over fist...what would a little till-swiping do to hurt them?*

Then her manager, Carl Witherspoon, began to take notice of the inordinate amount of overtime Beatrice repeatedly put in, staying way past everyone else and being the last to always leave. However, he told the police later on that he had only become suspicious of actual wrong-doing when she insisted on working from home and taking company files with her.

"You look exhausted," Carl said to Beatrice one afternoon. "Why don't you take some of that vacation time you've saved up over the year."

"No!" Beatrice replied, a bit too aggressively. "I mean, I'm fine."

"Nonsense," insisted Carl. "You know company policy. Use it or lose it, and you've certainly earned it, so take it—enjoy yourself on some exotic beach with your toes in the sand and drinking coolatas." The words out of Carl's mouth, although ambiguous enough, told a completely different story.

Beatrice began to panic. "I can't."

"Why not? The time's yours."

"I mean, there's too much work to finish," she said, grabbing a few files protectively to her chest. "I, um, need to get back to work. Excuse me."

"Leave 'em," he said, reaching out to grab them away. "I'll have Anne cover for you."

"No. Really...I'll do it," said Beatrice, her voice jittery, gripping onto the files. "But thanks anyway," she had said, guiltily scurrying off to her office and locking the door behind her.

"What the hell was that all about?" asked Gloria, one of Beatrice's managers.

"I'm not entirely sure," said Carl. "I offered to let Anne cover for her, take some of the work off her pile."

"I heard."

"Then you caught her reaction, right? I mean, could she be that worried someone will mess up her system?"

Gloria shook her head. "That or she's nervous about somebody finding irregularities."

Carl winced. "We're talking about Beatrice—she's one of our most highly regarded employees."

"I agree, she is, but I'm suggesting we watch our Ms. Aston more closely."

Carl nodded. "Okay. Fine. We watch her closely, but let's keep this between us for now. No use in sounding the alarms yet. If she is on the take, I don't want her to know we are on to her."

Gloria nodded. "I concur. No use making everyone in the office paranoid."

"So, it's agreed—what we've discussed stays between us for now. We'll observe everyone—examine all our employees—including any freelance workers we have coming in and out. This is too serious to start throwing accusations around without proof of any kind."

Over the coming months, the skimming of the office petty cash and other lower-level theft had been brought to Carl's attention. Then the numbers on some of the larger accounts didn't accurately match up either. All signs of a more severe fraud occurring.

Police records later indicated that Carl had first made a phone call to an outside investigator to get to the bottom of things—somebody who would do their job objectively with no personal feelings about the outcome, whatever it may be, one way or the other.

After that day with Carl, the walls closed in on Beatrice. What she had already stolen had exceeded her salary considerably. And although she may have initially started her life of crime with the intent to return every cent taken, it soon became apparent—*even to her*—that it would take a whole lot more finagling and cooking of the books to extricate herself from the larcenous cycle that she alone had set into motion.

Beatrice had been smart, but not smart enough.

She would never forget the day of her arrest.

What a mess.

The police came to the office unexpectedly one morning and went straight to Carl's office. Gloria and another woman, the new hire, soon followed. Everyone disappeared behind the closed door, as did her hopes of righting her many wrongs. For a minute or two, she had actually thought about running away, leaving before they came for her, but the police officer they had securing the exit crushed that hope as well. It hadn't taken long before they brought Beatrice in for questioning.

"Beatrice?" said Carl, moments later, peeping his head into her office. "There are some people here who would like to speak with you."

"Me?"

"Yes," he said, his ordinarily colorless face now a sickly pallid gray. "They have some questions for you."

"Questions? What kind of questions?"

"Please, come inside," he answered curtly, holding the door open.

Beatrice's heart raced. With trembling hands, she reached over to lock her desk drawer, but before she finished, a strange face entered her space.

"I'll take those, Miss. Aston," said the tall, suited man.

"I'm sorry?" Beatrice tried but failed to keep her shaky voice composed. "You have me at a disadvantage. And you are?"

"Detective James Lombardi, Fraud Department."

At that very moment, life as Beatrice knew it came to a stop.

The police were there to interrogate Beatrice, but they'd already known full well she was guilty—caught practically red-handed. By later that evening, they'd led her away in handcuffs.

Beatrice had embezzled close to twelve thousand dollars, making her crime a felony, with the potential of one to ten years in prison and a $10,000 fine. Fortunately for Beatrice, her employer didn't want to risk the bad publicity. Furthermore, since this was a first offense, the attorney, with her former employer's support, pleaded with the court to show leniency. Luckily for Beatrice, the judge acquiesced, offering to have the embezzlement charges dropped, and the case dismissed altogether *if* Beatrice agreed to return the money within a three-month period.

Beatrice didn't have to be told twice. She sold everything to raise the money, including her car, and her jewelry. Once the last repayment had been made, Beatrice, now unemployed, was free to relocate and seek employment elsewhere. To Beatrice's shock, a job opened for a proper job two counties over in a Municipal County office. Beatrice snapped up the job when offered, despite making only a third of what she had earned in the past.

After her arrest, Beatrice turned over a new leaf, staying on the straight and narrow to conceal her past indiscretions. She worked hard to seal herself away from judgment and potential scorn. To complete the transition, she drastically altered her appearance overnight, going from hot-to-trot to frumpy-and-forgettable. With head held high, she refused to become the brunt of anyone's insults or sympathy. She'd make it on her own and rebuild her life, one minuscule—but perfectly legal—paycheck at a time.

Then she faltered in her plan.

Alastair had been the first person in a long time to take any substantial notice of her despite her dowdy appearance and snooty attitude. At the time, Beatrice genuinely liked him, but halfway into their second date, the real

Alastair Brooke showed up. Snarling at the waiter, nitpicking endlessly about a perfectly acceptable meal, and then badmouthing any person the pint-sized, insidious jerk came into contact with.

Beatrice despised people like him and refused any further advances. Only then did she find out that Alastair Brooke had been one of her former company's clients. Somehow, without her knowledge, he had been made privy to her past scandal. Since turning him away, the little jerk had used the information to torment her, holding her dismissal paperwork over her head to make her toe the line.

In hindsight, Beatrice blamed her loneliness for accepting his invitation to dinner. For everything that transpired after—she blamed her utter stupidity.

CHAPTER 6

Irwin

THAT EVENING, Irwin joined Olivia and Harper upstairs in their apartment. He sat slumped at the kitchen table fidgeting in his seat, occasionally sneaking a quick glance in Harper's direction, watching her systematically destroy her umpteenth napkin, and sinking deeper into despair. Clearly, she required assurance. Perhaps, even a strong, supportive shoulder to cry on. Irwin opened his mouth several times, but closed it before uttering a single word, dreadfully incapable of finding the right thing to say. So instead, he elected to remain silent, mindlessly clinking a spoon against the rim of his teacup like a big, old, worthless grump on a log.

From the adjacent room, Irwin heard Cornelia snoring

like a chainsaw. Along with the snoring came intermittent loud snorts and grumblings. He imagined her battling with a gang of fictional characters kept sealed in her brain, all vying for space and attention.

Dementia had recently begun to tire Cornelia more often, causing his old friend to take frequent short catnaps while sitting in her chair. Then, more often than not, she'd jolt awake, clearly disorientated and uncharacteristically irritable. Tonight, she sat tipped over with her head cranked against the sofa cushion in an awkward position, her mouth opened wide enough to expose an impressive set of ancient tonsils. Bones, her trusty feline sentinel, lay snuggled across her full lap purring contentedly; unaffected by the unseemly racket. These days, the two devoted companions were hardly ever apart.

Olivia, on the other hand, refused to sit or relax, much too wired to stay in one place for long since Darren's arrest. All her scooting back and forth around the apartment in search of something worth fussing over made Irwin dizzy. Scurrying from room to room to tidy up, spinning in every which direction like a whirling dervish. Anything to keep busy and her mind off Darren wallowing away in some jail cell, and this time, for a crime he honestly didn't commit.

Harper reached across the table for a fresh napkin to annihilate. Irwin watched as her long, slender fingers mercilessly twisted the paper by the far corner, shaping it into the finest point. But no matter how tight she wound it, it would inevitably loosen as soon as the pressure lifted. Undeterred, she'd twist to initiate her torment again.

Harper glanced up at Irwin, "Must you?" she asked, thoroughly annoyed by his clanking.

"Oh." Irwin positioned the spoon at the edge of his

plate under Harper's fixed, disheartened glare. "Sorry." He rubbed his hands together, miserable that he had nothing helpful to offer—nothing to help alleviate the frustration. Not yet, anyway.

Harper banged the table with her fist. "Would you say something already?" she blurted out, clearly exasperated.

Irwin grimaced. "I don't know what it is that you want me to say?" he replied, his strained eyes meeting her stony stare.

"I don't know. Say something. Anything."

"Something. Anything," Irwin repeated, making a feeble attempt to wheedle out of Harper a smile.

"Funny, ha-ha," Harper groaned, flashing Irwin an exhausted pout. "You know, I'm sitting here trying to make sense out of this craziness, but no matter what I come up with—which isn't much—I still can't believe that any of it is really happening. I mean, I really can't."

"And yet, here we are," he replied in his usual deadpan voice.

Harper crumbled the remains of her latest dilapidated napkin into a ball and added it to the growing mound. "There's got to be something we're missing. Something we can do," she implored. "You know full well that with Dad's past record, they'll ship him back to prison in a heart-beat—guilty or not."

Harper's father, a former drug user, had done time for assault and battery, but over the past two years, he'd been out on parole, managing his responsibilities without a single hiccup. His parole officer, Jay, had even commented at his last check-in that Darren, by all accounts, had turned into a solid, model citizen; one of his few success stories to date. However, the accusation of being considered a cold-blooded murderer could quickly put a damper on even the most exemplary citizen's reputation.

"He needs a lawyer," said Harper. "A good one."

"I agree," Irwin sighed. "I plan on contacting my attorney first thing in the morning." Without thinking, he lifted his spoon again, but this time, Harper, without missing a beat, reached over and snatched it out of his hands before the next round of clanging could commence. Irwin humphed, crossing his arms defiantly across his chest, but didn't bother to resist.

"But I thought your guy only handled commercial real estate?" interrupted Olivia, busy emptying the dishwasher.

"He does," agreed Irwin, "but I plan to ask for a referral."

"Good idea." Olivia dried her hands on a dish towel. "Harper, I forgot to ask you earlier. Did you get a chance to move your father's things out of Christopher's apartment? He meant to do that before all this happened." Now that Christopher lodged at school, it only made sense for Darren to use his studio apartment down the hall temporarily.

Harper nodded. "I changed the sheets on the bed, left fresh towels, but didn't touch Dad's stuff in the second closet, or on his dresser."

"That's fine." Olivia checked the time on her way into the living room. "I wonder what's keeping that boy?"

A loud trio of knocks at the front door startled everyone.

"Anybody home?" In popped a familiar, most welcoming face. "I knocked but—"

"Christopher!" shouted Olivia, rushing toward him, arms spread open. "I was just talking about you. Irwin, Harper, it's Christopher!"

Irwin slid out of his chair to join the welcoming committee with Harper trailing closely behind. Never entirely sure what to do in any given social setting, he did what he usually did—nothing—waiting impatiently for Olivia to stop fussing. However, when she leaned in for a third hug, Irwin protested.

"Okay, now. Let the poor fella breathe," he teased, gripping Christopher's hand for a shake, and pumping it up and down.

Christopher laughed, then tugged Irwin into a bear hug. The two friends embraced, each offering the other a succession of well-placed-guy-pats on the back.

"You look good," said Irwin, holding Christopher's shoulders while he studied his face closer.

"Nonsense," interjected Olivia. "He looks too thin. Are you eating enough?"

"I thought I was," said Christopher, patting his flat stomach.

"Ignore the local food-pusher," said Irwin, winking—thoroughly enjoying having the whole clan back in the nest.

Well, almost the whole clan...

"It feels great to be home," said Christopher.

Home...

Irwin's lips curved into an almost perceptible smile. He still found it difficult to believe that this group of people, who, not long ago, were total strangers, were now more like his family.

"I've missed you guys something fierce," Christopher told them all, although Irwin noticed when Christopher's eyes lingered a second or two longer on Harper than on anyone else.

Never one to miss her chance at being included,

Cornelia pretended to slowly stir awake, stretching her neck, while dramatically fluttering her eyes open. She spread her arms wide apart, wiggling her fingers in Christopher's direction to indicate it was her turn for a hug.

Christopher laughed, leaned over, and placed a big, noisy smooch on her soft, awaiting cheek. "I've missed you, beautiful," he whispered playfully, pecking her again on the other cheek.

Cornelia beamed. "Glad to have you back home. Aren't we, Harper?" she said, shooting Harper a devilish side-wink. Then she squeezed Christopher's toned upper arms. "Oh my, my, my," she moaned admiringly. "Nice and firm. Just the way I like 'em."

Christopher blanched, beseeching Irwin for assistance.

"Behave, old gal. You're making the poor boy blush," he said.

Cornelia clapped. "Outstanding. That means I haven't lost my touch."

Meanwhile, Harper, still standing off to the side, played it cool. "Hey," she finally offered Christopher, offering him the limpest wave hello.

"Hey? Is that's all I get? Totally lame," he teased, scooping Harper into his arms for a big hug.

"Dork," she giggled through fits of spontaneous laughter, pretending to push him away.

"You know you missed me," he countered, still whirling her around.

"Missed you?" she laughed. "You're delusional!"

"Stop your lyin'..."

The rest of the threesome watched in amusement as Christopher gently lowered Harper to the floor, leaving one arm casually hooked around her slim waist.

Irwin, usually clueless in matters of the heart, finally comprehended the unspoken rapport brewing between the young duo. Unfiltered, he got ready to imprudently blurt something out when Olivia swooped in out of nowhere and—

"*Ouch!* He snarled at Olivia, rubbing his sore, freshly pinched forearm. "Would you kindly, *please* stop doing that?"

However, Olivia apparently didn't care—much too busy signaling Irwin with her eyes to shut the heck up.

Meanwhile, Harper, having difficulty maintaining eye contact with Christopher without blushing, jokingly poked him in his side. "You're ridiculous."

"Guilty as charged," said Christopher, lowering his arms and playfully exposing his wrists as if waiting to be handcuffed.

In that instant, the air evaporated from the room.

Christopher watched as his friends faces instantly turned grim and slowly dropped his hands to his side, confused. He glanced first at Irwin, who stood, head bowed, staring at the ground. Then glimpsed Harper, flighting to blink back tears, her hand covering her mouth to suppress a sob. "All right. What's going on?"

Olivia turned her face away to dry her eyes.

"Olivia—" sighed Christopher.

"Before we get into all that, why don't you put your things down?" she instructed, deliberately ignoring Irwin and Cornelia's glares. "Anywhere is fine."

Christopher slipped his knapsack off his shoulder and dropped it on the floor but made an extra effort to lean his computer backpack safely against the wall.

"Man, what a trip," he said ultra-cheerily to the depressing room, obviously trying to lift the mood. "Traffic's everywhere. Even I-80 was backed up for like six miles straight. Hard to tell if it was holiday traffic holding every-thing back or an accident. Luckily, I remembered the few side-roads Irwin showed me the last time, and got off the highway, and—" Christopher abruptly stopped mid-sentence. "Look you guys, I'm not always the sharpest tool in the shed—"

"No, that honor goes to Irwin," announced Cornelia.

Irwin rolled his eyes.

"Maybe," shrugged Christopher, "but even I can see that something's seriously wrong. What gives?"

Olivia eyeballed Harper, then shot Irwin another warning glare.

"Aw, come on you guys," Christopher frowned. "It's me. You know, Christopher? What's up?" He stared pleadingly at the four solemn faces around the room. "Is it me? Did I do something wrong?"

All four murmured a resounding, *No... Don't be silly...Not you... It's kind of complicated...*

"Ah, huh," muttered Christopher, clearly unconvinced. "Well, not for nothin', but it's got to be a whole lot more than complicated. I mean, honestly, you all look like death warmed over—no offense."

"Offense taken, young man," carped Cornelia, strug-gling to make her body sit up straight. "I'm eighty-nine years old. What the hell do you expect me to look like at eleven-thirty at night?"

"Cornelia!" chastised Harper gently.

"Cornelia nothin' —I can't be expected to look like a beauty queen all the time you know," she grumbled, play-fully sticking her tongue out at Harper.

"Ignore her," whispered Olivia. "Hey, I bet you're hungry."

"Famished. You don't know how much I've missed your cooking."

"Excellent," said Olivia, "because I've been keeping a plate warm in the oven for you."

Christopher yawned. "Sorry. Long day. I'm gonna bring my stuff over to my place. I'll be right back." Christopher's studio was located on the same floor, only a short distance down the shared hall.

"I'll give you a hand," offered Irwin.

"That works," said Olivia. "While you do that, I'll put on a pot of water. I think we can all use a hot cup of tea."

Cornelia rocketed to attention. "Tea? More tea?" she protested muttering under her breath, her pointer finger wagging in the air. "Screw tea. I swear, these damn people...forever plying me with tea," she complained. "At my age, I need the stronger stuff. Gotta keep this old ticker of mine running," she exclaimed, tapping her chest.

Christopher chuckled.

"Ha! So, you find that funny, do you?" Cornelia extended an arm for Christopher to hold. "Come here, you. Bring those sexy, young, toned muscles over and help an old lady out, would ya?"

Christopher

CHRISTOPHER GATHERED HIS THINGS. "Following you, Irwin," he said, unable to ignore how Harper leaned against the wall, clamping down on her bottom lip, deep in thought. Her beautiful dark eyes appeared tired and strained. He fought the overwhelming urge to reach out to hold her...comfort her. As if able to read his mind, she thrust her open palm in his direction.

"Don't," she mumbled softly.

Unlike Harper, who decided to attend college locally, Christopher had enrolled in a university located in Manhattan, New York. He had come dangerously close to changing universities a few times to remain close after Cornelia's outbursts increased and her health declined. In the process of scouting out a school closer to home, Irwin had somehow managed to catch wind of Christopher's plan and stepped in—nixing it cold turkey.

"No. Absolutely and unequivocally not," Irwin told him. "You stay put. We have everything under control. Between Olivia, Harper, and Darren and myself, we'll make sure the old gal stays safe and sound."

"But Irwin—"

"No, Christopher. I mean it. Your only concern right now is school—and graduating, of course." Irwin tilted his head and whispered into his ear. "Besides, that gadget you made will help."

"I'll be fine," said Cornelia, absentmindedly fidgeting with the heart-shaped neckless clasped around her neck. "You worry too much. Besides, it's not like I don't have more than enough bodyguards nosing around in my business as is," she grumbled. "Consider your services terminated. Thank you very much and have a good day."

Olivia stepped in front of Cornelia. "We promise, Christopher. We'll take good care of everyone while you're gone. Now please, go out into the world and make us proud."

Thinking back, Harper had remained strangely quiet during that conversation, not adding her usual two cents. Truth be told, although Christopher may have eventually acquiesced, Cornelia's waning health wasn't the only reason he wished to stick around.

IRWIN CAUGHT the coquettish exchange between the young pair. "Ah. I see," he muttered flummoxed. He lifted Christopher's computer bag over his shoulder. "Let's get you settled in and fattened up before we dump the world's predicaments upon your able shoulders."

"Thanks for letting Darren use your place while you were gone," Olivia replied with false cheerfulness. "The couch was getting uncomfortable for him."

"No problem." Christopher nodded. "Glad, to do it."

"By the way," added Olivia, "Harper moved most of her father's stuff out, but left his clothes in the second hall closet and in the extra dresser."

"That's fine, but she really didn't need to do all that. I don't need much space." Christopher snuck another glance at Harper, still unable to read her face. "You know, I'm more than happy to hear everything now."

"No, no, no," insisted Irwin, with a weary, gloomy sigh. "Trust me, son. This piece of news is best digested on a full stomach."

"And brandy," urged Cornelia, trailing closely behind the pair. "Better make mine a double."

CHRISTOPHER ATE and listened while the group, sometimes all talking at the same time, filled him on the latest debacle.

"It was awful," interjected Harper, viciously snapping a

cookie in half, leaving crumb droppings everywhere.

"Alastair's a first-class turd, but he didn't deserve this," grumbled Cornelia.

"And then the police came and arrested Darren! I mean, how stupid can they be? It's obvious Darren didn't do anything, but do you think that cop would listen?" Olivia exhaled a long, thick, raspy breath.

"Wait," interrupted Christopher, a forkful of food dangling in front of his lips. "Are you all telling me that Darren's in jail?"

"Correct," said Irwin.

Stunned, Christopher released his grip on his fork, sending it clanking against his almost empty plate. "Damn."

"And awaiting arraignment sometime tomorrow morning," explained Irwin. "Which is why I must find him a good criminal attorney. Somebody we can trust."

"—and afford," added Olivia.

"Never mind that right now, Liv," assured Cornelia. "We'll figure something out. Right, Irwin?"

Irwin nodded. "Of course."

"I don't know." Olivia lowered her gaze, wringing her hands. "Attorneys are expensive, and it's not like we can afford a whole lot."

Harper leaned in closer and gave her mom a hug. "It's going to be okay. Like Cornelia said, we'll figure something out."

"Uh, I might actually know somebody," interjected Christopher. "I mean, I did. Well, I kind of still do."

"Oh, my stars and garters, young man, which is it?" carped Cornelia, swiping a wafer cookie off Irwin's plate.

"Do. It's definitely a do. I do know somebody." Christopher paused. "Sorry. I'm just shocked right now.

What I'm trying to say but making a mess of it is—I heard through the grapevine that one of my former classmates, Taylor Maldonado, works here in town. Actually, the office is fairly close to the courthouse, if I'm not mistaken."

"A criminal attorney?" asked Harper.

"Yes. And a damn good one, excuse my French." Christopher inched his hand towards Harper's and squeezed. "Listen, Taylor was ahead of me in school. Got hired right out the box. Why don't I make a call first thing in the morning?" he glanced at his watch. "Ah, make that in a few hours."

"Thank you, Christopher. That would be wonderful," said Olivia, reaching across the table to clasp his wrist. "What a relief."

"Well, make sure to tell your friend, Taylor, that my father's innocent," exclaimed Harper, returning to her seat.

"I agree," said Olivia. "I might not have been able to say that same thing a few years ago, but I sure can now—and with no hesitation. Darren's not capable of hurting anyone anymore—even that imbecile, Alastair Brooke."

Irwin had to concur. For him, how Alastair died was not in question. It had only taken one naked mermaid statue smashed to the noggin to finish him off properly. And the where? Easy–the shop. That only left the why?

What motivated someone enough to kill Alastair?

Once Irwin discovered that, everything else would most assuredly fall into place.

"I better get some sleep," said Christopher, his stare fixed on a sulking Harper.

Bushed and ready to call it a night, Irwin rubbed his eyes, suppressing a yawn. "That makes two of us." He slipped his coat on. "Until tomorrow, everyone."

CHAPTER 7

Harper Crane

Two weeks ago, ...

For some time, Harper had been staying over at Cornelia's house frequently to help her store a few of her most prized possessions.

"What do you want me to do about the rest of this stuff?" asked Harper one evening a few weeks back, as she taped a labeled cardboard box securely closed.

"When the time comes, take what you want. Same goes for Irwin, Olivia, Darren—Christopher. Donate what you can, and toss the rest," said Cornelia, matter-of-fact, but inside, where fear kept her locked in a vice, she wanted to scream.

"That's not what I meant," objected Harper, visibly

saddened. "I mean, what did you want me to do with that stuff over there?" She pointed to the far corner of the living room at a pile of photo albums and stacks of framed photographs. "I can box the albums easily enough, but the frames have glass. I'll need tissue paper for those."

Cornelia hobbled over, leaned down, and picked up a small handmade clay dish shaped like a birdbath with a pair of delicate tiny birds perched on the rim. "This is one of my favorite pieces," she said, placing it tenderly off to the side. Then she lifted an antique framed picture, an old photo of her and her late husband on the day they married.

We sure were a handsome couple.

Cornelia bit down on her bottom lip until she tasted blood.

Harper labeled the next box with a permanent magic marker. "You looked stunning in your wedding dress."

Cornelia touched the filigree frame. "My mother made it for me. She was quite the seamstress. Everyone came near and far to our home when they needed a gown or something altered."

"Your husband looked handsome, too."

"Oh, yes. Always quite *the looker.*"

Unfortunately, he couldn't control his anger.

After a passing, cursory glance, Cornelia tossed the frame back on the pile, glass and all. "I don't think these old things will mean much to anyone but me."

Harper lifted the sealed box and stacked it carefully on top of the others. "They mean something to me."

Harper

HARPER FINISHED PUTTING AWAY the packing tape, markers, the bubble wrap, but especially the scissors while Cornelia napped. It had been a long and challenging day for them both. Cornelia's constant rummaging had become her latest endeavor. A coping mechanism which Harper supposed made Cornelia feel initially productive, but ultimately caused her to become progressively agitated and paranoid; stressing out over a supposed lost document, a missing set of keys, or 'stolen' financial papers. Once she fell apart over a missing piece of valuable jewelry she actually never owned. Unable to discuss the matter with either Irwin or her folks, Harper decided to speak to her psychology Professor, Dr. Flanigan, the next day.

"You said she's started to search for things?" asked Professor Flanigan, busy packing her briefcase, getting prepared to leave to her next class across campus.

"Not every day, but more than before. At first, I thought, no big deal, right? Until I realized Cornelia's need to re-organize things might be a part of her disease process. I'm not sure what I should do about it?"

"First and foremost, I'm not your friend's doctor, but I can tell you this—I went through something similar with my dad and his dementia. However, in his case, we lost him once he started making sorting and rummaging a constant, everyday thing."

"Cornelia's not that bad yet. Only once in a while, so far. Can I ask what you did about it?"

"I turned his insatiable urge into a structured packing and sorting routine. That helped reduce some of his anxiety and agitation."

Harper jotted the advice down on her phone. "That makes perfect sense, and that's something Cornelia might eventually enjoy as well."

"It's a better alternative." The Professor grabbed her coat off the hook.

"One more thing," rushed Harper. "I've noticed that Cornelia doesn't always remember to check expirations dates on her food, so I've been trying to remind myself to do that weekly; going through her cabinets and the refrigerator to make sure there's nothing in there to get her sick."

The professor nodded approvingly. "Good move."

"I also caught her the other day staring at some cleaning fluid. I got nervous she'd mistakenly grab it thinking it was a drink or something. That totally freaked me out."

"Perfectly reasonable reaction. I once caught my father ready to pop a raw shrimp into his mouth." The Professor checked the time. "Walk with me."

Harper hiked her backpack over her shoulder, taking long strides to keep up.

"I assume you've removed all the cleaning supplies since? Under lock and key?"

"For sure," nodded Harper. "I've been going around proofing her house, and anywhere else she spends time, but it's so hard to anticipate what she'll do or get into next."

"Unless you can watch over your friend 24-7, which is nearly impossible to do, there will always be something. For example, at one point, I remember having to contact the post office to redirect all my dad's mail to my house since he kept destroying anything he could get his hands on—bills, tax documents, letter and cards from family— you name it."

Harper sighed. "A friend of mine gave Cornelia a necklace in the shape of a heart, so of course she loves it, but it's really a GPS thing—I have an app on my phone."

"That's brilliant. I wish I'd have thought of that with my dad. He was forever wandering away—even after we got him in the adult center. Drove the nurses nuts."

"Cornelia does the same thing, or tries to."

"Do you have help?"

"I do. My parents and her best friend all help so she's never alone, but still..."

"Not easy," lamented Professor Flanigan.

"No," Harper exhaled heavily. "Not at all."

"Have you thought about the possibility of placing her in an adult living facility where they have round-the-clock care? I know it's not the greatest solution, but it might be the best one all around." The Professor shoved open the door to the back staircase with her shoulder, then held it open for Harper to step through. "We can go this way instead of crossing the courtyard. It's freezing out there. You were saying?"

"Actually, Cornelia's been pushing for that recently," said Harper, walking fast to keep up. "She makes jokes about it...that's her way, but I think she knows that eventually, she's going to need more help than we can give her—health-wise. So far, her biggest issue is forgetting words or names. That frustrates her. But most of the time, she's pretty lucid." Harper's cheeks turned flush.

"Sorry," said the professor, slowing her pace after noticing Harper breathing hard. "Then what's the problem?"

"We're the problem." Harper tensed. "We don't want to let her go. I don't want to let her go."

"That's a big problem, but one I fully understand. It's tough to hand over the care of a loved one to a stranger," voiced the Professor. "Again, not easy." She gestured with her hand for Harper to follow down the hall into the next classroom. "Listen, Harper, my next class is starting in a few minutes, so I'm going to have cut this short, but let me say this—there are no quick fixes for this illness. It's a ruthless, unforgiving, cruel disease for any person to experience, and equally as miserable and challenging for their loved ones. It did a number on my brother and me when we went through it. In all honesty, I'm only grateful my mom wasn't alive to watch it go down. It would have destroyed her."

"It's having a field day with us."

"I can imagine."

Students started filing noisily into the room. Harper smiled. "Thanks for your insight, Professor Flanigan. This really puts what I was feeling into perspective. I've been finding it difficult to talk to my family about it. Everyone's in denial...walking on eggshells these days, pretending that Cornelia's having an off moment, an off day or an off entire week, but she's getting worse, and this whole thing scares me. I don't want her to get hurt."

"And you're right to feel this way. Your friend's symptoms will continue to worsen as times goes on, and it is scary, even terrifying, which is why, in my most non-judgmental way, I encourage you and your family to listen to Cornelia if she's lucid enough to make decisions about her care. Pay attention when she expresses to you what she needs. And as hard as it's going to be to let go, respect her wishes and give her the gift of dignity. Give her the room and support to make whatever final life choices she can before her disease process robs it all from her."

That evening, Harper slipped out of the apartment to take a walk alone. She hadn't meant to go far, but once she started walking, she couldn't stop. Her unplanned journey eventually brought her across town to a familiar secluded spot. As if by rote, she marched through the wrought iron gates, down the still visible, snow-covered walkway, her boots crunching against patches of ice, passing row after row of names and dates, all elegantly etched on stone. When she finally reached her destination, she plopped down on a cold, hard bench. Within in seconds—if that long, her eyes welled up in tears.

Alone on that icy bench, she sobbed and sobbed until exhausted, but even then, no amount of shed tears could erase or alter the unbearable realization that Cornelia would soon slip away forever. It felt almost too much for Harper to face.

Sniffling, she dug into her coat pocket in search of a tissue. A soft crunching sound in the distance caused her to glance up. Walking towards her was a man sporting an ill-fitting trench coat and a floppy hunter's cap. "You have *got to be kidding me*," she grumbled, more relieved than afraid.

Irwin stopped a few feet from where Harper sat. "May I?" he asked, jutting his chin in the direction of the bench.

Harper scooted over to give Irwin room. The two sat side by side in comfortable silence, staring off into a distant nothingness.

"How did you know where to find me?" she finally asked.

Irwin gazed straight ahead, his tired eyes seemingly focused on nothing. He shrugged. "Where else do wounded souls like ours go to protest?"

Cornelia

MONDAY EVENING, *the night before court...*

After a long, distressing day and hours of exhaustive conversation, it had become glaringly apparent that nothing *more* would be gained by rehashing what had already been discussed, *ad nauseum*, so the group collectively decided to call it a night. Each lumbered off to their prospective beds to catch a few winks before the shop and courthouse reopened. Thankfully, tomorrow was Wednesday, Hump Day, and the only day of the week the bookshop opened late. Another of Harper's bright ideas.

"Are you coming back with me tonight?" Irwin asked Cornelia. As a result of the increased bouts of memory loss, everyone, except Cornelia, readily agreed that somebody should remain nearby her at all times—to keep an eye on things. Darren didn't hesitate to volunteer a few nights out of the week, as did Irwin and Harper, each taking turns to stay over regularly in Cornelia's guestroom.

Naturally, Cornelia preferred to remain in her own home, for the time being, surrounded by the things that meant something special to her, memories to indulge in before they scattered and ultimately disappeared.

"I'll stay here with the ladies if that's okay with you," she informed Irwin, tired of being asked the same darn questions.

Are you coming, Cornelia?
Do you want to eat, Cornelia?
Are you tired, Cornelia?
Don't wander away, Cornelia.
Cornelia, Cornelia, Cornelia....

.   .   .

"THAT'S FINE." Irwin slid his chair in and slipped on his coat, past ready to hit the road. He grabbed his cup and saucer to walk them over to the sink.

"Leave it, Irwin. I got it." In one fluid motion, Olivia lifted them from out of his hands to load in the dishwasher. She glanced over at Cornelia. "You know, you're always welcome to stay with us whenever you like."

"I'll take the couch," offered Harper, sealing the deal. She bolted from her chair to her bedroom to make sure she hadn't left anything out for Cornelia to hurt herself with.

As Cornelia's condition degraded, and her symptoms turned more disruptive, it was Cornelia herself who proposed putting her house up for sale—a lovely old Victorian situated in a desirable part of town, which would most assuredly fetch an excellent price when sold, or at least more than enough to cover any of Cornelia's extenuating healthcare costs.

Irwin, however, didn't want to hear it, and vehemently disagreed. Whenever she brought the subject up, he'd either deflect or try to talk her out of it. Becoming impatient, Cornelia continued to prod. In her opinion, the sooner this happened, the better. For now, however, all plans and discussions—*pro or con*—would be placed on hold while everyone tried to figure out how to get Darren back home.

"Cornelia? Do you have everything you need?" asked Olivia. She looked ready to topple over from exhaustion, her body pressed against the kitchen wall for support.

"I'm fine." A few months earlier, Cornelia thought it wise to keep a couple of extra outfits and a few personal care items packed in a duffle bag left in the shop's storeroom. "Harper? Be a dear and fetch my suitcase from downstairs. You know where I keep it."

"Sure thing."

"Stay put," said Irwin. "I'll get it. I'm heading down there, anyway." Irwin, tired himself, jiggled his keys in his hand. "Olivia, I'll swing by here in the morning to pick you and Christopher up for court. Let's plan for eight-thirty—nine the latest."

"I'll be ready," agreed Olivia.

"I plan on leaving earlier than that," said Christopher. "I want to speak to Taylor beforehand, see what our game plan will be."

Irwin nodded. "Understood. Harper? Can I count on you to handle the shop while we're out?"

Harper hesitated. "I was planning to go also. Show Dad my support."

"Unfortunately, we can't afford to close during this busy season, and I think your mother needs to attend," explained Irwin, apparently reluctant to speak further.

"Fine," she shrugged, understanding, but still disheartened.

"Uh, excuse me," Cornelia piped in, "but aren't you forgetting about somebody?"

"I'll need you to stay here with Harper." Irwin leaned closer to Cornelia's chair. "Give her a hand."

"Oh, fiddlesticks. Who are we kidding?" Cornelia complained, insulted. "Say it. You don't want me there. You think I'll do or say something to embarrass you." She fidgeted with her fingers, pouting. "It's fine. I completely understand."

"That's not it at all," explained Irwin, rather abruptly. "This is a difficult time, and Harper shouldn't be left here alone," he added.

"Right," Cornelia mumbled, not buying Irwin's bullshit story for a minute. "So instead, you opt to have the oldest inmate guard the asylum. Brilliant strategy if there ever was one."

Irwin shrugged, exasperated.

"Let me ask you something," inquired Cornelia, refusing to let the matter drop.

"I'm listening," answered Irwin, his weariness etched across his craggy face.

"Exactly how long do you all intend on babysitting me?" Cornelia looked around the room, staring each of her friends down.

"For the record, I'm not babysitting you," said Harper, not willing to get involved.

"I just got here," added Christopher, palms facing forward, following Harper's lead.

Olivia didn't bother to offer up an excuse but instead reached across the table to supportively squeeze Cornelia's hand.

"Nobody here is babysitting you," corrected Irwin, close to the millionth time.

"Nonsense, you big fibber," barked Cornelia, exasperated. "We all know that's not true. I keep telling you, let me sell my house at some ridiculously exorbitant price, and then dump me in one of those adult living centers here in town. I'll fit right in with the rest of the decaying, geriatric diaper brigade."

Harper groaned, shaking her head, discouraged.

"We've already discussed this," Irwin said, gently adjusting Cornelia's sweater around her now bony shoulders. "No one's dumping you anywhere, certainly not into one of those places. And unlike the so-called geriatric diaper brigade, you have us. We're your family, and we will take care of you."

Shoulders squared, Cornelia slammed her fist hard on the table, causing everyone present to flinch. "For Pete's sake, Irwin, don't you get it yet?" Cornelia stomped her foot, causing Bones to bolt from under her chair and take off clear out of the room. "You've all become quite adept at preparing my meals, making sure my old ass doesn't starve. You've even taken it upon yourselves to balance my checkbook and cut my damn weedy lawn. And nobody can beat you guys when it comes to filling in my frequently forgotten words or repeatedly explaining to me even the simplest concepts when I can't follow a basic darn conversation." Cornelia slouched, but her angry voice softened. She tapped a single finger on the table. "Olivia—honestly... how much time should you be expected to spend looking for misplaced items that aren't even lost or searching for the ones I've hidden—for what reason, God only knows why?"

Olivia crossed her legs under the table but remained silent.

"And Harper—sweetie, how many times a day do you have to rescue me from wandering off into rooms I have no business being in or get saddled with driving me to scheduled doctor appointments when you should be doing school work or hanging out with your friends? Gheesh." Cornelia's eyes moistened. "And please, don't any of you even get me started about Darwin."

"*Darren!*" they chorused in correction.

"See what I mean!" Cornelia smacked her forehead. "Anyway, that poor guy. He's been staying over at my house for months now, watching over me like some mother hen. 'Careful on the steps, Cornelia...' 'Sit, I'll make the tea,' he's always telling me, probably afraid I'll forget and set my house on fire." Cornelia exhaled and coughed. "Instead of playing Nurse Betty, Darren should be here, at home," she glared sternly at Harper, "humping your uptight mother."

"Cornelia!" admonished Olivia, shame faced.

Harper, her chin rested on her palm, appearing confused as to whether to laugh or cry, so she did both, wiping her nose on a crumpled napkin, while Olivia whirled around in her seat, looking away in embarrassment.

Cornelia leaned over and softly touched Christopher's forearm. "Christopher...I know this has been especially difficult for you, watching me deteriorate like this. You watched your mother go through this not that long ago, and now me."

Christopher rubbed his chin, then lowered his head and cupped his hands to shield his red-rimmed eyes.

Cornelia drew in a long, labored breath. She turned to face Irwin. "And you, my Irwin. Nobody could have asked for a better friend than you to have their back, especially when facing something as difficult as this shit. But truthfully, even you won't be able to handle it much longer, particularly when I start catching more infections or when I have difficulty swallowing—or worse—when I lose control over my bodily functions." She grasped her old friend's hand, fighting back the tears. "I love you too, you big, sentimental old dope, but one day, maybe sooner than later, you're not going to have any choice but to let me go."

Irwin squeezed Cornelia's hand tenderly in return. "Maybe so, old gal, but today's not the day."

CHAPTER 8

Darren Crane

DARREN SWORE his jailers kept the cells ultra-bright on purpose. Without windows, anyone inside could have easily imagined it being midnight. The temperature inside his cement chamber felt unusually cold. At times, closer to freezing. With no other place to rest, Darren sat on the only available seating—a hard, uncomfortable, narrow plastic plank; the length of an average bed, but without cushion. He pressed his back against the chilled, pock-marked cement wall covered in jerky initials and illegible dates, etched by past bored inhabitants.

Help me, God.

Only a few hours had passed, but for Darren, incarceration for any length of time felt like a grueling eternity.

Disoriented, he felt himself slip further into isolation, devastated by the all-too-familiar, unwelcome suffocating loss of control—the powerlessness to go, do, or be anywhere of his choosing. Being stuck in this godforsaken place had once again awakened a flood of painful memories which Darren would have preferred left buried and forgotten.

Man, what I wouldn't do to be home.

Home...the one place where everything, including Darren's relationship with Olivia, meant the world.

They had finally begun to communicate again, and not on a superficial level either. Long, open, often uncomfortable, but always honest discussions about how they both had gotten it wrong in the past. They agreed to put an end to the blame game which they had both latched onto, along with the unhelpful expectations held against the other. They spoke at length about all the mistakes, the missteps, and the selfish decisions they had each made, things they might have done differently...better—and the hurt they unnecessarily caused. Most of all, they gave themselves space to dare dream again about a future together—*if* they agreed to commit as a couple and make it happen. So far, no real promises had been solidified, no total commitments secured, but for Darren, they were getting closer every day ...and undeniably on the right track.

And then this happened.

Darren's thoughts turned to his daughter, and the incredibly strong woman she had become right before his eyes. He thought about how often Harper's steadfast relationship with truth and kindness had put him markedly to shame. How her selfless capacity to love and forgive increased the strength of his commitment to be a better man and father. Darren never again wanted to be the object for his daughter's disdain—or worse, her disappointment. Never her disappointment.

He sighed, wondering what would happen to Cornelia if he got sent back to prison. Sure, everyone would pitch in to cover for his absence, but the thought of Cornelia spending her last days struggling while he rotted behind bars unable to be by her side hurt more than he cared to admit. Without fully understanding how, Cornelia had become like a mother to him and Olivia, and a grandmother and confidant to Harper in every conceivable way. They'd grown close over the past three years...built a family where once there was none. But of course, that never prevented Cornelia from exerting her fierce independence and obstinance. She had put up one hell of a fight about him or anyone else staying at the house with her, staunchly arguing that she didn't need people fussing over her 'like I'm some sort of child.' She hated being such an imposition. Soon enough, however—a real wake-up call to the dangers of dementia had occurred. Nothing earthshattering, but enough of a kerfuffle to finally convince Cornelia that having somebody around made sense.

For the most part, the arrangement had worked. With Irwin, Cornelia enjoyed spending time in cerebral pursuits, solving simple puzzles or playing games. They'd often listened to classical music or discussed literature together, arguing the finer points, while dining on only a medically approved, nourishing, doctor-approved diet.

With Harper, however, Cornelia had a helper around the house. Harper took over all the light cleaning and organizing. The two claimed to be doing a bit of light cooking together, but Darren had long suspected they ate mostly takeout and fast food.

With Darren, Cornelia got to let her hair down. The two enjoyed watching old silly movies, black and white mysteries, and YouTube videos of people and animals doing the stupidest things, all while chowing down on all the foods the doctor explicitly ordered Cornelia to avoid. As Cornelia's designated bad influencer, Darren relished prepping his charge's decadent cheeseboards brimming with a variety of cheeses, sliced salami, grapes, dates, walnuts, and her favorite fig jam. On the side, water crackers and toasted slices of bread. He'd park the caloric tray before the television set, where they'd stuff themselves silly, while busy chewing and arguing the merits of today's fast-paced movies against the cinematic virtues of the past.

Darren chuckled to himself, grateful Cornelia's sporadic memory had so far never outed him to either Irwin or Olivia.

Ah, the conniption those two would have if they ever found out about all the stuff I allowed Cornelia to eat.

Darren knew he shouldn't have let her—*but damn it, what's life if you can't indulge once in a while?*

Staying at Cornelia's a few times a week had also provided Darren with a safe place to be other than locked in his head, pining away over Olivia, who slept less than a few feet down a shared hall. Over time, he began to open up to Cornelia about his feelings for Olivia and Harper, frequently asking her for motherly advice about how to win them both back.

"First off, you need to stop fretting all the time," Cornelia told him one evening while the two prepared a snack tray for a movie night marathon. Cornelia held a cracker in one hand and waved a slice of gouda in the other.

Darren watched as her eyes darted between the two, undecided as to which to indulge in first. "I'm trying," he explained, adding more cheese slices to the plate, "but sometimes, especially with Olivia, I'm not sure how she feels."

"Why? You don't think she loves you?" Cornelia sniffed the cracker, satisfied. Then tongue-tip-licked the cheese. "*Hmmm.*"

"No, I do, not that I've given her much reason to over the years. But I want her to fall *in love* with me again."

"Then be the man Olivia needs instead of the man you think she wants." Cornelia nibbled the cheese, then the cracker, then back to the cheese. "Damn, this stuff is good."

Darren ran a calloused hand over his face. "You make it sound so easy."

Cornelia shook her head, wagging a free finger at him. "Oh no, my friend," she mumbled, mouth half full. "Love that is worthy is never easy."

As their time spent together continued, and the trust between the unlikely pair grew, Darren looked to Cornelia for help in finding ways to expand his limited world view. Always a consummate reader and writer, Cornelia accepted the mantle of a challenge with vigor, managing to convince the ever-reluctant Darren to read for enjoyment.

"'Reading is the sole means by which we slip, involuntarily, often helplessly, into another's skin, another's voice, another's soul,'" recited Cornelia wistfully.

"Who said that?"

"Joyce Carol Oates. An American novelist. She wrote over fifty-eight novels, numerous plays, short stories, novellas, poetry, and, if I'm not mistaken, nonfiction as well. However, she was mostly known for how her work expounded on the evil and violence of modern society."

A corner of Darren's mouth lifted as he stuck his pointer finger in the air. "As Irwin would say, 'Intriguing.'"

Cornelia laughed.

Darren selected another book off the shelf sifting through an assortment of Cornelia's books in search for his next read. *"The Case of the Bulging Muscle?"* He flipped the book over and read the back blurb. Then turned it over to the front again. "What kind of title is that?"

Cornelia slapped her thigh, highly amused. "Funny story, that—"

"I bet."

"After writing a bunch of cozy mysteries, I decided I wanted to try my hand at something new. Something with a little bit more pizazz. Still keeping the plot quaint, mind you, and mysterious, but also *super sexy*."

"Hence, the title."

"Hence, the title. I thought at the time that I needed to catch the world's sleepy attention. Let's be real. You and I both know that 'prim and proper' is deathly dull. I remember thinking having the word *muscle* in the title would garner attention." Cornelia bent over to sort through a stack of books.

"Bulging was the word that got my attention," mumbled Darren.

Cornelia glanced up. "I'm sorry, what did you say?"

"Nothing." Darren slid the book back on the shelf, too intimidated to open it.

Cornelia transferred three books to one pile and then proceeded to move another three back, for no apparent reason. "By the way, how are you coming along with the last book I loaned you?"

"I'm done. I meant to return it."

"Next visit. And what did you think?"

"I actually enjoyed it." Darren reached for another book.

"That's what I like to hear. I hope you were kind enough to leave me a review."

"Leave you what?" asked Darren baffled.

"A review," she smirked. "Oh, *Darwin*, don't look at me like that," she scolded, switching to her teacher's voice. "A reserved, but non-pretentiously written appraisal about how brilliant I am, and how highly you'd recommend the book."

"Like where? Online?"

"No, tattooed across my ass," grouched Cornelia. "Of course, online."

"I guess I could do that, I mean, if you want me to, but I'll have to ask Harper to show me how. I'm not that great on computers yet."

"Nah. That's all right," teased Cornelia. "I was only pulling your muscle."

At the shop the following day, Darren tugged Irwin's sleeve, indicating that he wished to speak with him privately.

"She said that, did she?" Irwin sort of frowned, clearly feigning distress for Darren's uproariously uncomfortable sake.

"Stop smirking. I know you don't really care, but it's not funny."

"Indisputably."

"Seriously, Irwin, for an old lady, she's got one hell of a potty mouth."

Irwin patted Darren on the shoulder. "Don't knock it. Cornelia was magnificent in her heyday," he explained, jesting aside. "While perhaps her work was not as celebrated as let's say, a Fyodor Dostoevsky or Dorothy Sayers, Cornelia's extensive collection of writings were most assuredly deemed light years ahead of their time. Her writings were filled with complex stories and nuanced characters, many of which effortlessly explored a host of rarely discussed universal themes—sometimes through the use of parody."

Darren scratched at his five o'clock shadow. "Yeah, well, I admit, some of her stuff is pretty hilarious."

"Oh, without a doubt. And do you want to know why?" Irwin didn't bother to wait for an answer. "It's because as a satirist, Cornelia infused her wit and wisdom into her writing to ridicule the abhorrent inadequacies and failings of an impenetrable society. In doing so, she held objectionable institutions of biased thought accountable."

Darren scratched his head, confused.

"In other words, my unlettered friend, she wrote to expose idiocy."

"Ah." Darren shrugged. "Yeah, I can see that. For sure...but Irwin, I mean, *still*..."

"Listen. I am well aware of how our Cornelia can get a bit crude at times."

"Crude—that's one hell of an understatement—"

"Yes, but at least Cornelia's ill-timed attempts at witticisms, however socially abhorrent, suggest that those brain synapses are still active...connecting the dots. At this juncture, I don't want to do or say anything to discourage that." Irwin gripped Darren's shoulder. "Simply put, it's either we keep Cornelia sharp *or*—"

"—or we lose her," grieved Darren, shoulders slumped.

"Exactly." For both men, a world that didn't include Cornelia in it was, well, unthinkable.

"Yeah. I can see what you're saying."

"Besides," teased Irwin, "*The Case of the Bulging Muscle*' is right up your—"

"Don't!" Darren had warned, cupping his ears as his cheeks turned a pitiful shade of dark pink. "Just—don't."

DARREN TRIED to block out the noise to sleep. And he was doing a reasonably good job of it until an influx of angry, raised authoritative voices, followed by heavy booted feet prodding down the hall, stopped outside Darren's cell, startled him alert.

"Get your hands off me, pig," hollered a belligerent drunk prisoner, putting up quite the fight and refusing to be led to his holding cell. As a result, a terrible scuffle ensued.

"On your knees and face the wall!" shouted one of the officers. "Hands behind your back. Now!"

"Make me," the drunk man brazenly replied.

Darren cringed. *Fool.* Eyes closed tight, Darren rubbed his cold arms, contemplating whether or not to request a blanket. Even a state-issued, thin ratty one would be better than freezing. In its place, he tried to block out the jail-house mayhem by redirecting his thoughts out of this cell, straining his mind to oblige, sending him back to the evening before his arrest.

"HEY," murmured Olivia.

Darren glanced up, startled to find her standing

outside his door. More stunned when she unexpectedly poked her head into his studio/bedroom to chat.

"I see you're getting packed to go?"

Darren remembered how soft her voice sounded— inviting. However, he had also noticed how Olivia had intentionally remained outside the door. He had tried to play it cool that night, painstakingly careful not to barge his way into Olivia's world as he would have years back, only concerned about his needs and wants. Now he wanted more than anything to be absolutely sure he was being invited to return.

"Yeah," Darren blushed, collecting a few miscellaneous items from off the top of his dresser. "Did you need me to do something before I leave?" he asked, not sure what else to say or do.

Olivia leaned her head in a tiny bit further. "Do you think Irwin would mind watching Cornelia tonight?"

Caught off guard, Darren didn't know what to think. "Liv?"

Olivia wore a mischievous grin. "Unless of course, that would be a problem," she said, practically purring.

Pulse racing, Darren gripped the handle of his tote tighter, unsure of what to do next. "I, err, think it would probably be most likely, um, fine. Yeah, come to think of it," he babbled, "I'm positive, I think. It would be okay." He kept repeating himself, babbling. "I'll, uh, run down-stairs to, um...you know, speak to Irwin." He shoved his trembling hands into his pockets, hoping she hadn't noticed.

Olivia tugged the door open wider and smiled coquet-tishly. She took a single step forward. Without missing a beat, Darren rushed to hold her. He placed his hand gently on her back when she—

BOOM! Darren heard feet stomping down the hall, followed by a loud crash. Then a clattering of keys, and an exchange of angry words. More shouting coming closer, closer...

"Get off me," prattled that same intoxicated somebody as before, after his cell door slammed shut. "I have rights, you bastardos!"

Darren sighed. "Damn it, damn it, damn it..." He pressed his head against the cold, cement wall, refusing to open his eyes. Hot angry tears dripped down his scruffy face. Resting his clammy palms on his lap, Darren wished to God he knew what Olivia was doing and thinking right now, and if she'd ever trust him again.

Olivia

OVERTIRED, stressed out to the max, but too anxious to sleep, Olivia opted to lie on her bed curled under a heavy quilt, yearning for her body to rest. But her mind refused to let that happen. Instead, wild, unthinkable thoughts raced around in her head about the fate of her future. *Their future.* The future she almost made herself believe she and Darren might have had together.

She lifted her head slightly off the pillow, attempting to bend and fold it into submission, only to wind up scrunching it uncomfortably under her neck. She faced the window. On the ledge sat a plant, a lovely Pothos given to her by Darren as a housewarming gift some years back. Its dark, broad, green leaves had grown wild and impressively full. Its foliage bent toward the sun, while its new growth cascaded down to the floor. Olivia adored that plant and had dubbed her 'Rapunzel' —pruning her back ever so gently whenever her abundance became too unmanageable.

Staring into the dark, Olivia remembered the night before Darren's arrest, when she had brazenly invited him to share her bed for the first time since his getting out of prison over three years ago.

"Wow. That sure grew nicely," Darren said, nestled beneath Olivia's blanket, looking pleased to see where his housewarming gift now called home.

"She has."

"She? Your plant's a she?"

"Oh, absolutely." Olivia rolled on her side and laid her head on his warm, still familiar chest. "She has a name too."

Darren wrapped his bare arm protectively around Olivia's body and smirked, thoroughly charmed.

"Want to know what it is?" Olivia loved teasing and laughing with Darren. Thinking back, it had been his smile that she had first fallen in love with years ago.

"Do I have a choice?"

Olivia raised her brows, smiling.

"Would I be able to guess?"

Olivia brushed her lips ever so softly against Darren's cheek. "Probably not but give it a shot. You might surprise both of us."

Darren had laughed. "I'm so glad you have so much faith in me, Liv," he teased, cutting his eyes at her. "Okay, okay. Let me see...*green...long*...by the window...*Hmmm*. Sunny?"

"No." She nibbled his ear.

"Spider?"

She lifted her head in mock shock. "Seriously?"

"I don't know...Plant?"

"You're ridiculous."

"Hey, this isn't exactly easy, you know. Be kind and give me a hint or something."

"Fine," she said, propped up, leaning on an elbow. "The man wants a hint. Okay, think long, but not necessarily green, but definitely royal."

"Not green but royal..."

"Yes."

Darren pondered, and pondered, and pondered. "I got nothin'."

"Ugh. Rapunzel, silly."

"Rapunzel, silly? Hmm, never heard of her."

Olivia poked Darren in the side, playfully. "I told you, think long—Rapunzel's hair—super long. Royal—she was a princess."

"How the heck was I supposed to know that?"

"You never read the story of Rapunzel? 'Let down your golden hair' as a kid?"

"Nah. I was more into *Archie* and Marvel comic books."

"Now, you're dating yourself."

Darren kissed Olivia on the forehead. He pulled her closer to him. "To be honest, I always wondered what happened to it—pardon, my lady, I mean, Rapunzel," he said, jutting his chin in the plant's direction.

"That's because you thought I killed her, didn't you," accused Olivia, her face nuzzled under his warm neck.

"The thought did cross my mind."

"You!" she laughed, tickling his ribs.

"Stop, stop," he pleaded, practically snorting out his laughter. "Show some mercy!" he teased between laughter.

After a moment, Darren lifted Olivia's chin tenderly to meet his eyes. "Liv? I need to ask you something."

With one arm slung across Darren's bare waist, Olivia raised her head—looking deep into his dark, compelling eyes—at the same face she had loved for most of her life. "Anything," she whispered

"Tonight. You and me...*us*, to be exact. What are we now? I mean, are we, you know?" Darren ran his fingers through his short-cropped hair while exhaling a nervous breath. "Man, this is totally not coming out right at all."

"You're fine," she murmured, tracing the bottom of his lip with the tip of her finger. "Tonight," she kissed him. "Us," another soft, sensual kiss. "You and me—are we?" Olivia beckoned him closer with her eyes. "Yes."

Words would no longer suffice. Darren lifted Olivia's warm, inviting body onto his. Holding her face close, her pressed his lips against her neck, her chin...her cheeks...her lips, breathing her in. "Liv...," he moaned, as every sense of his being reawakened.

"*Shhh*..."

CHAPTER 9

Irwin

ARRIVING home to an empty house without even his idiot cat for company felt depressing. Irwin unlocked the back door and flipped on the kitchen light. He stood there, staring ahead at a room which looked exactly the way he had left it. Neat and boring. He removed his hat, folded it, and placed it in the basket. Then hung his coat and scarf on the wall peg. Lastly, he lowered himself down on a wooden chair to remove his shoes. He bent over and slipped on a pair of house slippers and an old, button-up, V-neck soft sweater. The whole Mr. Roger's routine took less than a minute.

Now what?

Yawning, he lumbered over to the refrigerator and

yanked it open. "My Lord," he spluttered, appalled. Irwin loathed food shopping. The mere thought of having to socialize with people, even if it only meant the cashier and occasional stock boy, left him spent and overwhelmed. Like most social introverts, Irwin had to work up the mental energy to leave the confines of his house and face strangers, which proved to be a daily struggle. He hated crowds, disliked small talk and despised small minds. For the most part, he found most human beings exasperating, yet his love for books and the written word won out, and he opened a book shop.

Shopping provided a whole new set of risks. After arriving at a store, he had to park, which meant selecting a spot as far from other beings as possible. Once parked, he had to give himself the usual pep talk before going inside. More often than not, he'd shut off the engine to steal a quiet moment in his car. There, he would observe the general frazzled populace busy running in and out to grab whatever they needed and then leave. Easy enough for most, but for Irwin, this necessary, albeit laborious task proved much too cumbersome. First off, there was all that cart pushing...searching up and down endlessly congested aisles filled to capacity with brightly colored, overpriced, ready-made food products. A total sensory overload. Most of the time, Irwin forgot the stupid food list at home and found himself battling brain fog. Staring at a bunch of boxes, bags, and cans, and incapable of remembering what the hell he came in for—all while acrobatically dodging attitudinal rushed shoppers, screaming babies, unruly children, and motorized customers hellbent on making food acquisition an endurance competition.

Unimpressed but too worn-out to care, Irwin slammed the fridge door shut. "Food's, overrated, anyway." Besides, he only made a concerted effort to shop and cook when either Cornelia or Darren were coming over. When alone, he barely bothered.

Exhausted and unable to keep his eyes open for too much longer, he hoped sleep would come easily, but undoubtedly not tonight. Not while he worried about Darren and his chances of being convicted for a crime he certainly had no part in. Then his thoughts landed on Olivia. She played tough to mask her fears, but Irwin knew better. And of course, there was the matter of Harper and Christopher's unrequited budding heart affair. The sexual heat growing between those two could easily set alight a forest fire. Lastly, Irwin's mind rested on poor Cornelia, whose increased memory lapses and frequent illnesses were forever a growing concern.

No longer interested in snacking, he flipped off the overhead light and plodded up the dark stairway, dragging his weary feet across the familiar creaking old floorboards. The hollow sound carried, thumping against the walls and echoing back and forth, before ultimately becoming absorbed. This dull, muffled sound only served to emphasize for Irwin the absolute solitude.

In bed, he rested flat on his back, eyes wide open, staring into nothing but darkness; his entire being weighed down by an indescribable loneliness. In the quiet of the night, he remained still, preparing himself for the onslaught of nightly intrusive thoughts to encroach, wishing he could discover some way to block them. But nothing he did seemed to fend off the memories. Even the promise of time healing his crushed spirit had failed him miserably.

Since his fiancée's death in a tragic car accident, the inability to stay asleep plagued Irwin night after miserable night. He'd eventually doze off, only to awaken a short time later tossing and turning; his covers twisted around his flailing, needy limbs. The next day, he'd awaken tired, angry at the world, and going through his paces too bleary-eyed under strain to care. Nothing so far had been able to deaden the empty pain of loneliness. Nor, did it appear, would anything ever erase the yearning.

Nowadays, whenever Irwin envisioned Gilly before him, she'd come mostly in short, indistinct glimpses, floating throughout his subconscious like a stunning apparition, albeit less detailed the longer time abated. He'd imagine her loveliness hovering above his heart... sadly, and forever out of his reach. When alone, if he concentrated hard enough, he could hear Gilly's voice rattling around in his head. Everything from the slight lisp of her 'r's' to the elongated staccato of her 't's.' Now, over time, that, too, had gradually begun to taper off. Now, despite the absence of clarity, Irwin welcomed Gilly's presence in whatever degree afforded him. And now, even during his most stressful dreams, she still managed to embody an absolute quietude and stillness he never imagined existed. It made the *missing her with all his heart* part all the more tormenting.

During the day, Irwin kept himself busy, surrounded by his newfound family and the unrelenting business of running a successful small town book shop. Cornelia consumed the remainder of his time. It took a lot to keep her safe and happy. He had truly appreciated when Darren proposed spotting him a few times a week over at Cornelia's. His offer couldn't have come at a better time, seeing that it allowed Irwin a small window of time to work a few shifts at the library for a much needed change of pace. On Fridays, Irwin continued to visit the graveyard in town to speak with Gilly.

Nighttime, however, offered Irwin no such reprieve. Without any distractions to pull him back, he remained utterly consumed by recurring memories of Gilly, reminiscences which never failed to expound on every aspect of their too short time spent together. Irwin had loved Gilly—as much in death as when their paths first crossed. He'd be forever drawn to the way her eyes had sparkled against the light. That throaty giggle of hers that brought him crashing to his knees in fits of uncontrolled laughter. When alone and feeling particularly vulnerable, he'd lie absolutely still, searching into his past to conjure up even a taste of her memory, but in doing so, he had paid a heavy, exacting toll. A price he swore he was more than willing to pay—and pay he did—every day and every single night since the love of his life left this world, slated for the next. Powerless to switch off the thoughts, he tired of trying and had all but given up.

Notwithstanding the agony of their existence, Irwin's memories yielded to human frailty despite his diligent and courageous efforts to curtail their departure. Gilly's legacy, no matter the strength of their heartfelt prominence, ultimately subdued in intensity, dimming unforgivably. Perchance, he often mused, somewhere within this wrenching theft hid a merciful blessing. Possibly, he'd tell himself, this diminution was the natural order of things— the way bereavement behaved. Perhaps, he'd deliberate, his expectations were at fault, unrealistic. Nevertheless, Irwin found the progression of grief and the insatiable loss unbearable and hard to reconcile against all that he held precious and dear.

Over time, Irwin would have to accept that eventually,

most everything he reminisced about Gilly would wane—fade forever into the background, displaced by life's demands. All excluding his undying love which he vowed to protect with body and soul. His feelings for Gilly would survive the ravages of time, unquestionably anchored and unwavering—permanently and eternally devoted.

Irwin gradually opened his eyes.

I miss you, Gilly.

But his body, refusing to comply, taunted him. He missed her warm, supple body pressed longingly against his. The smooth touch of her skin. The honeyed, alluring scent of her hair. The sweet taste of her soft, inviting lips. Irwin tugged the bedcovers over his shoulder, pushing his face harder against the pillow.

Why did you leave me?

He envisioned their limbs entwined...her head wedged perfectly asleep under the protection of his chin. If Irwin concentrated hard enough, he could almost conjure the memories of their shared hungry whispers...visions which held him captive to their absolute power to liberate even his most weighty doubts, thrusting them high and far into the indefinite like a blustery rain riding upon the wind.

But never more.

So many familiarities—*too many*—had been left incomplete.

Irwin squeezed his eyes shut as his heart raced, fitfully beating against a barrage of conflicting emotions. He wanted to fight back, stomping the unsolicited intruders down and away—driving them mercilessly forever into a place of oblivion. But not tonight. And not for a hundred, thousand other nights either.

In a fit of frustration, Irwin bolted straight up clutching his chest, frantically panting for air. He ran his aged, stiff fingers through what thinning hair stubbornly remained on top of his sweaty head; his scalp wet and clammy to the touch.

After hours of endless tossing and turning, and finding no position remotely comfortable, Irwin gave up. He checked the time, disheartened that it was still too early to rise, so he punched his pillow a few times before folding it in half to re-lodge under his head. Then he turned onto his other side, pressing his sweaty face once again against the damp pillowcase.

"Gilly...," he sighed. A single, salty tear slid down his already wet cheek, dribbling past his stubbled chin. "I need you," he repeated against the still of night until eventually drifting off into yet one more restless, lonesome slumber.

Morning...

Brrng

Irwin jolted awake, groping frantically for the shut-off button on the now blaring alarm. He swatted once, twice, but missed both times. On the third try, he slapped it so hard that he wound up sending the wretched contraption careening across the bedroom, only to roll far beneath a dresser.

"Oh, for heaven's sake," he grumbled, shouting his frustration into the pillow pressed over his face.

Brrng

"Fine, fine. You win." Irwin whipped the blanket off, dreading the cold air swirling surrounding him. "Ouch, ouch," he carped, as he wobbled tippy toed across the freezing, wood floor over to the dresser. He bent low... lower...as low as possible, oscillating his arm blindly, wiggling his fingers to coax the earsplitting clock out from hiding.

"Blasted torture machine," he complained, realizing that nothing but a full on-the-knee retrieval would suffice.

The clock continued to torment.

Brrng

"Shut up!"

On top of not sleeping well, he now had to contend with this utter ridiculousness. Irwin swore he would have gotten rid of this wretched noisemaker had it not been a gift from Harper.

"This is for you," she had told him about a month ago.

"What's this?" he asked, violently shaking the nicely wrapped box package.

"Stop doing that and open it."

Irwin hated surprises but detested receiving gifts even more. Gift receiving in particular meant sentimentality, and sentimentality required empathy, and empathy meant responsiveness, and responsiveness required sensitivity— all of which Irwin perceived as too cumbersome and awkward.

Scowling, but resigned, he painstakingly undertook the task of peeling off the tape starting from the far edge of the paper, careful not to rip it unnecessarily.

"Are you kidding me right now? Rip it off."

Irwin ignored Harper's youthful impatience and continued his laborious task. "It's a box," he announced finally, underwhelmed.

"Wow, Irwin, there's sure no fooling you." Harper nibbled her lip. "Open it."

Irwin rubbed his forehead but obliged. "It's an alarm clock."

"Affirmative."

"I don't understand."

"What's to understand?" Harper smiled, apparently enjoying herself.

"First and foremost, why would you feel compelled to gift me this particular contraption? Need I remind you, Harper, promptness is a sign of professionalism and character. As a punctual person, I clearly have an impeccable sense of time and pride myself on never being tardy."

Harper inched closer, giving Irwin a lopsided grin. "But that's not why I got it for you."

"Then what, pray tell, is its purpose?"

"Its purpose, Mr. Grumpy, is as an aide-mémoire."

"An aide-mémoire?" Perplexed, Irwin tilted his chin sideways.

"Aww, come on Irwin, even *you* can't be this dense."

Eyes narrowed, Irwin, his brow knitted, began fidgeting with the clock's knobs and dials.

"Oh, man, I can't believe you don't remember." Harper leaned over, sticking her face close to his. "Fine. I can see you aren't purposely being insufferable, so I'll attribute this perplexing memory lapse to old, *old*, age." Yanking the clock from Irwin's fumbling fingers, she started pushing this button and pulling that knob to set the proper time and date, before handing it back.

"Thank you, I suppose."

"You're welcome. Hey, don't forget to read the note." Before wrapping the gift, Harper had taped a quote to the top of the box, scripted in her awful penmanship.

"What note?"

"This note," she pointed, tapping the paper.

"That's a note? It looks more like playschool hiero-glyphics." Irwin cleared his throat and began to read it aloud.

"The greatest gift you can give someone is your time because when you give your time, you are giving a portion of your life that you will never get back." Anonymous

Harper, bouncing from leg to leg, grinned in anticipa-tion. "Do you get it now?"

Irwin shook his head. "I do not."

"It's our friendiversary," announced Harper. "Today marks the third year of our friendship."

Irwin whistled. "Has the torment lasted that long?"

"And," said Harper, disregarding Irwin's sidebar comment, "I wanted to let you know how much you mean to me."

Irwin's head drooped...his shoulders slumped. He jiggled the dial on the clock feigning interest, while all along refusing to look Harper in the face. Instead, he merely nodded. "I see."

Harper nudged him playfully in the shoulder. "Does that mean you like it?"

"*Ahem*," he cleared his throat again. "It means I don't hate it."

Harper laughed.

"—however unnecessary," he added in his usual brusque manner.

Harper's eyes sparkled as she leaned over to peck the top of Irwin's head. "Gifts seldom are, Mr. Grumpy, but they're sure a lot of fun."

Brrng...

"Damn it!" Irwin crouched down on all fours, erupting into a host of profanities as he bent his stiff body down to retrieve Harper's bright idea for a friendship gift. With his chest practically touching the floor, he stretched and stretched his arm, wiggling his fingers under the dresser—"Son of a gun!" He missed again.

Brrng...

"One of these days I'm going to lose my blasted hearing!" He scuttled to his nightstand, groped inside the drawer, and came up with a pencil usually kept bedside for tackling late night crossword puzzles. "Ah, ha!" he snarled. "You're mine now, you blasted, sadistic contraption!" Irwin managed to crawl back over to the dresser, doing his best to plot his next move over the earsplitting noise assaulting his ears. After a few more failed attempts, he eventually coaxed the noise maker forward, inching it closer until finally locked in his grip. Once dragged out, he slammed the off button as fast as humanly possible.

"Fun my ass."

Fully awake but already utterly irritated past the point of no return, Irwin stomped his way into the bathroom, doing his best to ignore the winter chill hovering in the air. He turned up the thermostat to high, refusing to undress until his teeth stopped chattering. Besides showering and getting dressed, Irwin still needed enough time to swing by the shop to pick Olivia up, prep the register, and check in on Cornelia before heading to the courthouse. If he had any hope of grabbing a cup of coffee and a slice of dry toast before starting his day, he'd have to get a move on. Most of all, he trusted Harper could handle Cornelia on her own today.

On second thought, he frowned, *who knows what those two might get into if left unsupervised?*

Wrapped in an oversized towel, Irwin twisted the shower knob and waited impatiently while the ancient old house kicked into gear. Each morning the old pipes complained, commencing into the most raucous symphony of knocking, banging, and clanking, which wouldn't end until he turned off the hot water. Steam clouded the bathroom, with condensation building up on the mirrors and walls, but Irwin didn't care. His achy body needed to feel the hot water pressure knead his old bones back into compliance.

Irwin hoped that everything would run smoothly for a change, especially concerning Christopher's law buddy. *If not*—well, for the time being, Irwin adamantly refused to accept the likelihood of that most unsettling possibility.

CHAPTER 10

Harper

TUESDAY MORNING, 6:00 am...

The anticipated snow had fallen overnight, leaving behind a beautiful mess to contend with. It started first as flurries, then came down in bigger, heavier flakes, plunging to the ground in large batches the size of dense white clumps, drifting and casing every visible surface. On the street below, barely anything dared move except for the occasional *snap* of a weighted tree branch, or a municipal plow.

Upstairs, the apartment remained still. Cornelia, currently inhabiting Harper's bedroom, sounded deep asleep—if the snores and snorts emanating through the walls were any indication. Olivia, unable to relax, had pushed herself last night to sheer exhaustion, finally knocking off after two am.

And Christopher?

Full of apprehension, Harper warily glanced down the hallway, staring at his closed door. So close, yet so far away...

Enough. Refocus.

Staring down the empty corridor, she mulled over everything discussed the previous evening. So many expressed tears and frustration, but nothing compared to the show of love.

Her jaw went slack.

What do I know about love—except for what I've read in steamy romance books?

What do I compare it to?

For years, Harper had watched the tumultuous relationship between her parents rise and swell, but as of yet, culminating into nothing more than a few flirtatious volleys—or so she assumed. Then again, there was Irwin...

Irwin loved Gilly—still does, and look where that got him.

Harper drew her knees tight against her chest, hugging herself.

Are my feelings for Christopher love or infatuation?

A sadness transformed her face as she shuddered, thoroughly annoyed with herself.

What am I doing? What kind of daughter thinks about this when their dad is locked away in a jail cell?

Dad.

Harper prayed her father would be okay, safe. While she knew her feelings, she didn't have to imagine how frightened her mother felt; not after watching her face when thinking about the possibility of her husband doing yet another stint behind bars—this time possibly for life.

Will Mom be able to handle it?

Harper thought about the hidden envelope. Any possibility of accepting the scholarship and going away to college had all but disappeared. *The school will always be there*, she told herself, adamantly refusing to move far from either Cornelia or her mom. Not now, and certainly not with what both women now faced. They'd need her to stay more than ever.

And there was Irwin...

No longer a spring chicken himself, Harper feared he'd take an emotional plummet into depression if things didn't get straightened out and soon.

"And what about Christopher?" she whispered to the empty room.

Ugh... No, no, no. Stop it. Stop thinking about him.

But Harper couldn't help it. She'd fallen hard. Closing her eyes, she imagined his wispy, chestnut brown hair splayed across his pillow as he slept. She visualized how his chest looked rising and falling with each intake of sleep-filled breath. She wondered about what he dreamed about...

Better yet—who?

"Stop it, Harper," she groaned, pounding her thigh, eyes wide open.

"Ugh."

Who am I kidding? He's gorgeous. Kind. Smart. There's no way he's alone. He's got to have somebody in his life by now, she thought glumly. Most likely beautiful and successful. Probably a corporate woman accustomed to having her name engraved on fancy office doors.

Would Christopher ever notice me as something more than a kid or a friend? See me as his somebody?

She desperately wanted him to notice her. Want her.

Dream about her. Desire her, but that was plain silly. She scowled. *We're friends. Great friends. Nothing more. Shoot, we're practically siblings—minus the being related part.*

Aren't we?

Harper lingered on the couch a bit longer before finally pulling off the blanket from around her shoulders to pad softly across the cold living room floor. She drew back the curtain. She recalled hearing a few trucks rumble through earlier on, but now the streets below were once again coated with a new sheen of virgin snow.

Was it this morning? Late last night?

Hard to tell. The roads needed to be cleared and sanded again. Parked cars lined up on either side, encased under several feet of snow. As temperatures outside continued dropping, it threatened to turn to ice.

I should get out there and shovel while I still can.

Harper sighed. The curtain slipped through her slender fingers, only to flutter closed. She turned and traipsed back to the couch, not exactly in a rush to get this dreaded day started. Added to her pent-up frustration—the decision that only Mom, Irwin, and Christopher would go to the courthouse, while she and Cornelia were left behind to man the shop. Christopher's lawyer friend had agreed to meet them at the courthouse.

I hope this guy knows what the heck he's doing.

Eye's still heavy, she drifted back to sleep. Moments later, the house burst to attention. First, she heard the unmistaken sound of somebody already bogarting the shower. Then the clinking of cups, spoons, and utensils hastily being set on the kitchen table. The definitive proof of burgeoning life came in the form of Harper's pajama sleeve being frantically tugged.

"*Psssst. Psssst.* Harper?" whispered Cornelia. "Hey, Harper, you awake?" she asked, poking her in the shoulder.

"I am now," she grumbled, pulling her arms out from under her warm blanket to stretch. "Hold up—" she squinted, "why are you in my bathrobe?"

"Because it's colder than a witch's tit in here."

Goosebumps rose on Harper's exposed arms. She quickly gathered the blanket and tugged it tighter around her shoulders. "Point taken."

"Good. Now that you're awake, I wanted to run something by you." Cornelia plopped down on the sofa. "I was thinking."

"Dangerous, but please, feel free to continue."

Cornelia plucked Harper's arm. "Hush and listen, wise guy," she whispered.

"Why are you whispering?" whispered Harper in return.

"Because if your nosy mother hears what I've got to say, she won't be happy."

Harper smiled and leaned in slightly closer toward Cornelia. "Then, I'm all ears."

"Thought so. Now, *here's the thing...*"

Harper listened carefully to Cornelia's idea, intermittingly nodding in agreement, but careful not to interrupt her lucid train of thought.

After Cornelia finished, she leaned back against the cushion, clasping her hands. "So, doll, what do you think? You in?"

Harper's smirk loomed large. "Oh, yeah."

Christopher

IN HIS STUDIO apartment down the hall, Christopher stared at the bedroom ceiling, fully awake. Sleep came in sporadic spurts, leaving him feeling restless and disturbed. Last night's news about Alastair Brooke and what happened to Darren had been upsetting, to say the least.

Christopher checked his watch. Almost seven, but still too early to phone Taylor.

I'll give it ten more minutes.

Christopher's thought about Harper only a few feet down the hall. How, up until recently, he never considered her as anything other than a cute kid, more like a baby sister—until last summer. Then something drastic had changed. She changed. At nineteen, soon to be twenty, Harper had turned into a drop-dead gorgeous, brilliant woman, and one hell of a constant distraction. Christopher couldn't stop thinking about her. But he had to, so after returning to campus, he had tried his hand at the dating scene. Eventually, he met Elise. Attractive and intelligent, but neither witty nor the slightest bit adventuresome, Christopher didn't put much stock in the relationship ever going anywhere. However, what had been the colossal cardinal sin in his eyes and the ultimate deal breaker was when she bragged during one of their dates about never reading for enjoyment.

"Like never?" he had asked, half his dinner still on his plate.

Elise sipped daintily at her drink. "I wouldn't necessarily say never but reading outside school is not my thing. I'd rather do something fun."

Not your thing? Rather do something fun?

Christopher hadn't known what to say to that at the time but recalled staring at Elise like she had two heads—both empty. In response, Elise misread his indignation and began to giggle, finding the whole topic of conversation hilarious. For him, the rest of the evening was a bust.

After the meal, Christopher didn't dawdle. He politely paid the restaurant tab and put the lovely Elise in a cab, bidding her a friendly, but final, goodnight. When he returned to his apartment a half-hour later, he texted Harper on the off chance.

`Hey,` he typed and waited.

`Hey back—Wats up?`

`What are you up to?`

`Binging out on a fab book. U?`

Of course, you are, he smiled.

`Home.` He typed, then quickly added. `Have to study for a final`

`Same`

`Harper?`

`Yes?`

His fingers lingered and hesitated over the keyboard.

I miss you. I can't stop thinking about you.

`—nvm ...gotta go. Give the fam my love`

`Will do`

WORDS. They had escaped him. His feelings for Harper? Haunted him. This trip, he told himself, would be different. This trip would tell Christopher everything he needed to know.

CHRISTOPHER TOSSED AND TURNED, pulling the blanket over his head.

"*Ugh*," he groaned into his pillow. It was useless. Nothing he did managed to get Harper out of his system, and now, he wasn't entirely sure if he wanted to.

The holidays couldn't have come at a better time, or so Christopher hoped. He had planned to go back and ask Darren and Olivia for permission to pursue a relationship with Harper.

Christopher wasn't sure how Harper felt about him— she was always sending out mixed messages. One minute, she would be sarcastic and detached, watching him from a distance, but not saying a word—the next, talkative, funny, perhaps even coquettish, but always so gorgeous and smart. When they did talk, they really talked, and about everything. He admired Harper's ability to expound on any topic under the sun, but as smart as she was, she never came off as arrogant. More like in a sort of 'come with me and let me show you what I've learned' kind of way. Ever-more endearing, always engaging, and utterly fascinating.

Harper's gorgeous.

Christopher craved to run his fingers in her long, wild, wavy brown hair. Feel her flawless, creamy skin next to his. In his dreams, he'd envision slipping her out of those crazy signature outfits she wore—most of the time with work boots. Christopher even dug the unique jewelry Harper chose to embellish every available limb. Unlike Elise, whose face relied on gobs of makeup to portray confidence, Harper wore little to nothing, living self-assuredly in her skin.

And then there were Harper's parents. He cherished how her mom forever fussed over him and already treated him like one of the family.

And then there was Darren. From the start, Harper's father couldn't have been more welcoming. He had gone out of his way to be kind. Sure, they'd kid around a lot, exchanging off-the-cuff, snide jokes, but nothing meanspirited. Darren had also proven to be a surprisingly good sounding board for Christopher, and a great person to discuss guy stuff with, mainly since most of those topics made Irwin blush. Not that Irwin didn't try. He'd mumble and grumble under his breath, excruciatingly embarrassed until becoming thoroughly exasperated. Eventually, he'd give up the pretense of trying, desperate for retreat, leaving Darren and Christopher rolling over in stitches.

But Irwin, for all his idiosyncrasies, had been the friend-catch of a lifetime.

When Christopher's mother died, he never dreamt that he'd be able to finish school, no less excel. Then he met Irwin—in the cemetery of all places! Christopher chuckled remembering that afternoon—the day that significantly changed the course of his life.

He'd been visiting his mom, explaining to her his predicament with school, his job, when Irwin showed up all decked out in a long dark trench coat and wearing the goofiest hunter's cap—the kind with the floppy ears. Irwin had been carrying a large bouquet of flowers, looking like some villain out of an old black and white silent movie. But what really took the cake was when he bolted behind a tree to hide so Harper, who Christopher thought at the time was his daughter, wouldn't see him.

Harper.

She'd been only seventeen at the time but deeply troubled. Standing at a headstone, pouring her heart out. Much like Christopher had been doing moments before. It had been heartbreaking all around.

Then, after Harper left, he and Irwin—this complete stranger—got to talking. Somehow the topic of school came up, and Christopher told Irwin everything—about not having enough money to finish school...his being unable to pay rent because his part-time job didn't pay enough to make ends meet or continue to work around his crazy school hours. No longer able to afford the apartment he and his mother had shared, Christopher, at the time, had been seriously jammed up, overwhelmed, and not sure what to do next.

Over the next few weeks, the two men bumped into one another a couple of more times, always at the cemetery. Christopher found Irwin fascinating, sardonic...if not a bit lonely, but what happened next totally blew him away.

Somehow, out of the blue, and completely unexpected, Irwin had tracked him down.

"What the hell?" mumbled Christopher, doing a doubletake. "What are you doing here?" he asked in quiet amazement, stunned to see his cemetery buddy waiting outside his classroom.

Irwin handed Christopher an envelope.

"What's this?"

"An envelope."

"I know that, but I mean, what's it for?"

"It's for you."

Christopher brow furrowed. "I meant, what's it about?"

"Perhaps you should read it before asking redundant questions."

"Is this for a party?"

"Bite your tongue." Irwin rolled his eyes.

Christopher laughed. "Okay." He pulled a slip of paper out to read. "Uh, this is for later today—"

"Your insight leaves me speechless."

"I don't know—"

"There's nothing not to know. I expect you on time." And with that, the old man disappeared.

Christopher watched Irwin march away, head held high and forward. As usual, the old guy had his hands stuck in his trench coat pockets, taking long, deliberate strides, while the ear folds of his hunter cap flapped in the wind.

"Who was that?" asked one of Christopher's buddies.

"That, my friend, is an enigma."

"An egg-what?"

"Not an egg—oh, forget it." Christopher walked fast, almost running down the hall, late for his final class.

"Egg or no egg, I dig the old dude's hat," laughed his friend, toggling to his side.

Christopher grinned. "You're probably the only one."

LATER THAT SAME AFTERNOON, Irwin had presented Christopher with a job opportunity paying double what he currently earned with the promise of a schedule that would work around his classes. On top of that, Irwin threw in an apartment above the book shop at a ridiculously low rent. The same studio that had housed him comfortably—stress-free—through a year of school before he transferred to a law school in New York City. In fact, when Christopher graduated, he did the math and figured out that his old friend Irwin had saved all Christopher's rent payments, only to give him the entire amount back, plus some, as a graduation gift—no strings attached.

Who does that?

Not only that, but Irwin hadn't hesitated to take him into the fold, treating him more like a grandson than a boarder. Cornelia as well, and since then, Christopher's life had steadily moved in the right direction.

Christopher checked his watch.

Time's up, buddy.

My friends need me, and I'll be damned if I let them down.

Christopher dialed Taylor's number. He let it ring six times before a sleepy, legitimately irritated voice answered.

"This had better be important, asswipe."

"Homicide," said Christopher. "Arraignment—today. The guy's not guilty. Has a record, on parole, like family. Not broke, but close to it. You in?"

"Name?"

"Darren Crane."

Christopher heard the phone jiggle, shake, then clatter to the floor.

"Shit! Stupid phone." grumbled a half awake Taylor. "Did I lose you?"

"No. Astonishingly, I'm still here."

"Where were we, oh, right. How sure are you that your guy's innocent," probed Taylor "And don't pull my chain, Christopher."

"Affirmative. He 100% didn't do it."

Taylor deep-groaned, before running through a few other colorful expletives for good measure. "Fine."

"Seriously?" asked Christopher, relieved. "You'll take the case?"

"I didn't say that. First, I'll need to talk to your guy; feel him out, but I will be at the arraignment."

"Trust me. After you speak to Darren, you'll see he's a good guy."

Taylor laughed. "I don't care if he's Mother Teresa's doppelgänger. I don't have to like the dude. I only have to believe him."

Christopher sighed, relieved. "I owe you, big time."

"No shit."

CHRISTOPHER NEEDED to hurry if he wanted to meet up with Taylor before Darren's arraignment. He tore out of bed, tossing the bed covers and sheets to the side. He snatched the towel left for him on the chair and sprinted out the bedroom for the shower, determined to take care of business and bring his friend home.

Harper & Cornelia

THE PLAN, if one could even call it that, had been simple enough. Wait until Olivia and Christopher left for the courthouse. Then head downstairs to the basement, using the key to get through the metal door that connects the attached buildings. Lastly, snoop around Alastair's store to see what, if anything, they could find. Simple enough.

"What do you mean you don't have the key?" humphed Cornelia.

"Exactly what I said." Harper squinted at her. "Irwin's got it, and I don't know where he keeps it."

"Did you check the drawer by the cash register?"

"Yes, and nope. It wasn't there."

"How about the cubby behind where your mother hangs the bags?"

"Did that too. *Nada*."

Cornelia frowned. "How about under the register."

"*Under* the register? Why would she put it there? That thing's heavy."

"True." Cornelia hummed. "Oh! I got it! Look in the drawer again, but this time, lift the draw liner up."

"The gray one?"

"I don't know what color the damn thing is—lift it up."

Harper hurried to the front of the store, opened the drawer, and lifted the mat.

Hot damn.

"Bingo!" she shouted, waving the key elatedly in the air. "How did you know?"

"Not exactly sure," Cornelia shrugged. "Either I came across it during one of my many snack explorations, or—I remembered seeing Irwin put it there. Be glad I remembered."

"It could have been my mother." Harper flipped her hair over her shoulder and scraped at a dry blob of tooth-paste on her tee-shirt. "She's always moving stuff around."

"Possibly. Olivia does tend to think she's so slick... hiding stuff as if I—a seasoned mystery writer—won't find it."

"Simply preposterous," Harper giggled.

"Utterly ludicrous."

"Patently absurd!" roared Harper, laughing.

"Damn straight," agreed Cornelia, winking. "Now, let's go."

"Um, one more thing."

"What's that?"

Harper wiggled the key in the air. "What exactly are we looking for?"

"No clue, babycakes, but we'll know it when we find it."

"That's good enough for me," Harper nodded. "I'm right behind you."

CHAPTER 11

Darren

DAY OF ARRAIGNMENT...

This place. The noise. The assaulting stench of unwashed, anxiety-riddled bodies contained unnaturally close together. He could find little reprieve from the stale heavy air or the endless permeated whiff of fear. A collective despair seeped and oozed from every corner of the building, slithering down every wall. Intermittent screams heard echoing long into the night, disrupted only by the random muffled sob. Either one provoked within Darren a desperate and inconsolable urge to flee.

Restless, he tried leaning on his side when an unusual sharp pain seared through his left shoulder blade, shooting straight down his leg. He winced in discomfort, but kept his mouth shut.

Show no fear.

Darren clenched his jaw and squeezed his fists to fend off the pain. His nerves were getting the best of him.

When first arriving, the correctional officers had ordered him to turn over all his clothing, which then got inventoried. They checked the condition of everything handed to them, searching through pockets and beneath loosened hems. Once cleared of contraband, Darren was provided with a receipt to sign along with a copy for his records for any items retained. Then they hauled him to a holding cell located at the courthouse. No one except a lawyer would be permitted to see him, but since Darren didn't have a lawyer, all he had to look forward to was a long wait.

"Crane. Follow me," ordered one of the guards a few hours later, unlocking his cell.

"What for?"

"Your lawyer's here."

"My lawyer?"

The heavy-set guard stared across at Darren, shifting impatiently from one foot to the other. "So, you haven't met her yet, huh? You're in for a real treat. Let's go."

Less than ten minutes later, Darren was escorted into a small enclosed room with a phone and a chair. Through the thick plexiglass window, he saw a stunning woman already waiting, presumably his attorney. Christopher sat next to her.

Christopher?

Grasping a single phone in his hand, Christopher pointed to the phone on Darren's side of the wall, indicating for him to lift up the receiver, then turned to make the introductions. "Darren, this is my friend, Taylor Maldonado. One of the best attorneys in town." He promptly handed the phone off.

"I won't argue with that. Please, call me Taylor. Sit, Mr. Crane. We have a lot to discuss and no time to waste."

Darren pulled out a chair and sat, facing his friend and attorney.

Taylor got straight down to business. "Christopher assures me you're innocent."

"I am."

"Yes, well, isn't everyone. However, from going over your paperwork, I can see this isn't your first rodeo with our illustrious court system. Care to expound?"

"I did time for a crime I did commit. Guilty as hell. Did six years, and still on parole when this bullshit happened."

"Any issues with parole that I should know about?"

"None. Since my release, I've kept my nose clean."

Taylor nodded. "Okay, Mr. Crane. Let me hear your side of the story and do yourself a favor by not leaving out any details no matter how trivial you may think they are, even if you believe they will incriminate you. Got it?"

Darren agreed.

"And Mr. Crane—" Taylor added, resting her chin on her hand.

"Darren."

"Darren. Let me make myself perfectly clear. I'm here today on your behalf because of our mutual friend over here." She gave a slight chin nod toward Christopher. "—who I have a lot of respect for. However, the minute—no—make that the second you think you can sugarcoat something or bullshit me, I'm out of here. No second chances. Understood?"

"Perfectly."

"Excellent." Taylor leaned back, flipped a few pages over on her legal pad, glanced up, pen ready. "Begin."

Darren recounted his story, leaving no stone, pebble, or grain of sand unturned. Taylor listened, periodically jotting down notes, and only interrupting for clarification. After a solid thirty minutes, their time was up.

"That's about all I need from you for now," she informed him. "Remember, the way you conduct yourself in the courtroom tomorrow matters, so I suggest you stand straight. No slouching, no mumbling, and keep from looking hard or guilty."

Out of nervousness, Darren laughed.

"This isn't remotely funny, Mr. Crane—*Darren*. That means no mean-mugging anyone. Stay as calm as possible. Make eye contact when necessary. If the judge asks you a question, don't hunch, stoop, or put your hands in your pockets. Before you answer, call him 'Your Honor.' Appear interested in whatever's going on but keep your comments to yourself. You need me to know something, jot it down. I'll make sure a pen and paper are available."

"Understood."

"I want you to look open, friendly, approachable, but absolutely no weird smiling, smirking, or blinking at anyone."

"Got it."

Taylor relaxed. "I had this client once—a real character. He came to court dressed like one of the Goodfellas. Black shirt, black tie, and he wore the same exact navy-blue jacket over his black slacks every single day. He even kept his greasy hair slicked back."

Darren smirked. "Gold tooth?"

"No, but because he was entirely too thin—probably

drug-related, he appeared even more emaciated. Couple that with horrible skin, and *voila,* a full-fledged criminal. Oh, and to compound matters, he had the most annoying, creepy laugh. The moron kept giggling at inappropriate times, tugging at my sleeve during the hearing like a toddler."

"—and as a result, he was found guilty."

"Oh, no. I got him off, but only barely."

Darren nodded. "Impressive."

"Hardly. I did my job, and Mr. Crane, and I expect you to do yours." Taylor rose from her seat, game face back on. She gathered her things. "I understand you have friends and family coming tomorrow?"

"Uh, my, um, Olivia and Irwin."

Taylor turned her head toward Christopher to clarify.

"His wife and employer, but Irwin's more a friend."

"Ah." Taylor leaned over and wrote something on her pad.

Darren rested his hands on the ledge. "Personally, I wish they wouldn't come."

"Why is that?" Taylor stopped writing and glance up.

"I don't want them to see me like this."

"I disagree," she said. "It's important for the Magistrate to see you have people who care enough to take the time out of their busy lives to sit through this madness on your account."

Darren shrugged, not entirely sure he agreed.

The guard poked his head inside. "Time's up, Crane. Let's go. Put a move on it."

Christopher

"WHAT DO YOU THINK?" asked Christopher, once alone with Taylor in the lobby.

Taylor leaned against the hall wall. "If you're asking me if I think your friend is sincere, then yes. I believe him."

"That's great."

"Now we need to get the judge to believe him as well." Taylor lowered her voice. "I won't lie to you, Chris, this is an uphill battle, especially because of Darren's priors. We need to either get the coroner's report which will show that the cause of death was not murder to clear him, or a miracle happens, and the police find who really did it before we go to court." She straightened. "His being on parole doesn't help."

Christopher stiffened, knowing Taylor was right.

"In any event, tomorrow's all about bail. Frankly, I don't think we have a chance in hell."

"Why is that?"

"I know the prosecutor. A real hard ass who thinks everyone's guilty until proven innocent. We've clashed before, and honestly, I don't see today's hearing going any differently. Bottom line, your friend's chances of being released on bail for murder are less than zero."

Christopher crossed his arms over his chest, none too happy with the news. "His family is going to be disappointed."

"Temporarily."

"Meaning?"

"It means, my friend, that I'm freakin' exceptional at my job."

"And?"

"And from where I stand, the police don't have a shred of evidence except a fingerprint on a supposed weapon with a perfectly logical explanation. Also, Darren has umpteen witnesses to confirm his whereabouts prior to the attack. Additionally—the motive. What's his motive? The reason? The history? But again, tomorrow's hearing is only about bail—not any of this."

Christopher nodded. "Darren did threaten Alastair on the sidewalk."

"Did anybody hear him?"

"Only the entire block."

"Yes, however, the fact that he threatened Alastair with a bear attack works in our favor. I'll chalk it up to verbose male posturing."

Christopher wasn't so sure. "I don't know. He's done time for assault before. They're bound to bring that up."

"Oh, they most certainly will—I would." Taylor switched her briefcase to her other side. "But I'll be ready for them."

"And in the meantime, as your 'intern'—what do you need me to do?"

"Keep Darren calm. Make sure his family doesn't do anything stupid. I'll need to speak with each one of them, individually, but not today or tomorrow. Monday, the latest. Hopefully, by then, we'll get the coroner's report back so we can see precisely what we're facing."

"And when he doesn't get bail?"

"It'll either get carried over to a Preliminary Hearing where his case gets waived to the Court of Common Pleas by our defendant; or, after the hearing, if the charges are either dismissed or bound over to court by the Magistrate District Judge. Either way, we'll know soon enough."

"Got it."

"Oh," she snapped her fingers. "And his parole officer? I appreciate you getting this letter from him," she tapped her briefcase, "but I'll want to speak to him directly unless you want to handle the interview? It'll save us both time if we team up on this."

"Not a problem."

"Good. I'll meet you at the Magistrate's."

"Anything else?" asked Christopher.

"Yeah," said Taylor. "Pray."

CHAPTER 12

Beatrice

DESPITE THE MARATHON shower taken the evening before, Beatrice had another, but this time to clear the cobwebs from her foggy head.

As much as she preferred to stay home and hide from the world, Beatrice decided the best thing to do was to act as if nothing out of the ordinary had occurred. Containing her nerves and keeping up appearances would prove difficult, but in all probability, the smartest course of action. Regrettably, her only option, until of course she was discovered as the real culprit. Beatrice shuddered, envisioning the police officers surrounding her home, breaking down the door, handcuffing her while they read her the Miranda rights. She could see herself being dragged and shoved down the steps and tossed into the back of a police car, carted off to the jail like a common criminal. Her eyes filled with tears. Then another horrible thought clobbered her.

I still don't have the news clipping.

She reached up and clenched her throat, feeling her pulse going buck-wild.

If the police find it before I do, they'll have a motive.

Face flushed and nostrils flared, she fought to regain control. Breathe," she instructed herself, leaning over the sink to comb through her still damp hair, twisting it carelessly into a sloppy bun at the base of her neck.

If I find where Alastair hid the paper, I still might have a chance to walk away from this—as long as Cornelia's memories don't return.

She slid her black reading glasses on, rubbed her parched lips with balm, and squeezed exactly two modest squirts of perfume to cover the stench or guilty perspiration on each wrist before slipping her jacket on. Fighting the shakes, Beatrice snatched her briefcase, filled mostly with a bagged lunch and a half-way finished romance novel and headed out the door—completely forgetting about the discarded, blood splattered clothing bagged in her hall, ready for the garbage heap.

Beatrice proceeded to lock the front door.

I can do this.

Her neighbor, the retired teacher from next door, must have heard her leaving.

"Good morning, Beatrice," greeted Mrs. Carmichael, popping out a head crowded with over-sized curlers. "Nippy today."

Beatrice suppressed a sneer. "Sure is, Mrs. Carmichael." They had this exact same conversation with little deviance at least twice a week. "How are you feeling this morning?" she asked, hating herself the minute the words left her mouth.

Mrs. Carmichael tugged her old, frayed at the hem blush pink housecoat tighter around her body as if bracing for a tornado. "Oh, you know me, not one to complain."

No. Never you.

Beatrice shoved her keys into her coat pocket.

"Same stuff, different day, I say." Mrs. Carmichael shuffled over to where Beatrice waited. "I'll tell ya, though, my arthritis been acting up something terrible over the past few days."

"Has it?"

"Oh, my, yes. Must be a storm brewing. My guess headed from the south. I can feel it in my bones."

Mrs. Carmichael's bones worked harder than most weathermen.

"A storm? When?"

"Oh, by the feel of things, probably by early evening. It's gonna be a big one. You might want to stop at the grocery store on the way home as a precaution and pick up whatever incidentals you'll need to hold you over for at least a few days I'm thinking."

"Good idea." Beatrice agreed, although, in truth, she had no intention of heeding her nosey neighbor's unsolicited advice.

"If you do decide to stop at the store, Beatrice, would you mind picking me up a carton of orange juice? And a loaf of raisin bread. I love having a slice for breakfast or for my mid-afternoon snack. A habit I picked up from my father, God rest his soul. The man always had to have a slice slathered with jam with his oatmeal every morning—along with a strong cup of coffee, black, no sugar."

Beatrice nodded.

"He was a machine."

"I can only imagine."

"And would you pick me up one of those lotto tickets while you're at it? Here's my numbers." She handed Beatrice a filled-out slip of paper. "I'll make sure to pad this month's rent to cover the cost."

"Sure thing, Mrs. C." Beatrice knew full well the promised reimbursement would never quite materialize, but she gave up caring a long time ago.

"You're a sweetheart. Thanks."

"Not a problem." Beatrice turned to leave.

"*Brrr*, cold out here!" Mrs. Carmichael shifted from foot to foot, blowing hot air into the palms of her hands. "You know, you can't be too careful these days. Not in this crazy world."

Beatrice gave a half shrug. "I suppose not."

"It's important now more than ever to take precautions. Be prepared for the worst and hope for the best is what I always say."

Since when?

"True," Beatrice tensed her shoulders.

"I mean, let's face it. One day you're here, minding your own business with not a care in the world, and then the very next, poof, you're gone."

Beatrice gasped and spun to face her boarder. "What did you mean by that?"

"Hmm," said Mrs. Carmichael, in a loud, conspiratorial whisper. "I suppose you haven't heard the news, then?"

Beatrice gulped, but the lump jammed in the back of her throat made swallowing difficult. "No. What news?"

I feel sick.

"A shopkeeper on Main Street got murdered yesterday.

Come to think of it, I believe you might know the guy I'm referring to."

Oh, God.

Beatrice's knees banged. "Me?"

"Yes. Now that I think of it, I'm almost sure of it. Small, compact man, awful mustache, pasty skin? Owns—or rather owned—the old antique shop."

"Alastair Brooke." Head swimming, a rush of bile rose in Beatrice's throat.

"You see! I knew you would know. Small world."

Beatrice pressed her lips closed, fighting the urge to stifle the woman.

"Well," continued Mrs. Carmichael, "it turns out somebody, they don't know who yet, killed him, and in broad daylight no less. I mean, can you believe it? Here of all places." She clasped her throat. "Mind you, I never had occasion to go into that store. Too uppity for my tastes, but perhaps you have—with him being your friend and all."

"I-I—" Beatrice rubbed her temples, trying to focus.

"I never liked how dark and gloomy he kept his place," *tsked* Mrs. Carmichael. "Much too grim. And with my allergies and all that dust. A recipe for disaster, if you ask me."

Stop talking.

"There had to be a ton of that stuff floating around," touted Mrs. Carmichael, oblivious to Beatrice's increasing distress. "—the dust I mean. Anyway, I best go inside. It's getting a bit too nippy to be standing out here with just a bathrobe on."

Despite dipping, frigid temperatures, beads of sweat slid down the back of Beatrice's neck, soaking the inner edge of her coat collar. A lightheadedness rushed over her.

Mrs. Carmichael opened her screen door. As she

tugged, a single undone curler slipped and sagged, looking ready to escape. "I mean, what's the world coming to these days?"

Beatrice tried to respond, but only managed to squeak out a high-pitched garbled, "*Youdon'tsay?*"

"Hmmm, from what I heard, he died pretty quickly."

"Heard? From who?" mumbled Beatrice, conscious of her labored, slowed speech. "The police?"

"No, not exactly, but it's common sense, right?"

Eyes glazed, Beatrice could only manage to stare. However, she must have looked dolefully confused because Mrs. Carmichael pointed to her temple.

"The head. Or rather the human skull. It's not meant to be knocked around like a golf ball, you know."

Ugh.

Beatrice swayed side to side. She reached out an arm, groping for anything to lean on for support.

"Are you okay dear? You look awfully pale." Genuine concern traversed Mrs. Carmichael plump face. "It's my fault. I probably shouldn't have said anything, but it's been splashed all over the news."

Beatrice's eyes fluttered...

"And to think, here we are, us gals alone with a cold-blooded murderer running about."

The world went still.

It took only a millisecond before Beatrice's knees buckled beneath her, sending her body cascading down the side of the house until she landed butt first, flat on the porch.

"Beatrice!" screamed Mrs. Carmichael, rapping her repeatedly on the cheek. "Oh, Beatrice, you poor thing. Can you hear me?" she fussed.

Beatrice's eyes flitted open. "Please," she moaned, pinching the bridge of her nose. "Stop hitting me."

"Oh...sorry about that, but you scared the bejesus out of me." Mrs. Carmichael pressed her hand flat on Beatrice's chest.

"What the hell are you're doing?'

"Checking for a heartbeat."

"I'm obviously alive," she snapped, flicking the annoying woman's hand away. "I'm a little dizzy, is all."

"Here, let me at least help you sit up." Mrs. Carmichael darted to the side and leaned over, gripping Beatrice underneath the arms. Beatrice acquiesced and let the woman help her up.

"I don't think you're in any condition to go to work."

"I'm fine," Beatrice puffed

"Don't be silly. The flu's been making its rounds, knocking folks out."

"It's not—it's not the flu," insisted Beatrice, tempering her voice.

"How's your throat? Does it hurt to swallow? Any swollen glands?"

"My throat is fine..."

"Then what about your ears? Any pain in your ears? That can cause dizziness as well."

Oh, my Lord, make this woman go away.

"My ears don't bother me either," grumbled Beatrice.

"Sometimes, it can start in the ears, and before you know it, the infection works its way down to the throat. The piping's all connected inside." Mrs. Carmichael's housecoat blew up, exposing a blue trail of varicose veins on two, thick, pale legs.

Beatrice, doing her best to block out the woman's relentless yammering, wiped away a pool of saliva forming in the corner of her mouth. "I'm fine, Mrs. C. Really. But thank you." Beatrice slowly rose to her feet, gesturing that she could manage by herself. "I didn't get enough sleep last night."

"Now, now," said Mrs. Carmichael, her fluffy slippers slapping against the wood porch. She guided Beatrice by the elbow over to a small deck chair. "Sit and catch your breath for a minute."

"Thanks, but I'll be okay."

Mrs. Carmichael *tsked* in disapproval. "Hmm, are you sure about that? I mean, about going to work?"

Beatrice struggled to concentrate, weighing her limited options. She tucked a fallen lock of loose hair behind her ear before attempting to stand. "I'm sure," she mumbled, exhaling a long, drawn-out, wearied breath. "What choice do I have?"

Beatrice

BEATRICE PRESSED her cupped eyes against the shop's glass, searching for any indicator the store was open. Besides all the lights on inside, she hadn't thus far, seen anyone.

Maybe I got the time wrong.

She rechecked the signed on the door.

Great. Opens at ten on Wednesdays.

Frustrated, she wiggled the doorknob again as if by some miracle, it wouldn't be locked like the last two times she checked. Beatrice peered through the window again, but this time, she noticed Cornelia's stupid cat stretched out on a cushioned chair, cleaning his paws.

Sensing her presence, Bones quickly turned his head toward her, twitching his tail. Pupils dilated, he flattened his ears against his head, glaring. Then, as if ready to pounce, he arched his furry back, baring his incisors. *Hiss.*

"Ah!" she screeched, jerking her head back, startled. "Stupid cat," she grumbled, grateful for the separation of glass.

She turned around, ready to give up, but in that instant, she caught movement inside. Inching closer, and careful not to press her entire body against the window frame, she peeked inside.

Now, what do we have here?

She watched the girl who worked there, Harper-something, rifle through the drawers behind the cash register.

What's she up to?

Beatrice crept closer, straining her neck as far as it would go, but still not enough to see past the tall counter blocking out whatever the girl searched for. And then, there it was—"Ah-huh." Beatrice murmured, cracking a slight smile.

A key. But a key to what?

Wherever it's to, it must be pretty important since the silly young woman could be seen bouncing up and down, waving her find in the air. Beatrice heard her shout something to somebody else.

Why a key?

Could she have gotten locked out of her apartment?

No. That doesn't make any sense.

The last time Beatrice had been inside the book shop, she had clearly noticed two doors. One that led upstairs to the apartments, and another, presumably, to either a basement or a storage room.

—unless...

Beatrice would need to check out a few things, but if her hunch was correct, all buildings in the township kept plans—schematics—filed with the administration. She strained her neck higher to take one last quick peek and—

"Can I help you?"

"*Gah!*" Beatrice yelped, practically vaulting far enough away to almost slip and fall.

Irwin reached out and caught the tumbling woman before she landed splat on the sidewalk.

"Oh, Mr. Abernathy!" Beatrice gasped. "It's you."

Irwin helped steady her.

"Thanks."

"Are you, all right, Miss Aston?"

"Yes, fine," she sputtered, totally taken off guard and embarrassed. "Gosh, sorry. I, um, well, to be honest, you scared me," she said, realizing how suspect she looked.

Irwin nodded, his expression blank.

"I came by hoping to get something from the shop, but I must have gotten the time wrong."

"We open late on Wednesdays."

"Yes, I see that now."

"Was there something in particular you needed?" he asked.

"*Err*, I'm looking for a book on—um, baking. Baking cupcakes," she nodded too fast. "Lots and lots of cupcakes. In lots and lots of colors." Beatrice drew her scarf closer around her mouth.

Irwin checked his watch. "The shop doesn't open until ten, but I can help you. Why don't you step inside where it's warm?" he insisted.

Beatrice leaned away, twisting her body towards the street. "No, um, that's all right. I can come back at another time." She looked at her wrist, bereft of a watch. "I'm already late for work, and I should really, uh, go." She felt Irwin dissecting her.

"Nonsense," he said. "You're already here. Come inside, grab whatever book you wanted. I'll ring you right up and send you on your way."

"That's very kind of you, Mr. Abernathy," she said, her mouth forming a confused smile.

Irwin unlocked the door and held it open for her to enter before him.

It hadn't taken Beatrice long to realize how idiotic she'd sounded, concocting such a stupid story.

Of all the stupid things to say—cupcakes. What the heck do I know about baking?

Her eyes darted side-to-side, uncertain which direction to head in. Beatrice hesitated, taking a small step forward then pausing, only to start again and stop. To mask the absurdity, she strode with determination toward the right side of the shop.

"Miss Aston." Irwin flipped on a succession of lights. "We keep the cookbooks and anything pertaining to baking to your left, two middle rows down, last aisle."

Good grief...

"Ah, that's right. Thank you, Mr. Abernathy," she replied, muttering under her breath the rest of the way. "Silly me."

Meanwhile...

"Don't walk so fast," huffed Cornelia, gripping her cane with one hand and the back of Harper's shirt with the other.

"We're almost there."

Harper and Cornelia successfully navigated their way through the dimly lit laundry room and around the bend to the far back metal door linking Alastair's store.

"It's sure dark and cold in here," complained Cornelia. "I can hardly see a thing."

Harper groped her way forward. "I thought there'd be enough light from the laundry room to see." She waved her hands, feeling for a switch. "We should have brought a flashlight."

"I sort of remember there being a light somewhere," mentioned Cornelia. "One of those—"

"*Eek*!" screamed Harper springing backward. "*Ewww!* Something popped me in my face," she yelped, swatting at the air.

Cornelia laughed and pulled the long, twine cord. "And God said, 'Let there be light.'"

"Oh." Harper blushed. "How was I supposed to know?"

Cornelia pointed to the door. "What's that?"

"I don't know. Looks like something stuck to the door." Harper stepped closer. "Oh, no."

"What?"

Harper sighed. "You're not going to believe this."

"Try me."

"It's a note."

"A note? What kinda note?"

"A note addressed to us."

"Oh no, is right," groaned Cornelia, ripping it down to read aloud.

To My Dear Miss Marple, and her trusty sidekick,
Harper-Nosy-Crane:

While I appreciate the two of you wishing to help, your
ill-timed bungling assistance shall not be required.
Therefore, promptly return the key to its proper place,
and we will pretend that this latest kerfuffle never
happened.

Much appreciated.
Sincerely,
Irwin

"Dagnabbit," grumbled Cornelia. "Foiled again."

"I'd really wish you'd stop saying that."

"What else do you want me to say?"

Harper yanked the chain, leaving the two of them standing in the dark. "Let's get out of here," she said, headed back to where they started. Harper shoved the door open. "Give me the key. I'll put it back."

"I still think we should have gone inside," said Cornelia, brooding. "Who knows what illuminating clues we'd find."

"I doubt that."

"Why? For all you know, Alastair hid something—maybe something his killer wanted."

"Like what?"

"Like maybe a suitcase full of George Washingtons."

"Dollar bills?"

"Uh, okay. Make that Jeffersons."

"Negative."

Cornelia grew frustrated. "Lincoln, Jackson, then—"

"Nope. Still wrong."

"Oh, I know. Hamiltons!"

"Benjamins," Harper smiled. "And why would Alastair

keep a suitcase full of money in the store? That doesn't even make any sense."

"True. Maybe rubles."

"Rubles?" Harper sucked her teeth. "You and your whodunits. One of these days they're going to—uh oh. Irwin—" she shrieked, hiding the key behind her back. "Look, Cornelia, it's Irwin."

Irwin sat relaxing on Cornelia's favorite chair, his hands clasped on his lap. He gave the pair an amused, knowing smirk, then unwrapped a piece of chocolate and popped it into his mouth.

"H-E-double-hockey-sticks," grumbled Cornelia, elbowing Harper forward.

"Ladies." Irwin crumpled the wrapper in his palm and tossed it in the can.

Harper reddened. "We were, um..." She jiggled the key in the air. "But you already know that."

Irwin plucked at the cuff of his shirt.

"Why are you here?" asked Cornelia. "I thought you were supposed to be at the courthouse."

"I am, but Christopher called and left me a message. He said that they don't hear his case until right before lunch, so I decided to hang out here for a few extra minutes." He checked the time and glanced at Harper. "Is your mother ready?"

Cornelia trotted over to the stairs, opened the door, and yelled.

"Olivia! Irwin's here."

"I'll be down in a minute," came the reply.

Harper returned the key back under the mat. "How'd you know?" she asked.

Irwin relinquished his seat. He put his hat on, zipped his coat closed and adjusted a wool scarf around his neck.

"I suspected you and your crime partner over there would try something."

Cornelia returned in time to overhear. "Nobody likes a know-it-all, Irwin," she said, rolling her eyes.

"Excuse me." Beatrice nipped her head out from behind a bookshelf, an oversized cookbook clasped in her hands. "I don't mean to interrupt, but I think I'll take this one."

Beatrice

BEATRICE PAID for the cookbook she'd probably never use, careful to avoid making eye contact with Cornelia. After leaving the shop, she headed to the office to do a bit of snooping.

I need to get into his store and look around, find that paper.

If what she suspected was correct, she'd have no choice but to find a way to pinch the key from beneath the bookshop's mat and return it without anyone the wiser.

But how?

Irwin

BEATRICE ASTON ... pondered Irwin, not generally perplexed. *A skilled liar she isn't.*

After spending decades listening to people invent all types of excuses as to lost or supposed stolen library books, he'd gotten pretty adept at detecting a fibber. He found that typically, before speaking, the liar in question would first try to pretend they were calmer than they were, often keeping their hands flat at their sides like toy soldiers. Other times, they would tell their convoluted tales speaking particularly slow, keeping their facial movements to a minimum, as if making it up as they went along.

"So, what you're telling me is, somehow, somebody stole your book?" he'd ask, his eyes glued to the culprit's face.

Then, more often than not, the person would emphatically repeat 'yes' —under the delusion that Irwin believed them. Meanwhile, they would subconsciously be shaking their head 'no.' Another probable sign of deceit.

While Beatrice certainly portrayed an outward aura of calm, her strained efforts to convince Irwin were for naught. He had kept an eye on her bumbling her way through the store, nervously puttering about as if caught red-handed at something.

But what exactly?

Irwin had also noticed how uncomfortable she became any time he moved closer, recalling at one point how she kept arching away or stepping to the side, her hands firmly placed on the opposite side of where he stood, as if ready to bolt and run.

Something is up.

Irwin didn't trust Beatrice. Something about her aloof, bordering on rude—personality had never sat right with him. However, until today, Irwin never would have described Beatrice as a blatant liar. *Yes,* he thought to himself, *something apparently is going on—something she wants to hide.*

Then again, Irwin mused, he could be over-reading something less nefarious into Beatrice's behavior, knowing full well that individual deviations weren't necessarily a guarantee that somebody was actively trying to be deceptive. However, in Beatrice's case, there had been a mixture of unusual reactions in direct response to his inquiries. Most noticeably, her body movements. Those alone had been enough to betray whatever innocuous words coming out of her mouth. Another red flag that she wasn't exactly being forthcoming.

Irwin decided he needed to pay closer attention to Miss Beatrice Aston moving forward, hoping that catching her in a bald-faced lie would be as easy as her making one nonsensical slip-up.

CHAPTER 13

Olivia Crane

OLIVIA'S STOMACH had been bothering her all morning; cramping spams...butterflies. Nerves. Her left eye, weary from lack of sleep, twitched, which had made applying her mascara this morning an acrobatic feat.

The short ride over to the courthouse had been uneventful. Had it not been so blustery and frigid outside, they would have walked. Luckily, the pair arrived early enough to secure a parking spot relatively close to the building, making the brief hike through the ice tundra less cumbersome.

I should have worn boots, she thought, cautious as to where she stepped. Her gaze cast downwards, making doubly sure not to slide or bust her ass on a patch of uncovered ice.

"Here we go," grumbled Irwin, holding the heavy, ornate door open for her.

Only a small handful of folks were already waiting inside. Olivia notice a somewhat despondent looking group of people whose collective glumness and apprehension soundlessly encouraged a general use of hushed voices. However, not less than ten minutes later, the dam of silence broke, and people noisily flooded in from all directions. Stern-faced court officers without a drop of levity in their step, led in an endless stream of defendants—all wearing their version of a long face through various halls and into different courtrooms. Each prisoner, one behind the other, shuffled more than walked, hindered from making any sweeping movement by either leg or handcuffs. Sometimes both. They moved in procession, solemnly forward as if inwardly bracing themselves to face either the short—or long-term consequences of their committing varying degrees of offenses. Their harried attorneys showed up in spurts, most gripping leather briefcases in one hand and thick files in the other. Some were already inside the courtroom while others stepped out of jammed-packed elevators in a mad search of their clients. Administrative workers also disembarked from lifts or from the staircase, quickly commandeering their designated places. Everyone moved about, clear about the role they played in getting everyone ready for today's latest version of the Greatest Show in the World.

Irwin, new to the workings of a brutal, and often taciturn justice system waited on the wooden bench calmly observing the mayhem beginning to unravel around him, while Olivia, more familiar with how the system worked, couldn't sit still.

"Olivia, please," sighed Irwin.

"Sorry. I'm nervous," she said, leg bouncing. Her fidgety fingers wound and twisted the cord attached to the "Visitor's Pass" tag she wore around her neck. "This place brings back too many bad memories. The sooner today is over, the better."

The noise level quickly swelled as more defendants showed up. Lawyers in three-piece suits sauntered in, heads rotating side to side, mouthing the names of their clients, while others already seated bent or twisted over wooden benches to speak to their charges, some of whom they had obviously never met before. Three people stood at the front of the room, conversing in lowered voices over the contents of a cardboard box, overflowing with files.

"Who are they," asked Irwin, his chin jutted in their direction, "and what do they do?"

"They're court officers," answered Olivia quietly. "Their job is to sift through all those dockets you see in that box to make sure they have the correct defendant files to hand-off to the judge whenever he's ready."

Irwin blinked. "They seem utterly perplexed."

As if on cue, a bullet-proofed-vested, surly-looking armed court officer traversed the aisles, stopping momentarily to stare long and hard at Irwin before walking away.

"What in the hell was that all about?" snorted Irwin, not at all appreciating the eyeball dressing down.

"Patrolling for cell phones and other contraband."

"Contraband I understand, but cellphones? Rather redundant since they insisted on taking ours away."

Upon entering the courthouse, all visitors were required to surrender their cell phones.

"Can't we simply turn them off?" Irwin had said to the court officer after walking through a metal detector.

"Sorry. No phones inside." The court officer dropped each cellphone into a plastic bag. The officer then handed Olivia and Irwin identification slips for later retrieval, and a lanyard visitor pass. "You'll get this back when you leave."

Olivia shifted uncomfortably on the bench. "Not everyone is inclined to follow the rules, Irwin. Some people don't listen and sneak them in any way," she explained. "Hence, why we are in a courthouse surrounded by handcuffed individuals all here due to some infraction of the law. Everything from simple misdemeanors to serious felonies."

Irwin, the consummate people watcher, a long-standing habit he had picked up during his years as a librarian, couldn't help but stare at a woman wearing a county issued jumpsuit, handcuffed four rows ahead, using the edge of a bench to scratch her back. When she glanced up and noticed him watching her, she snarled, flipped Irwin the bird, and finished her performance with an aggrandized, lip-synched version of, *Fuck You.*

Unfazed, Irwin didn't bat an eye but instead leaned into Olivia to lodge another complaint. "I find this entire process lacking a certain level of proficiency," he muttered, clearly not impressed.

"You can say that again, old timer," said a craggy voice from behind them, busy scribbling 'The system is rigged' in permanent magic marker on the back of the wooden bench. "It's a circus, and any minute now, the ringleader will be here to start the show."

"I assume our *neighbor* is referring to the judge," murmured Irwin in Olivia's ear.

Olivia wriggled in her seat, cursing the dress she selected for court. The same outfit she had changed in and out of at least five times before ultimately throwing in the towel. She reached down to tug the hem, willing it to stretch longer and feel less confining.

The morning had been rushed. A madhouse. Everyone vying for first dibs in the shower, anxious to get their day started and over with. Olivia had walked in on Christopher hunched over a bowl of cereal at the kitchen table, dressed handsomely in a suit shoving food into his mouth while jotting notes on the back of a discarded envelope. On the way to get ready, she'd passed Cornelia and Harper hanging out on the couch busy chatting, but still not dressed. They'd had their heads joined, whispering conspiratorially, but halting their conversation as soon as she showed up.

"Hey, Mom." Harper waved innocently.

"Harper...Cornelia. How did you ladies sleep?"

"Like the living dead," said Cornelia.

"Walking dead," corrected Harper, stretching. "Me, too," she lied.

"Uh, huh." Olivia side-eyed the pair. "Well, I'm next in the shower. Christopher's done and in the kitchen. When I'm finished, you two can decide who goes next."

"Sounds good," Harper agreed a bit too readily.

Cornelia smiled, but not a real smile. More of a conniving smile, like the two of them were up-to-no-good-smile. Of this, Olivia felt confident, but Irwin would arrive soon, and she didn't have the energy, time, or inclination to figure out what. She moved swiftly down the hall, rushed.

"Where did I put my hairclip now?" she muttered, rummaging through her dresser drawer, positive she'd seen it a second earlier. "Darn it! Where are my earrings?" She lifted her hand to tuck a loose strand of hair back in place when her fingers brushed over the petite hoop earring already in place. "Oh, man," she moaned. "I'm seriously losing it."

What's next?

"Shoes." Typically, a pair of sneakers would have sufficed, but not today... not for court.

Ugh ... court.

Olivia slipped on a pair of black flats; her stand-in shoe whenever forced to dress up. On top of getting washed, ready, and hunting for misplaced items, she also had to gather a few of Darren's things, making sure she remembered everything on Taylor's list: a pair of dress slacks, a white long-sleeve dress shirt, a tie, belt, dress socks, and a pair of shoes for Darren to change into for court.

Since moving into the apartment, Olivia had made it a policy to never go into his bedroom, and she certainly had never rifled through his personal things before. Today, she had no choice.

Forgive me, Darren.

Despite having a perfectly good reason for being there, Olivia moved guardedly around the small room, conscious of being in Darren's space, opening up his closet, his drawers. She slid open the middle drawer and found a pair of black dress socks. From the closet, she collected a pair of shoes, slacks, shirt, and tie. Olivia checked the list. "That's everything," she muttered to herself, anxious to leave. Then something caught her eye. A small, square, faded, much-handled photo tucked into the corner of his dresser mirror.

I haven't seen this for years.

A snapshot taken of them when they were kids...teens. She laughed, pleasantly surprised he had kept a copy.

Olivia had assumed the photo, along with most of the others, had been lost or ruined in the many moves since then. To see this one displayed prominently on Darren's mirror brought back a host of memories—all good ones. She bent over to take a closer look and smiled. There they were, young and dumb…sitting on the grass at their high school without a care in the world, Olivia nestled on Darren's lap. The photo had captured the two of them grinning about something they must have found amusing—what—she couldn't recall.

We had a lot of laughs back then, before—

Those were happy times, innocent times—unfettered or tainted by a future of mistakes. She rubbed the photo with the tip of her finger lightly over Darren's adorable baby face perched playfully on her shoulder—*he was always the one to ham it up for the camera.*

"What were you grinning about?" she murmured, studying her lost, stuck in the past expression in his vanity mirror. She slipped the photo out from its resting place and flipped it over. There, inscribed in Darren's slanted handwriting, 'Me & Liv 4-Ever,' enclosed in a heart.

We were so young—with an entire lifetime of dreams ahead of us.

Olivia took one last long look before returning it.

To the outside world, they appeared as a cohesive family unit. Privately, Olivia and Darren had worked exceptionally hard to implement healthy boundaries between them; deliberately done to make it easier to unpack and navigate the complicated feelings growing between them.

From the living room, she overheard Irwin speaking with Harper and Cornelia.

"Olivia!" shouted Cornelia a moment later. "Irwin wants to know if you're ready."

"Coming." She quickly gathered Darren's clothing into her arms and made a silent prayer that the outfit she had selected would still fit, especially since the last time the man had dressed-up was at Harper's high school graduation, three—almost closer to four years ago. She sighed.

Time sure seems to fly when your aspirations are about to crash and burn.

HOURS TICKED by and still no Darren. Court officers busied themselves with pulling out names off an endless docket, while defendants sat and waited...and waited. One big dude, easily over six-feet tall, eventually gave up and fell asleep, leaning onto the shoulder of the much smaller guy stuck sitting next to him who appeared reluctant to push the big fella off. The big man snorted so loudly during the previous proceeding that one of the court officers had to march over to shake him awake.

"Next!" yelled the annoyed, exhausted judge at the proceeding parade of defendants being ushered inside.

"I wish I could text Harper." Olivia twirled her thumbs. "We've been cooped up in here all day. She must be worried sick, wondering what's taking us so long."

"I'm wondering what's taking us so long myself."

Olivia shifted in her seat, unable to find a comfortable position.

"For heaven's sake, please stop fidgeting, Olivia," hissed Irwin.

"Sorry."

"You need to relax. It's going to be okay."

The woman sitting next to Olivia bent forward and scrunched her overly plucked eyebrows at Irwin as if to say, 'You really think so, huh, buddy?' She then leaned back once again, crossing her arms over her chest, cackling.

"Dreadful," mumbled Irwin.

"I don't know how you can stay so calm." Olivia reached into her purse and pulled out a small tin. "Mint?"

Irwin opened his palm. Olivia tapped a few pieces into Irwin's palm.

"Ma'am?" Olivia asked the woman seated next to her.

"Sure. Don't mind if I do."

Olivia poured more than a few into the woman's extended hand, saving two for herself. "My Lord, we've been here for hours. When will it be Darren's turn?"

"I have absolutely no idea." Irwin shrugged. "My rump is numb, my bladder is in distress, and I have lost all track of time and humanity while here."

"Aren't you wearing a watch?"

"I am, but I adamantly refuse to recheck it. Far too tormenting."

CHRISTOPHER WAITED IN THE HALL, periodically peeking inside the courtroom to check if they had arrived.

Inside the courtroom were a wide assortment of folks. Defendants wearing expensive suits while others remained in prison jumpsuits. Some had loved ones who'd showed up, while the majority sat unaccompanied, forced to face the music alone. Nevertheless, despite the variety of exteriors on display, everyone here shared one thing in common, and that was despair. The fear of the unknown. In some cases, the indefinite.

Where could those two be?

He could have kicked himself ten ways to Sunday for not being more precise about where Olivia and Irwin should meet him. He decided to peek in another court-room down the short hall, this time relieved to find them. "Psssst…," Christopher waved to Irwin and Olivia.

"Look. There's Christopher," muttered Irwin. "He wants us to go out in the hall."

"Come with me. Hurry." he motioned and quietly closed the door to wait in the hall.

Olivia and Irwin stared at one another, confused, but grabbed their coats and followed Christopher out into the hall as instructed.

"What's the matter?" asked Olivia. "Why haven't they brought Darren out?"

"You're in the wrong place—my fault. I assumed you knew where I meant."

"I don't understand," said Irwin.

"Darren's going in front of the District Magistrate. If we hurry, we can get there in time. They usually do the hearing by video from the jail, but since you guys are involved, Taylor persuaded the judge to give permission for you both to sit in on the hearing, but we have to hurry."

CHRISTOPHER, Irwin, and Olivia slipped into the room and took a seat. The Magistrate glanced over but didn't say a word to them.

Within minutes, Darren appeared on the video screen in his orange jumpsuit. A young, stunning young woman dressed to the nines carrying an expensively stylish brief-case strode over to the defendant's table, commanding her space with an air of confidence that ignited the room. The woman dropped her small bag on the table and lifted out a sizeable file, highlighters, and a pen.

"Who's she?" whispered Olivia, tugging on Irwin's sleeve.

"Mary Poppins," murmured Irwin, only half-joking.

"I wonder what happened to Taylor?"

"Shush."

"Why isn't Darren wearing his suit?" she whispered to Christopher.

"This is only the hearing," he quietly explained. "The suit is if we go to court."

Although uncuffed, Darren had two straight-faced, armed guards present, standing behind him.

The court officer shouted for quiet, and the room obeyed. "Commonwealth versus Darren E. Crane, docket 3578 Criminal 2019," said the District Attorney, Aaron Carter.

Darren and his attorney rose. The judge then ordered the court reporter to read the charges against Darren, including the alleged date, time, and place of the offense.

"Ms. Maldonado, has the defendant been made aware of all criminal charges against him?" asked the Judge, sifting through a small stack of stapled papers.

"Yes, Your Honor."

The judge spoke loudly. "A plea of not guilty will herein be entered into the court record."

"We're here to set bail on this matter," said the ADA. "The Commonwealth is asking for a secured bail in the amount of one million dollars since this is a capital murder case,"

Taylor cleared her throat. "Your Honor, Mr. Crane is here with support from friends; he is taking this case very seriously. He has been living in Monroe County for years, has a steady job, and currently reports to probation where he has had no problems, and indeed has done everything requested of him. My client denies his involvement completely, and that he showed up after the incident and fully cooperated with police—however, we understand the severity of the crime means there must be a secured bail. We would ask for $10,000 with the standard conditions. Mr. Crane, do you have anything you wish to say?"

From the screen, Darren shook his head "no."

"Your Honor, the defense requests that the court set bail for Mr. Crane. We contend that because Mr. Crane is anchored into this community, and has family in the area and employment, he is not, therefore, a flight risk."

"I disagree, Your Honor," interjected the prosecutor. "Mr. Crane might have family and a job, but he also has a violent history. A history that landed him a prior conviction which "If I may, Your Honor," interjected Taylor, "I would like to submit to the court a notarized letter from Mr. Crane's probation officer stating that he feels that Mr. Crane is in fact, not a high risk."

The prosecutor cleared his throat. "If the court pleases, I'd like to remind Ms. Maldonado that this is a homicide case, not a traffic violation."

"Which I am acutely aware of, Mr. Carter," interrupted Taylor. "Which is why I contend that the county's resources would be better spent searching for the actual killer instead of imprisoning the person responsible for reporting the crime."

"That will be enough," said the judge.

"Holy hell," whispered Olivia.

The judge shuffled through Darren's paperwork. "Mr. Crane, because the charge is murder, the court is unwilling at this time to grant bail. Therefore, I hereby order you to remain in custody. However, if anything changes, your attorney is certainly more than welcome to request a later bail hearing."

Darren put on a brave front as if this was no big deal.

Olivia's heart sank as she watched the officers lead Darren away. "I don't understand. Are they going to deny him bail just like that? They can't do that, can they?"

"Come. Let's wait outside for Christopher and Ms. Maldonado," instructed Irwin, guiding Olivia out of the courtroom. "They'll explain to us what happened."

"I already know exactly what happened. The system railroaded my husband," shouted Olivia.

"Amen," hissed a toothless woman wearing a tee shirt that read, 'Disorder in the Court.' "You tell 'am."

Olivia's eyes locked onto the prosecutor hoisting his bag over his shoulder to leave and took off after him.

"Olivia," called Irwin, too late.

"You piece of vile dog shit," she hissed at Carter.

"Excuse me." The District Attorney turned to see who spoke.

"You heard me."

Carter sneered, clearly irritated, but in control. "I suggest you take your friend out of here," he informed Irwin, "before I call that officer over here and have her arrested."

"You'd like that, wouldn't you," snarled Olivia, madder than a hatter and losing control.

Carter leaned forward and warned. "I was just doing my job."

"So, locking up innocent people is your job, is it? Did they teach you that at law school or was that something you picked up at Nazi training camp?"

Irwin sighed.

Carter lifted a finger, about to signal the court officer for assistance when Taylor swooped in out of nowhere, seizing Olivia by the arm like a long-lost sister. "That won't be necessary, Jim," she replied, sporting a too wide, ingratiating smile. "Mrs. Crane, please come with me. We have a lot to discuss."

"But—"

"Now, Mrs. Crane." Taylor placed her arm firmly around Olivia's shoulder. "Please," she whispered into Olivia's ear. "Not another word. Darren doesn't need you locked up as well."

Olivia's hawkish stance softened enough for Taylor to lead her out of the building without any further incident.

Jim Carter watched the women leave, his eyes fastened onto Taylor's curvaceous ass. "Hot temper on that one," he commented to Irwin.

"Excuse me," Irwin glowered, not at all comfortable with the DA's insinuation about Olivia nor his randy demeanor toward Ms. Maldonado, "but Mrs. Crane happens to be one of the kindest, most caring people I know, nevertheless, she does tend to get herself rather worked up, particularly whenever provoked by human canine excrement. Good day."

CHAPTER 14

Harper

HARPER UNLOCKED the register and popped open a roll of dimes. She glanced at the wall clock and sighed. "I wonder what time they'll be back?"

"I hope soon. I'm starving." Cornelia shifted in her chair. "What's Olivia making for dinner?"

"No idea," shrugged Harper. Maybe we should get takeout? I could go for some egg drop soup, and I know Bones is fiending for Shrimp Lo Mein."

Cornelia drew her shawl around her shoulders. "I'm starving. What's Olivia making for dinner?" she asked again.

Never say remember.

Harper sighed. Lapses in the middle of the conversation happened more frequently now, but Harper did her best not to draw attention to it. "Maybe, takeout."

"Bone's would love Shrimp Lo Mein."

Bones stretched, flexing his sharp claws. Then positioned himself on a floor pillow with his feet tucked underneath his body.

"Good idea."

"Can I ask you something?"

"Sure," nodded Cornelia.

"Don't you think Irwin's been sort of depressed recently?" asked Harper.

"He's probably concerned about Darren. He knows your father didn't whack Alastair."

"True, but I got the feeling that it's more than that. I don't know. Irwin's been sort of moody lately."

Cornelia sighed. "Perhaps."

"Maybe because of the holidays? Do they bring back memories of Gilly?"

Cornelia leaned back, appearing to gauge her response. "You have to understand, Harper. For Irwin, Gilly was a one-of-a-kind type of love. Beautiful, and I'm not only talking about the outside but the kind of exquisiteness that radiates from within a person when their heart is always in the right place." Eyes downcast, Cornelia let out a tired, ragged breath. "I'm probably repeating myself, but Gilly always made time for anyone who needed her, no matter what. And she was always the first to offer help."

Harper stopped counting. "I'm sorry. I shouldn't have brought this up. I'd forgotten how close the two of you were."

"Best of friends."

"You must miss her a lot."

"Oh, most definitely."

Harper closed the drawer. "I wish I could've met her. And her daughter."

Cornelia shrugged. "I didn't know Dakota as well as I did Gilly, but she seemed like a lovely girl on the few occasions we spoke. I do remember how proud Gilly was of her though. They enjoyed a close mother and daughter relationship, much like you and your mom." In an instant, Cornelia's facial expression transformed. Her eyes seemed to glaze over as if disappearing into a fog of distant memories.

"Cornelia?" Harper rushed to her side. "Are you okay?"

"What?" Cornelia's jaw poked out defiantly as if clamping down on a door of hidden emotions just waiting to bust wide open. "I'm sorry, what were we talking about?"

"Gilly," whispered Harper.

"Ah, yes, Gilly. She always made time for anyone who needed her, no matter what," reiterated Cornelia. "And she was always the first to offer help. You would have liked her."

Everyone understood how important Gilly had been to Irwin. How her sudden, tragic death had left him permanently wrenched precariously between existing and longing. But Harper never realized until this minute how devastatingly hard it must have also been for Cornelia—losing such a close friend so unexpectedly. "I'm sorry, Cornelia. I'm a jerk for even bringing it up."

"Oh, no, don't be silly. Sometimes the only way to keep those we've lost and miss close is to remember them when we can, speaking kindly of them with our lips and praying for them in our hearts."

A small smile tugged at the corner of Harper's mouth.

Man, for somebody on the dire cusp of losing her entire memory, Cornelia sure never forgets what's really important.

Harper reached for the broom and dustpan.

Now, if only she could remember who she saw next door.

Harper

"Soon. I don't care what mountains you need to move, it just has to be soon," Cornelia whispered urgently into the phone while Harper ran upstairs to prepare them a snack.

"I understand that perfectly well, Rodney, I truly do, but time is of the essence...Yes...I see." Cornelia leaned forward, craning her neck toward the back of the store, making sure she wasn't being overheard. "Fine. Fine. Do what you have to...No, everything's the same...The paperwork? Oh, yes, that. Just use what I filled out last year. That'll do... Listen, I'm counting on you to take care of all this loose end stuff...Ah, huh." Cornelia heard Harper clumping down the back stairs. "I gotta go...Yes, yes. I do understand but—"

Harper, hands full, shoved the door open with her hip. "I come bearing delicious, nutritious morsels of nutrients," she announced, balancing a tray of food and drinks. Without turning, she kicked the door shut with the heel of her boot.

Cornelia cupped the phone. "Yes, but, I-have-to-go," she hissed, as Harper approached.

"Who are you talking to?" mouthed a suspicious Harper, eyes squinted.

Cornelia stuck her finger in the air for Harper to give her a second. "Okay, President Obama," bellowed Cornelia into the phone. "Give your lovely wife Michelle and the girls, my love. Uh, huh...yes, most definitely. Oh, and please let 'em know I'm eating all my vegetables—except for cauliflower. I despise that pale, cruciferous vegetable." Cornelia nodded. "Okay then, yes, Mr. President...you too. Thanks for calling. Bye now." Cornelia hung up the line and slipped the phone into her sweater pocket.

Harper's mouth fell open. "Cornelia? Are you making pranks phone calls again?"

Cornelia stared straight ahead, feigning bewilderment. "Huh? I'm sorry, Harper, what did you say?"

Harper stared down at her friend, currently sticking her pointer finger into a donut, trying to scoop out globs of grape jelly, not entirely convinced whether or not Cornelia was screwing with her. "You were just on the phone."

"Who was?"

"You were."

"Me?"

"Yes, you."

"Who was I talking to?"

Never be condescending...

Harper, on the verge of hyperventilating, audibly counted back from five before speaking. "Apparently, President Obama."

Cornelia mischievously grinned ear to ear, fanning herself. "Oh, how nice. I must be awfully important to get a call from the likes of him."

Harper hung her head in defeat. "I give up."

Unencumbered by Harper's expectation of reality, Cornelia applauded. "Jelly donuts! My favorite."

Later that afternoon...

"WHAT THE HELL is going on at the courthouse already?" grumbled Harper, checking the time. Outside the sun had started to hide, the temperatures had dropped, and people rushed home to escape the chill. The morning had seen a sudden rush of customers, as did the early part of the afternoon, but now, as the quiet of the evening approached, a new batch of intrusive thoughts impeded Harper's peace of mind. To keep busy, she grabbed a rag from the backroom utility closet. "Don't you think some-body should have called by now?" Harper sneezed, breathing in a fresh scattering cloud dust from the air.

Cornelia polished off the last chocolate and returned the empty dish to the front desk. "Refill."

"Jeez, Cornelia! You ate the entire thing?" Harper lifted up the bowl, stunned.

"Not the entire thing. Most of the entire thing."

"That's a ton of sugar."

"What? Afraid I'll get sick?" Cornelia belched. "Give me a break, Harper, and stop policing me. I barely remember what I ate ten minutes ago, no less how much."

"What about what the neurologist said?"

"Who? Dr. Latimer?" Cornelia grumbled. "That guy... he's a first-class killjoy. Lives to ruin my life."

"Well, Mom's gonna kill me. She specifically told me before she left not to let you eat all of that."

"Then it's a good thing we follow the code."

"What code?" Harper stopped dusting, looking confused.

"*The code*. You know, —What happens in the bookshop

stays in the bookshop." Cornelia winked. "Besides, Olivia doesn't have to know everything. Now, be a doll and refill the thing."

Harper rolled her eyes, ready to argue, but stopped, realizing there was no point. For the time being, Cornelia seemed to be doing pretty well, however, the reality that most Alzheimer's patients failed anywhere from three-to-nine years after their diagnoses scared her down to the core, especially since Cornelia already had three years in.

Harper located a fresh bag of chocolates from beneath the front desk and ripped it open. She poured another impressive round into one bowl, saving the rest for a second. "Fuck Alzheimer's," she proclaimed, popping a milk chocolate square of pure deliciousness into her mouth and handing the rest to Cornelia.

Cornelia winked. "Amen, sister. Couldn't have said it better myself."

Harper laughed and returned to the desk. "In all seriousness, I'm terrified they're going to send Dad back to prison."

Cornelia humphed, unwrapping another candy. "Don't be silly," she mumbled, mouth full. "He's not going back to prison."

"Oh? How can you be so sure?" Harper picked up the decoy candy bowl, trying to decide where to put it.

"For starters," Cornelia licked her fingers, "because he didn't do it."

"I already know that."

"And for two, I know who did."

Harper nearly dropped the candy dish on the floor. "What!"

"What-what!" yelped Cornelia, bouncing out of her chair, her head turning side to side... "What happened?"

"What did you just say?" repeated Harper.

"What did who just say?"

"Not me, you!"

"Say about what?" Cornelia asked, turning flustered.

"About who did it?" Harper banged the candy dish down on the counter. A few of the chocolates tumbled over the side, one landing on the floor. Harper rushed to Cornelia's side, crouching down low enough to look into her friend's eyes. "Cornelia," she said as calmly as possible, "you said you knew who did it. Those were your exact words."

"Did I?" Cornelia frowned, pursing her lips in deep concentration. After a moment, she shook her head, thwarted. "Sorry, kid. I'm afraid I've hit another blank wall, but no worries, it'll come back to me...eventually."

Encourage, don't lecture.

"We don't have *eventually*, Cornelia. My dad's in jail now."

"What's he doing in there?"

"Oh, for shit's sake," grumbled Harper.

"Kidding," Cornelia giggled. "Lordy, lighten up, will you? Stop with all the doom and gloom."

Harper sighed.

"Look, if I know something, it's still in here," indicated Cornelia, tapping her forehead. "...somewhere."

Request, don't demand.

"Try to remember, Cornelia. *Please*. This is really, really important. I need you to think hard. What happened yesterday?"

Cornelia peered forward, her eyes motionless. "I...*remember*..."

"Yes—"

"Looking for Bones." Upon hearing his name, the lazy

cat stretched his paws and yawned. Arching his back, Bones rubbed his furry body against Cornelia's shin.

Encourage, don't humiliate.

"Good. That's great. Keep going."

"And...I *remember*...going next door."

"Okay. Awesome. Now we're getting somewhere." Harper leaned in closer. "Did you go inside? ...Maybe into Alastair's store?"

"I object, Your Honor. The prosecutor is obviously leading the witness."

"Cornelia!" Harper bit down on her lip, her patience all but slipping.

"Sorry...Hmmm, yes. I think so," nodded Cornelia. "I sort of recollect Alastair's stupid bell clinking. You know, I have to tell you, I've always hated those loud things. I mean, for heaven's sake, why does every shop owner feel compelled to put bells on their doorknobs? Is it a rule? Why not something nicer? Softer... maybe chimes," she shrugged. "I like chimes."

"Concentrate, Cornelia," Harper bounced on her knees. "You're doing fantastic, but I need you to keep going."

Cornelia squeezed her hands into tight balls. "You know what? I think I bumped into something." She bolted straight up. "No! *Wait!* It wasn't a something...it was a—"

"Go on."

"A...a—somebody! That's it. I bumped into a *somebody*!"

"Who? Who?" Harper repeated. "Tell me who—"

Clang

The shop's front door opened, and Cornelia glanced up.

"Beatrice!" hollered Cornelia, rather proud of herself. "*It's Beatrice!*"

Harper looked over her shoulder, following Cornelia's line of vision and recognized Beatrice Aston standing at the front of the store.

"It's Beatrice," Cornelia repeated, jabbing Harper repeatedly in the ribs with a finger. "*It's Beatrice!*"

"I know who it is," grumbled Harper. "I can see her. She's standing right there."

"No, no, no. You're not listening to me. I said it's *Beeee-atrice!*"

Harper stood, shushing Cornelia. "Good afternoon, Ms. Aston. Is there something I can help you with today?"

"Good afternoon. Ah, yes, well, I *um*, funny story," Beatrice said, somewhat befuddled. "I *err*, got to work and realized I needed a new calendar. Silly me. I forgot to pick it up when I was here earlier."

"It's Beatrice," whispered Cornelia, nudging Harper in the back, only to get shooed away.

"Nothing too cumbersome or fancy," continued Beatrice. "I'm thinking something with enough space so I can jot a few notes down, but still compact enough to fit into my handbag." She lifted her purse, for example.

"No problem. We've got plenty to choose from over here," said Harper, pointing.

Beatrice twisted her fingers but made no move to follow Harper's direction.

"While you're looking, can I offer you tea? Or maybe a cup of coffee?" asked Harper. "I have a fresh pot ready."

"I'm sorry, what did you say?" asked Beatrice, her attention glued onto Cornelia picking off every last piece of lint from of her obnoxiously red and green, reindeer sweater.

"I asked if you'd like tea or coffee," Harper repeated. "I can also make you a hot chocolate if you prefer."

"Oh, no, that's kind of you, but just the calendar."

"Righto. Follow me." Harper leaned into Cornelia and planted a soft kiss on her forehead. "You stay put," she whispered. "I promise I'll be right back." Then she leaned further down, reaching under Cornelia's chair to give Bone's sleepy head a rub. "You too, big guy. No more gallivanting for you."

CHAPTER 15

Beatrice

BEATRICE RUFFLED through the shelved calendars, picking one, pretending to read the inside, then turning it over, only to exchange it for the next one, totally disinterested. She strained to listen, to see if Cornelia had begun to show any curiosity or acknowledgment of her presence. So far— not a peep.

A few people entered the shop. One, a man by himself in his mid-sixties, maybe early seventies, apparently familiar with the shop. He darted straight to the sci/fi section without uttering a word to anyone. A young mother with two young kids in tow headed to the children's area in the far back.

"I want a book on octopuses," whined one child,

tugging his mother's arm, his pink nose brimming with snot.

"How many books can we get?" asked the other sibling, older than his brother, but visibly less congested.

"One each," replied their harried mom. "So, make it a good one."

Beatrice peered around the shelf to better observe Cornelia and Harper, hoping the two women would leave the front of the store long enough for her to sneak behind the counter to retrieve the key. The problem, however, was that the shop wasn't all that large, and sounds—any sounds—carried. The music played in the background wasn't all that loud, but Beatrice hoped it would drown out enough of the incidental noises.

Reluctant to draw undue attention to herself, Beatrice lingered about, watching and waiting, sure she wouldn't be noticed if she appeared busy. She inched forward, situating herself close enough to easily eavesdrop on Cornelia and Harper's conversation, which so far consisted primarily of what to have for dinner, the need to vacuum the shop before closing for the night, and if they should ask Irwin to grab takeout.

"Text him again," said Cornelia. "I'm starving."

"You're not starving. We ate lunch a little while ago."

"Is it my fault I have a supersonic fast metabolism? Call him again."

"I did, but he's still not answering." Harper's fingers raced across the screen. "I'm texting Cristopher for an update. Maybe he can fill me in. This waiting is killing me."

Overwrought with guilt, Beatrice crouched, biting her bottom lip.

They're so close. To get past, I'll need to be quiet, move slow, blend in, and do what everybody else is doing.

Heart racing, Beatrice exhaled slowly, inhaling only through her nose instead of her mouth so as not to be heard.

I can't believe I'm doing this. This is nuts. What if I get caught?

She rolled her head, trying to quiet the looming fear, unable to fathom those dire consequences.

Happy thoughts. Only happy thoughts...

Her nervousness increased the longer she waited for the right opening. She tried to conjure up ideas to deter her nervousness.

I am no longer hiding behind a bookshelf, ready to thieve, she told herself, *but sunbathing on a tropical island beach on a hot, sunny day*.

She stepped tentatively forward and heard a low, but distinct *squish*.

"Damnit!" she hissed, glaring down at her stupid rubber winter boots. Not the smartest footgear to wear when attempting to be all James Bond stealthy. Any other time she would have smacked herself for not choosing something quieter to troll around in.

Harper's phone vibrated. "Eureka. They're done and, on their way, back."

"With takeout? Bones is famished," said Cornelia, stymied by the zipper on her pants.

"I didn't ask."

"Then get those fingers of yours moving, babycakes. We're in dire need of sustenance over here."

Bones purred in agreement.

"Fine," Harper half shrugged. "I'll ask Christopher. I'm not sure what condition Mom or Irwin are in." Harper's fingers moved like lightning across the screen. "They said they'll be back shortly...Oh, Christopher messaged. He said cool about Chinese food."

"Cool on the vittles." Cornelia stood. "Now to use the lavatory," she announced loudly. "My bladder's ready to explode."

"Miss? Um, excuse me?" interrupted the harried young mother. "When you have a minute, would you direct me to a book on ocean fish? I see reptiles, insects in general, mammals, but nothing specifically on ocean life."

"Sure thing. I'll be right there," replied Harper, smiling. "Cornelia, will you be all right on your own for a few minutes? I'm not leaving—I need to get a book for a customer."

"I'm fairly certain I can still find where the damn bathroom is, Harper. Sheesh, calm the hell down, already. Cut me some slack." Cornelia snatched her cane and hobbled slowly toward the backroom while Harper dashed right past Beatrice's aisle toward the children's section.

Now or never.

Although a nervous wreck, Beatrice's adrenaline kicked in. Pumped up, she moved with lightning speed, determined to capitalize on the momentary diversion long enough to accomplish her mission. She brought the calendar along under the pretext of an innocent customer in case she got caught.

Practically leaping out and tiptoeing like a cartoon character from *Tom and Jerry*, Beatrice successfully covered the short distance to the front of the store within seconds. She snuck around the counter, crouching low as she quietly opened the drawer, her eyes darting everywhere. She lifted the mat and—*Bingo*.

Beatrice pocketed the key and returned the mat,

exactly how she found it. Book still in hand, she positioned herself on the other side of the register as planned, appearing to be waiting to pay—and just in time, too.

"I'll be right with you," shouted Harper, rushing to the front of the store. "Sorry about that, she said sweetly. "Is that everything?"

"Oh, yes. Most definitely," nodded Beatrice, trying not to pant.

"Did you find everything you were looking for?" asked Harper as she accepted Beatrice's payment and rung up the sale.

"Absolutely. I got exactly what I came for." Beatrice rebuttoned her coat, gathered up her bag, and barreled for the door. When she pushed it open, she wound up walking straight into Irwin. "Oh, no. I didn't mean to—Are you all right?" she said, dropping her bag, panic-stricken.

Irwin picked Beatrice's bag off the ground and handed it to her. "I'm fine, Miss Aston. Are you okay?"

"Yes. Yes, I'm fine."

"We really need to stopping meeting this way, Miss Aston," jested Irwin.

"What? Oh, ha, yes. I see what you mean." Beatrice pushed past Irwin and practically ran smack into Olivia.

"Whoops!" Olivia swerved to the side, clipped by Beatrice's shoulder.

"Oh, my goodness. I don't know what's wrong with me today," prattled Beatrice. "Please excuse me." And without further ado, Beatrice scooted away, shaking inside the entire way home.

"That was weird," commented a drained Olivia. "My goodness, that woman is so uptight."

Irwin glanced out the shop window and watched Beatrice carelessly crossing the busy street on green, then becoming flustered with oncoming traffic blaring their horns in protest. "I'd have to agree. Miss Aston looked entirely overanxious." He squinted over at the register. "...if not a bit fixated."

Irwin

"MA!" Harper greeted Olivia with concerned hugs. "You look upset. Where's Dad?" When no answer followed, Harper looked at Irwin. "What happened? Irwin? Where's Dad? Why isn't he with you?"

"Unfortunately, the judge did not grant your father bail," explained Irwin.

"And why the hell not?" Harper's voice rose two octaves.

"Shush. Lower your voice. We have customers," admonished her mother. Olivia peeled off her coat and scarf. "Look, I've got to get out of these clothes before I do anything else. The shop closes in thirty minutes. By then, Christopher should be back with dinner. We'll talk about everything, then."

"And until then— what happens to Dad?"

"Harper—I mean it. Not. Now." Olivia trudged away, one defeated step after the other.

Harper watched her mother leave, then glanced back at Irwin. "And that's it? I've been waiting all day to find out what happened and all I get is a, "Not now, Harper? Are we kidding?"

Irwin, hung his coat on the peg, contemplating how best to answer. "It's been a long day."

Dismayed, Harper threw her hands in the air. She grabbed a stack of misplaced books and slammed them down on the floor, shoving them one at a time onto their correct shelves. "Psssst, Irwin," Harper motioned, giving him a weird slight head nod to move closer and out of Cornelia's earshot.

"What?" he whispered, leaning in as close as possible without actually bending over.

Harper tilted her head and cut her eyes to Cornelia.

Irwin frowned. "What did she do now?"

"She didn't actually do anything this time, but while you were gone, she's started to remember a tiny bit of what happened."

"Oh?"

"Yeah. We were this close." Harper pinched her fingers virtually together for emphasis, "She had a name at the tip of her tongue until Beatrice the Ball Breaker walked in and ruined everything."

Irwin winced. *Beatrice again...*

"You really should stop calling her that." Irwin remembered back to his childhood days, third grade to be exact. For Irwin, that year would live forever in juvenile infamy, and all because of his beloved grandmother, Ethel Chamberlin Abernathy. Irwin's grandmother loved him, but the woman displayed little patience with fools and less with people she disliked. Their next-door neighbor, a snarly middle-aged woman with a perpetual frown on her lined face, and a cigarette lodged precariously between her thin evil lips turned out to be one of his grandmother's favorite targets. She abhorred, *Ronda Rotten Crotch*. (Mrs. Robinson, to be exact.)

—"Ronda's at it again. It's seven in the morning—on a Saturday, no less," carped Irwin's grandmother, Ethel

Chamberlin, "and the human ashtray is already out there mowing her lawn, disturbing the entire neighborhood."

—"Irwin, after Ronda Rotten Crotch finishes exposing her ass crack to the world, would you mind going outside and retrieve the mail."

—"It's March, for heaven's sake. You would think Ronda Rotten Crotch would be smart enough to take down her dismal display of holiday nightmare already."

Having grown up hearing the derisive nickname so often, Irwin naturally assumed that *Ronda Rotten Crotch* was, in fact, the woman's real name. His grandmother's running commentaries were such a regularity that he never gave them much thought...until that awful, awful day, when Rhonda—a substitute bus driver by trade—replaced Irwin's bus driver.

"Good morning, Mrs. Rotten Crotch," said Irwin innocently enough as he stepped onto the bus, a lunch box in one hand and his schoolbooks in the other.

Rhonda's face instantly froze then retracted, morphing into what Irwin thought at the time as the nastiest shade of a crimson death red. She snarled, frothing at the bit, and baring canine shaped incisors. She ordered him to the front seat right behind her and then proceeded to glare at him in her mirror at every opportunity until they arrived at the school. That's when she personally hauled him in front of the principal, knees trembling, and forced him to recount in cringe-worthy detail every last word said. The rest is history, although as far as Irwin was concerned, that single incident scarred him for the rest of his life and had since remained one of Irwin's most unpleasant childhood memories. Although, in hindsight, it had also single-handedly convinced him to disregard the common lazy practice of crudeness and vulgarity. In its place, he used verbose and extensive persuasive vocabulary laced with sarcasm to land his points.

"Ms. Aston," replied Harper snippily. "Feel better?"

"Considerably," agreed Irwin, not ready to revisit that particular childhood trauma.

Harper stomped her foot. "I can't believe it. We were so close, too."

"It'll come to her. Eventually."

"Do you think so?"

"I do," said Irwin, "but don't hound her into remembering. The doctor warned us against that. 'Never say, remember...agree, but don't argue...divert instead of trying to reason, and always distract instead of shaming.'"

Harper frowned. "Shoot! I forgot. I did sort of push her. I only wanted—"

"I know," offered Irwin, patting her shoulder. "A natural response, especially under the circumstances. Nevertheless, this brings me to my next point, which is, we need to keep an extra eye out on her."

"What do you mean an extra eye? What happened?" Harper's eyes grew large with concern. "Wait, do you think Cornelia's in danger?"

"No. Not necessarily in danger, but if she actually spotted someone, that somebody might not want to be discovered."

"Shoot. I never thought of that," nodded Harper, her face draining of color. "Maybe we should warn her?"

"Not on your life. It'll only make her upset, and then she really won't recall anything." Irwin leaned over and whispered, "But from this point moving forward, Cornelia doesn't go anywhere alone. Got it?"

"Understood."

"What are we whispering about?" whispered Cornelia,

shoving her way into the middle of their conversation, winking naughtily at Irwin.

Quick on her feet, Harper walked over to the desk and grabbed the candy dish. "Irwin's drilling me about where Mom hides the rest of the chocolates," she elaborated rather convincingly. "He's almost as bad as you."

"I don't blame you, Irwin," said Cornelia. "Those damn things are addictive." She reached up, took another chocolate, and popped it into her mouth. "So good," she moaned. "Do you know that in one of my books, *Delicious Deadly Bites* the murderer kills off his rival by feeding her chocolates laced with arsenic?"

"That sounds gruesome," said Harper, cringing.

"Oh. It most certainly was," agreed Cornelia. "Deliciously so, especially because the murder victim had been known for having quite the insatiable sweet tooth."

"Did the killer ever get caught?"

"Of course, he did. My detective, Jacque Findley, always got his man, and by pure genius, really."

"How's that?" asked Harper, genuinely interested.

"Well, Jacque Findley, being the magnificent detective he was, somehow convinced the police to analyze the metal content in the cocoa by a process called dry-ashing. Now, if I can remember correctly, which is hit and miss these days, they dry-ash samples at a super high heat, close to 800F. Then they follow it up by initiating a process where they inductively couple plasma atomic emissions with spectrometry."

Irwin and Harper stared at Cornelia dumbfounded.

"What the who?" Harper finally mumbled.

"Pretty impressive, huh? I've always loved how that sounded," Cornelia chuckled, licking chocolate off a finger. "'Plasma-atomic emission spectrometry' —Gotta love it."

"Well, I'm totally impressed," Harper grinned. "How the hell did you remember all of that?"

"Heck if I know. Anyway," Cornelia directed her comment to Harper, since Irwin, having already heard the story reiterated a hundred times before, had already made himself scarce. "It's basically a test, or rather an analysis to see *if* and *how much* the contents of the item in question—chocolates in this case—had been contaminated. One of Jacque's most fascinating cases."

"Book," corrected Irwin, seemingly popping in out of nowhere. "A fascinating *fictional* case," Irwin gently reminded her.

"Oh, yes. You're right, Irwin" mumbled Cornelia. "Fictional. Absolutely fictional," she said, walking toward her chair with a piece of toilet paper stuck to the heel of her shoe trailing behind her.

"Uh, Cornelia," winced Irwin, pointing down.

"What is it?" she shrugged.

Cornelia glanced down and laughed. "Would you look at that? I've left a paper trail."

"Look at the funny lady," giggled one of the children standing next to his brother. "She's got poo-poo paper on her shoe."

"Knock it off," hissed their mother, physically dividing the cackling twosome. "Sorry about that." She plopped her selection of children's books on the counter and began digging in her bag for her wallet. "I'll take these, please."

Harper stomped over and snatched the toilet paper off Cornelia's shoe. Already annoyed, she balled it up and tossed it in the trashcan, glaring at the two kids with an expression capable of melting glaciers.

"Thanks, doll," said Cornelia, oblivious. "Where's Darwin?"

"*Darren,*" Irwin corrected as a matter of course, "will not be joining us tonight. He is otherwise...detained," he said, choosing his words carefully.

An older gentleman waiting in line cleared his throat. "*Ahem.*"

"I can ring you up," offered Irwin. "Harper, why don't you take Cornelia upstairs. I'll finish up here."

"Are you sure?" Harper asked, eyes drooping.

"Absolutely," nodded Irwin already finished ringing up the next order. "Next."

Within minutes, the shop emptied. Irwin turned the window sign to closed, leaving the door unlocked for Christopher, who was expected back any minute now. Once alone, he opened the drawer behind the counter and lifted the mat, not at all surprised to find the key missing.

"As I suspected."

CHAPTER 16

Christopher

CHRISTOPHER BARRELED up the stairs holding four weighted grease-stained bags. "Food delivery," he announced. "I got a little of everything. Shrimp fried rice and extra crunchy noodles for Olivia, here you go. Fried Tofu Chop Suey for Harper, extra packets of hot sauce, bless your gut." He dug into his bag and pulled out another carton. "Shrimp Chow Mein for Irwin. No worries, Irwin, I made sure they didn't dare cheap out on the shrimp this time. And for you, Cornelia, egg drop soup and two vegetable rolls." Christopher glanced around to make sure everyone got their food. "And for me, my standard shrimp and broccoli."

"Meow."

"Ha! You didn't think I'd forget you, Bones?" Christopher pulled out another pint. "For my old pal, Bones. Where'd you go, my man?"

Bones pawed at Christopher's pant leg, impatiently.

Bones made a mid-pitch meow while circling Christopher's legs, waiting impatiently for his human buddy to empty the entire contents of deliciousness into his awaiting food dish.

"Eat up, everybody," said Christopher. "There's plenty. The last bag has extra shrimp rolls, noodles, rice, and," he reached in with two hands and emptied a pile of fortune cookies on the table. "Dessert."

"Thanks, Christopher," murmured everyone gathered around the table, some with mouths already full. Paper plates got passed around, and all immediate conversation focused solely on the acquisition of grub.

"Thanks."

"Can you hand me one of those?"

Hands moved swiftly across the table, reaching for a bit of this or scooping up a lot of that, while duck sauce, hot sauce, and soy sauce were squirted from clear, impossibly awkward plastic packets.

"Try this, it's delicious."

"Does anybody want some of mine? I won't be able to finish all of it."

"There's enough for tomorrow's dinner as well."

After a few short minutes of serious chomping and eating, Harper wiped her mouth and broke the ice. "So, I've waited long enough. What actually happened today, and please don't sugar coat it. I need to know everything."

"In a nutshell," said Christopher, half a shrimp roll in hand, "the judge denied your dad bail because of his past conviction. That's not unusual under these circumstances.

However, Taylor thinks that we will be able to redress this in the next few days."

Harper nodded. "Are the police looking for anyone else other than my dad to lay the blame on, or are they convinced he did it?"

Christopher reached for the rice. "Taylor thinks they're waiting on the autopsy report. From there, they'll decide what to do next."

"I see." Harper tapped her plastic fork on her paper plate.

"In the meantime, I plan to speak to your dad's parole officer and anyone else I can, in case this goes to court."

"Court?" Harper yelled. "This is ridiculous! Christopher, my dad, found the body—by mistake—searching for a cat! That's it. There's nothing more to this," she stammered. "How hard can this be to prove?"

"Taylor and I agree with you. All they have at this point is a bunch of circumstantial evidence, if that much, but it's your dad's past that clouds his innocence."

"His past? Seriously?" Harper snorted. "Like no one here has a past." Harper snapped the fork in two. "And does *Taylor* believe my father is innocent?"

"Yes. She does," nodded Christopher.

Irwin and Olivia kept mum, their heads turning side to side as if at a tennis a match.

Harper glared at Christopher, busy chowing down on his meal, clearly unfazed. "And while my father rots away in a jail cell for a crime he didn't commit, does your *friend* Taylor plan to do anything about it?"

Christopher glanced up, bewildered. "About the bail?"

"No—about getting him out for good!" shouted Harper testily. "I mean, *your friend* is a lawyer, right? Lawyers are hired to get their clients out, aren't they?"

Christopher wiped his mouth, looking uncomfortable. He glanced first at Irwin for help, then at Olivia. "Under the circumstances, Taylor did the best she—"

"Right." Harper exhaled. "My mistake."

Exasperated, Christopher leaned back in his chair, glaring at Harper. "Circumstantial evidence or not, this isn't the easiest kind of case to initially prove—"

"Apparently not," said Harper, staring down at her plate.

"You know what, Harper," snapped Christopher, "Taylor did us a favor. She didn't have to come today at all, but in my opinion, take it for what it's worth, her being there made a difference—granted, maybe not in terms of bail, but at least now the DA knows he can't railroad your father back to prison without one hell of a fight."

Irwin cleared his throat. "Well perhaps we might—" but Olivia pinched his arm to shut up.

"*Ouch*," mouthed Irwin, teeth gritted, rubbing his arm.

Unconvinced and thoroughly irritated, Harper squinted at Christopher, ready to battle again when Irwin interrupted. "Do you have an idea about when the autopsy will be done?"

Harper heatedly crossed her arms over her chest. "Yes, Christopher, what does *Taylor* have to say about that? I'm all legs. I mean ears." She tilted her head, sneering.

Christopher tossed his shrimp roll on his plate. "What's your problem?" he demanded of Harper.

"My problem is this—you told us you had an experienced lawyer *friend* willing to help my father out. Not some college girlfriend willing to throw you a bone."

"Harper! Enough!" yelled Olivia, banging her fist on the table. "I'm sorry, Christopher," she said. "That was completely uncalled for."

"Was it?" Harper tossed her napkin on the table. "I'm not hungry anymore." Pouting, she shoved her chair backward and stomped out the room.

"What the hell was that?" mumbled Christopher, utterly perplexed. "What did I do wrong?"

Cornelia burped. "Excuse me," she said, wagging a finger in the air. "If I may?"

"Please. Go ahead," fumed Christopher. "Enlighten me, because clearly, I don't get it."

Cornelia put her fork down, leaned at the edge of the table, and whispered, "What you just witnessed has absolutely nothing whatsoever to do with either Darren or Taylor."

Christopher looked at Olivia vexed.

"Nothing," verified Olivia.

"Full agreement," affirmed Irwin.

Christopher looked imploringly around the table in each of his friend's faces. "Then, what was it? What was that all about, because I never saw *that* coming."

"Christopher, Christopher, Christopher..." mumbled Cornelia. "For such a brilliant young man, you really are quite a dope."

"Super dense," agreed Olivia, smirking.

"Impenetrably dense," added Irwin. "Worse than me."

"Sad," nodded Cornelia in agreement, "but painfully true in this case."

"Fine. I'm thick-headed. Dense. A dope." Christopher flung his arms up. "So, tell me what I did wrong?"

"I thought you'd never ask," Cornelia grinned. "What you have witnessed is called jealousy. Pure and simple. Our Miss Harper, despite what she may say or do, is infatuated with you. I'd be comfortable even calling what she feels, love. Would you agree, Olivia?"

"Most definitely."

"And, I venture to say, she has been in love with you for some time now." Cornelia held up a finger. "Everyone knows it but you."

Christopher cocked his head. "Hold up...do you mean—?"

Cornelia signaled Christopher to slide his chair next to her and waited to speak again until their heads were closer together. "The question is, do you feel the same way about Harper? Yes or no?"

"Well, I, um...to be honest, I intended to speak with Darren—"

"Stop. It's a simple question. Yes or no?"

Irwin smirked, thoroughly enjoying himself.

Christopher threaded a hand through his hair while staring into Olivia's stern face. "Olivia," he began, "this wasn't at all how I planned on speaking to you or her dad, but I might as well just say it. I'm in love with your daughter."

Olivia smiled wide, covering her mouth with her hand. "Oh, thank goodness!" she blurted out, relieved. Cornelia gave Olivia a high-five, and the two women laughed. Irwin leaned back in his chair and reached over to pat Christopher approvingly on the back.

"Like I said, "stammered Christopher. "I had planned to do this differently. I wanted to ask you and Darren permission to speak with Harper about this. I mean, I've known you guys for years, and I didn't want to step out of any boundaries or be disrespectful. You're my friends—shoot, my family. I didn't want to do anything to upset anyone."

"Yes, fine, blah, blah, blah. We get it. Chivalry isn't

totally dead," grumbled Cornelia. "But what do you plan to do about it now?"

"Shouldn't I wait to speak to Darren first?"

"NO!" came the resounding group answer.

"Don't you dare," threatened Olivia through clenched teeth. "Don't you worry about Darren. I'll speak to him. You march yourself right in that room this instant and speak to my daughter. Tell her how you really feel. And don't waste time playing games, either. Trust me...I should have said a lot of things to Darren before all of this stuff happened." She started to tear up and sniffled.

"Olivia—"

"I'm fine, Christopher. Please, do as I ask. Go speak to my baby. She's hurting. She needs you."

Christopher looked at Irwin. "And you're okay with this?"

"Indubitably," winked Irwin. "However, I think it's only fair that I should inform you in Darren's absence, that if you ever hurt Harper or dare break her heart, we will both hunt you down and skin you alive."

"Noted." Christopher rose from his seat. "And what about you, Bones? You have anything you'd like to add to the conversation?"

Upon hearing his name, Bones stopped indulging in his meal. He lifted his furry head and started slowly blinking, sending Christopher 'kitty kisses' —his way of showing affection and letting Christopher know that he trusted him.

"Thanks, my man," said Christopher, blinking slowly back. "Okay, then. Nothing to it but to do it. Wish me luck."

"You won't need luck," advised Cornelia. "Only some regular old honesty."

Harper

GOOD GOING, Harper. You sure made a first-class ass out of yourself tonight.

An embarrassed Harper sat on her bed, knees pressed against her chest, rocking.

Knock, knock.

Oh no.

"Harper...it's me, Christopher. Can we talk for a minute?"

It serves me right, she sobbed.

Christopher pressed his ear against the door. "Please open the door."

"Why?" came the muffled response.

"To talk."

"To talk about what?"

Christopher leaned his forehead against the door. "Please open the door and let me come in. I have something important to discuss with you—privately."

I bet.

"Harper?"

Harper grudgingly slid off her bed. She leaned over her dresser to check her face in the mirror. "Ewww," she muttered, before patting away a streak of tears adorning her red-flushed face.

Here it comes. The proverbial letdown.

Harper adjusted her tatty old sweatshirt adorned with hot mustard stains, smoothed down her threadbare sweatpants, fussed with her hair, and then gave up. She cracked open the door. "What is it?"

"Can I come inside?"

She hesitated, "Fine." Harper waved Christopher in, inching her body to the side with only enough room to let him safely pass.

"Can I sit down?" he asked, pointing to the chair facing her bed.

"Go ahead."

Christopher patted the corner of her bed. "Can you sit here?"

"Why?" she half-shrugged, hugging herself; wishing the humiliation to be quickly over with.

"Because I'd prefer talking to your face." He tapped the mattress again. "Please."

Stomach in a knot, Harper unenthusiastically acquiesced, plopping on the bed across from him, legs crossed. She leaned on her knee, dropping her chin onto her clammy palm. "Talk," she hissed, eyes cast downwards, refusing to look at him. In Harper's head, she tried to prepare for the speech, while pulling at the fringe on her blanket with her other hand.

"I love you."

That's not the 'Let's be friend's' speech?

Harper choked. "What?"

"I love you, Harper Crane."

She stared, mind racing. "You mean like a sister, love me—"

"No. Not like a sister."

Harper stared him down. "A good friend?"

"Nope. Not as a good friend, either, although I do consider you a good friend."

Thinking for sure this was going to be a disaster, Harper tried to grapple with what she thought he might be implying. Eyes wide open, she barely uttered a word.

"I am *in love* with you, Harper," he added, waiting for her to say something.

"But I thought you and Taylor were—"

"No. Like I told you, she's a friend, a colleague, but nothing more."

Harper pressed her lips together, dumbfounded, and now beyond ashamed. She usually didn't react so viscerally, but the jealousy had taken over. "I said some awful things..."

Christopher reached over to hold the tips of her fingers. "Already forgotten."

Harper sobbed. Anger, she understood. Dismissal, she expected. Compassion—still tricky.

"Please don't cry." He used his sleeve to wipe away her tears. "You don't know how long I've wanted to tell you how I feel, but I didn't know if you felt about me the same way—"

"Until I made an ass out of myself."

Christopher laughed, "Well, yeah. That helped clear things up."

Harper giggled through sniffles. "I'm sorry. I didn't mean to act like such a jerk. I know your friend was only trying to help."

Christopher smiled. "I told her all about you."

"What? That I'm an asshole?"

"That too," he teased, "but that you're also a beautiful, kind, compassionate asshole...and a super intelligent woman." He paused. "I hope you don't mind?"

"I-I don't mind," whispered Harper shaking her head, and blinking rapidly. "What did she say?"

"She told me, and I quote, "don't be a dumbass, chicken-shit Chris, and tell the girl how you really feel."

Harper burst out laughing. "She said that?"

"Cross my heart."

"Taylor sounds like a nice person."

"She is." Christopher extended an open hand. "And smart, and one hell of a good attorney. If there's any way to get your dad home, she'll find it." He reached over and held her hands.

Harper didn't fight him.

Christopher kissed Harper's fingers. "I had planned to come home and do this the right way—I wanted to talk to your parents first, and make sure they were cool with this." He explained. "I know it's old fashioned, but I really care about how they feel, and I didn't want to do anything to ruin our relationship. You know what I mean?"

Harper nodded. "Totally."

"Man, never in my life... and all this other stuff going on. To be honest, I—"

Harper reached up and drew Christopher's face close to hers. Holding her breath, she leaned over and kissed him passionately. Hungrily. Exactly the way she had dreamt about for the past two years. "I am *in love* with you, too," she whispered, their lips still touching.

Outside in the hall, three sets of ears tussled for space by Harper's door.

"Give me some room," grumbled Cornelia.

"Hush," reminded Irwin.

"Be quiet. I think Harper's saying something," hissed Olivia.

Cornelia stepped over Irwin's shoe and planted her ear on the door. "I can't hear anything."

"She told him that she loves him, too," whispered Olivia, beaming, and silently clapping.

"Shush," ordered Irwin again, lifting his shoulder to

lean in closer. "I think I hear foot—" his head whipped back, "steps. Uh, oh."

The door flung open.

"Unbelievable!" yelled Harper, her hands clasped on her hips, laughing. "You know what? You guys refuse to quit."

Irwin gulped, red-faced. Olivia made a feeble attempt to crouch behind an already shrinking Irwin. Cornelia bit her cheek and stared contritely at the ground, scratching her head. Even Bones, that moggy coward, took off dashing down the hall and around the corner to make his quick escape.

"Foiled again," grumbled Cornelia.

Christopher grinned, thoroughly amused. He embraced Harper from behind, resting his chin on the nape of her neck. "I don't know about the rest of you guys, but I'm starving."

"Me, too," muttered Irwin, being the first snooper to hightail it back to the kitchen. Olivia followed, nipping at his heels, while Cornelia toddled away, keeping a close third.

Harper watched the three disappear and sighed. "You know, you're stuck with them if you still want to be with me."

Christopher kissed the delicate curve of Harper's neck. "I wouldn't want it any other way."

CHAPTER 17

Beatrice

THAT EVENING, Beatrice sulked at the kitchen counter; the absconded key displayed prominently in front of her. She flipped idly through the lovely crisp pages of her newly purchased day planner—a journal she'd now never have the opportunity to fill.

"What am I doing," she groaned, recalling how Cornelia had periodically kept staring at her from her perch when she first arrived... repeating her name, and poking the Harper girl.

Cornelia knows. And it's only a matter of time until she tells.

Beatrice slid the book to the side and buried her head onto her folded arms,

"I'm doomed," she thought bitterly.

This wasn't how Beatrice pictured her life turning out. When she left home at eighteen, she planned for adventure, excitement...later on a career. And of course, falling madly, deeply and forever in love.

Beatrice fiddled with the key, recollecting reading somewhere how inmates say that after being in prison for a while, their days start to blend into one. And before they know it, those days add up, turning into months, and months morph numbly into years. Despite never having met her goals, she still couldn't begin to fathom dithering away behind bars, locked in a cement tomb in the middle of nowhere for the rest of life.

"Serves me right. A prison of my own making."

A trickle of tears escaped from the corner of her stinging eyes, leaving streaks down her cheek. Overwhelming guilt threatened to choke her, but nothing—*nothing*—would compete against the onslaught of frightening images racing through her head. Their existence a constant, discouraging reminder of the awful fate which awaited her once Cornelia's memories of that dreadful afternoon returned.

This is no way to live.

BEATRICE, forever the fighter, didn't indulge in self-pity for long. Fortified by having the key now firmly in her possession, she began to plot and plan her next move. Logistics were kind of her thing, and in a matter of minutes, she had worked up a fairly concrete plan of attack—almost. She still needed to figure out when to sneak into the bookshop's basement undetected. Not an easy feat.

Without a doubt, when the store was at their busiest,

making sure to dress lowkey and play the part of the everyday book shopper. With the holidays winding down, and people flooding the shops, it wasn't as if anybody would actually notice if she went missing for a spell or realized if she left for good. In a pinch, she'd use the "Where's the bathroom?" excuse, then conveniently take a wrong turn right through the adjoining shop's door.

Once inside Alastair's, Beatrice would have only a little window of time to search around. However, with the days growing shorter and becoming darker earlier, she'd have to be especially careful not to flick on lights. Beatrice opened her utility drawer and retrieved a penlight; a much smarter choice for snooping as opposed to a bright flashlight. She clicked it on and off a few times, to test the battery.

"Ugh," she moaned, shoulders slouched. "Who am I kidding? I'm no burglar." She tossed the penlight into her bag. "A liar, sure. An embezzler? Not entirely on purpose. A cold-blooded murderer? Still up for interpretation—but a robber? Never."

She grabbed a pad and began sketching out a diagram from what little she remembered about Alastair's shop's layout, only because a recent google search said that all successful snoopers did that.

All this heartache over a single, old newspaper clipping—it wasn't fair. Beatrice bulleted a list of what to do in succession.

- Sneak downstairs undetected.
- Use the key to break in.
- Search for clipping and destroy. Stay no more than fifteen minutes tops.
- Find an alternate way out of Alastair's shop, maybe through the back door? Check.

- Return key before they detect it missing.

"*Oh, no,*" she hissed.

Wait—wait. It's not like anybody knows I took it, so why return it at all???

- Screw returning the key!

Beatrice sighed and leaned back in her chair, gutted by shame.

I can't let that man take the rap for something I caused, but I can't go to prison either.

In a fit of frustration, she crumpled the list into a ball and tossed it across the white, perfect kitchen. Head pounding, she slid off the stool and staggered to the cabinet in search of something to quell the massive throbbing headache refusing to budge. She popped three aspirin, followed by a swig of cold tap water.

What if the police already found the clipping? Maybe I'm already under investigation?

Fear gripped and seized her hostage. From out of nowhere, reeling lightheadedness caused her to become unsteady on her feet. Through clouded vision, Beatrice managed to lean her shaky body against the counter for support, although every stab at moving made her legs wobble like jelly. Seconds later, the next wave of nausea slammed her hard and fast. Gagging, she clenched her spasming stomach. She doubled over, ready to puke. Mouth cupped, but with no time to waste, she made a dangerously unstable mad dash to the garbage pail, barely making it in time. Clutching the sides of the pail for dear life, she vomited, violently hurling what little she'd eaten over the past few hours.

Every time Beatrice dared lift her head, under the mistaken notion she was done, another spasm would hit, thrusting her perpendicular to the can.

This went on until she had next to nothing left to disgorge. Once the nausea lessened, Beatrice slowly crept up for air, gulping and panting. She placed her vomit-stained face under the faucet, basking in the fresh spill of running water pouring over her flushed face. The headache from before continued to ache, albeit now, much less severely. Never in her life had she experienced a fear quite so debilitating as this except for that time when she got caught embezzling, but even then, her arrest had come as too much of a shock. There had been no time to mull over fate or become paralyzed by the pending devastating consequences. Those, Beatrice soon learned, came later—

"I can't go through that again," she sobbed to an empty house. "I just can't."

Irwin

CORNELIA DECIDED to spend one more night at Olivia's, but this time, Irwin, who had a lot to contemplate now that his suspicions had been confirmed, appreciated the time alone. He sharpened his pencil, half-tempted to fill Christopher in, but decided against getting the future attorney deeper involved. Besides, if his hunch was correct, Beatrice would try something sooner than later, although, for the life of him, Irwin couldn't figure out why. "Miss Marple made it look easy," he muttered. He jotted down a few outstanding questions.

—Why risk stealing the key?

—Or trying to go into Alastair's for that matter?

—And what did Alastair have that Beatrice needs back so badly?

The next day...

AS ANTICIPATED, the store got crazy busy the next day. Olivia, unable to step away for a split second, looked harried, busy ringing up one customer after the next. She had Harper working the floor, while Irwin took over running back and forth, stacking and replacing books. For once, even Cornelia cooperated by remaining in her chair, enjoying herself by handing out candy canes. Bones hid far under her chair, doing his best to ignore the human deluge.

Beatrice showed up at noon. Irwin watched as she idly poked around, selecting a random book here and there, but it was her eyes darting around the room that gave her away the most. He studied her every move, especially whenever she moved closer toward the storeroom.

With lots of people coming and going, the aisles quickly overflowed with shoppers, many juggling stacks of selected books and various other cool book paraphernalia. As usual, Harper had the music on a bit too loud, but only Irwin seemed bothered by it. Small children, looking for a sweet, gravitated to Cornelia.

"One for you, and two for me," she smiled, playing the role of the naughty candy elf.

Across the store, Irwin noticed Harper pleading with an older customer.

"Mr. Feinstein, you have to come down from there,"

she told him. "The shelves weren't made to support a person's weight."

"I need to get my book," he fussed. "Where's that other fella? Dwayne or Darwin, I think his name is. He's the one who usually helps me."

"His name is *Darren*, and he doesn't work today," answered Harper, growing increasingly irritated. "But I can help you get whatever you need."

The old man stared at Harper. "You're not much taller than me, young lady."

"Then I'll get somebody else to help you, but please, come down from there before you get hurt."

The old man scanned the room when his beady eyes locked onto Irwin. "Fine. I'll come down, but make sure you get anybody but *that guy*," he announced loudly for all to hear, unmistakably referring to Irwin. "What a meshugenah."

"A what?"

"A meshugenah—a crazy person. Not right in the head." Mr. Feinstein's shaky legs stepped down. It took all Irwin had not to kick the bookcase over.

In the last aisle behind Cornelia, Beatrice lingered. Irwin pretended not to notice when she inched her way toward the back of the shop. At one point, he deliberately headed to the front of the store carrying with him a large empty box. But before doing so, he first made sure to leave the basement door slightly ajar in the hope it would give Beatrice ample incentive to make a move.

After Irwin dropped the box on the floor, he peeked up in time to catch Beatrice stealing one last glance over her shoulder before slipping through the downstairs door, undetected by anyone but him. Irwin, wanting to catch the woman red-handed, waited a few moments before following in hot pursuit. He strode past Olivia swamped at the register. Then veered down the next aisle to avoid Harper and her galling customer, and finally past elf Cornelia, who just so happened to glance up when Irwin breezed by.

"Now, what in the blazes is that man up to?" she murmured under her breath, smelling a rat—or was that a candy cane? She sniffed the handful in her fist to make sure.

Irwin had purposely brought a pair of leather loafers with him to wear, supposing they would make less noise than his usual metal-tipped winter boots. Preferring not to flip on the light and give himself away, he worked in the dark, holding the basement banister tightly, sliding his hand as a guide. He made sure to be careful to place his feet strategically on each step as soundlessly as possible. Once at the bottom landing, he tiptoed and turned the corner, excited to find Beatrice with her back facing him, hissing angrily.

"Work, you stupid thing."

He moved stealthily toward her side. He noticed something protruding from her mouth. As he got closer, he realized she had a penlight wedged between her lips as she wiggled, jiggled, and turned the decoy key, but to no avail.

"I can't believe this is happening."

"Believe it," announced Irwin, flipping on the overhead light. He wiggled the real key in his hand.

"Ah!" yelped Beatrice, scared, and momentarily disorientated. She clasped her chest, hopping from foot to foot. "Holy moley," she panted, gasping for air. "Heavens above. You scared me!"

"What exactly do you think you're doing, Ms. Aston?" Irwin, an old timer at deciphering body language, used the element of surprise to take note of Beatrice's response, using it to gauge whether or not the woman was capable of telling the truth.

A jittery Beatrice looked left, then right before clearing her throat to expound. "I can explain," she said, her words escaping in a raspy, guilty whisper.

"Before we get into all of that, where did you get that from," he asked, nodding toward the key still clenched in her hand.

"I took it from the drawer upstairs."

"You mean you stole it."

"Yes."

"Why?" he drilled, listening for any sudden change or inconsistency in either Beatrice's tone or mannerisms. So far, so good.

Beatrice leaned back on the locked door, utterly mortified. She blew out a slow, despondent breath. "It's a long and complicated story."

"Then I suggest you make it short and simple."

Before Beatrice began her tale of woe, a set of rushed footsteps approached, accompanied by a clunk-clunk. "Hold on," shouted Cornelia, hobbling her way over, cane leading the way. "Don't say another word until I get there."

Irwin squeezed the bridge of his nose. "Damn it all." "I can't believe you'd start without me." She stood next to Irwin.

Irwin bit his bottom lip.

"Beatrice, Beatrice, Beatrice," toyed Cornelia. "You sure had me going for a while, but I remember it all now." She pointed her cane at the dismal woman. "It was you. You're the one I bumped into at Alastair's shop."

Shoulders slumped in defeat, Beatrice nodded. "Yes. It's the truth. You were coming in as I was leaving."

Cornelia scrunched her nose and barred her upper set of dentures, doing the worst piss-poor impersonation of a corrupt cop. "Did you assassinate Alastair?"

"Absolutely not," answered Beatrice.

"Castrate him? Cut his guts out?" Cornelia snarled.

"Cornelia—" admonished Irwin, exasperated. "Enough. Please." He stepped in front of Detective Tracy, endeavoring to regain a modicum of control over the bizarre turn of event. "Ms. Aston—did you or didn't you kill Alastair? A simple yes or no will suffice."

"I'd like to know the same damn thing," demanded a heated Harper, stomping onto the scene. She flashed Irwin an annoyed glare, then wiggled herself between him and Cornelia, throwing one arm protectively around her tiny shoulder.

"Not you, too," Irwin grumbled, disheartened at his evidently poor reconnaissance skills.

"Hercule Poirot, you're not," said Harper, shooting Irwin an amused, albeit sardonic grin.

Irwin sulked.

"Besides," Harper added, still furious, "weren't you the one who lectured *me* on not leaving *you-know-who-alone?*"

Cornelia glanced up. "Should I assume I'm the you-know-who?"

"No offense," added Harper, tenderly squeezing Cornelia's shoulder.

"None taken," nodded Cornelia.

"Ms. Aston?" Irwin cleared his throat. "If you would please—"

With nothing left to lose, Beatrice told her sordid story, starting at the beginning before her arrest. She explained in embarrassing detail how stupid she'd been, *borrowing* a bit here or there from the company's coffer without it being noticed. How at first, she only took enough money to cover a few of her most outstanding bills, but later on, expanded her thievery out of pure, senseless greed.

"And after you finished paying back the money you stole—was that when you decided to move here?" questioned Harper, no longer hostile, much to Irwin's chagrin.

"Yes," nodded Beatrice. "I stupidly thought I could start over here and make a fresh start. Find a decent job, buy a small house...and basically, mind my own business. And for a long time, that's what I did, until..." her voice trailed off.

"Alastair," prompted Cornelia.

"Yes. Alastair." Beatrice continued to explain to her three enraptured listeners about how Alastair came across the newspaper clipping and then tried to use it to blackmail her. "He told me that if I didn't agree to marry him, he'd expose me."

"What a total slime bag," mumbled Harper.

A weary Beatrice nodded. "Alastair wasn't the nicest person, but he still didn't deserve to die like that."

Irwin noted that Beatrice never repeated herself the way most liars did, nor did she attempt to wriggle out of the truth, saying the same thing three different ways without actually revealing anything she didn't want them to know. Her explanation didn't feel scripted either, which if it had, would have been another clear sign she wasn't telling them the entire story. For now, at least, she was telling them the truth.

Beatrice lowered her gaze, her gaze fixed on the cement floor. "For what it's worth, I'm deeply sorry."

Irwin frowned. "That's not worth much in my book, Ms. Aston, seeing how you've systematically allowed my friend to remain locked up in jail, facing prison for a crime he didn't commit."

"You're right. There's no excuse for my actions." Beatrice answered bluntly, and then she started to cry. Harper and Cornelia rushed over to Beatrice, and the three women began yammering at the same time.

Irwin watched the women, stunned.

Now they're comforting her?

He clapped his hands together, signaling for everyone to be quiet. "Let me ask you this, Ms. Aston—why go through all of this? What are you so afraid of?"

"Are you kidding, Mr. Abernathy?" Beatrice sniveled. "I got caught embezzling and misappropriating company funds. Do you think for one minute I'd be allowed to continue my job here if that news ever got out?" She stared hard at Irwin, aghast. "I'm alone, Mr. Abernathy. Unlike you and your friends, I don't have anyone to turn to. Since I pulled that stupid stunt, I've tried to make amends. I did everything humanly possible to do everything above board and honestly. If this gets out now, I'll lose everything I've worked so hard to repair, including my home."

"And that's enough of an excuse to kill somebody over?"

"No," Beatrice said. "Absolutely not, but in my defense, I wasn't actually trying to kill Alastair. At least, I don't think I was."

Irwin's lips pursed in disbelief. He tilted his head and stared at the woman, waiting for more of an explanation.

"Don't get me wrong," reasoned Beatrice. "I fully admit throwing the statue at Alastair, but only with the intent of knocking some sense into the little creep."

"That makes perfect sense to me," said Cornelia.

"Me, too," agreed Harper.

Jaw set, Irwin pulled out his cell phone.

Harper stared at Irwin. "What are you doing?"

"I'm calling the police."

"Don't do that." Harper reached out to snatch it away, but Irwin spun away too fast.

"Come on, Irwin," pleaded Cornelia. "Don't call the police, at least not yet. Can't you see Beatrice is upset? Why can't we try to help her get the news clipping back? Between the four of us, we should be able to find it."

"That's assuming it's even in there." Irwin clutched his phone, his resolve slipping.

"We certainly won't know unless we take a look," answered Cornelia.

"Well, I'm in," announced Harper. "It's not like fifteen more minutes will change the trajectory of my life."

"Same here," agreed Cornelia. "I mean, what's the worst that can happen if we get caught? I get tossed in prison? Shoot, I won't even remember why."

Harper crossed her arms, waiting. "Whaddya say Irwin? You in or not?"

"Oh, for heaven's sake," he grumbled. "Fine. Anyone else looking to do a stint in prison? Follow me."

"Oh stop," poopooed Cornelia, not buying into Irwin's melodrama. "Let's go pop next door and take a quick look-see."

Irwin snorted. "Breaking and entering aren't popping in for a quick *look-see,* Cornelia. Contrary to present company's opinion, breaking and entering is highly frowned upon in civilized society, and explicitly against the law."

"Mere details," she grumbled, dismissing his complaint. "I vote we go in and help."

"Me, too." Harper nodded. "I vote, yes," she said, waving her hand high in the air.

Beatrice glanced at the faces waiting for her vote. She inched her hand up midway. "I *really* need to get that paper back. And then I promise, I'll call the police myself," she paused. "I'll admit to fighting with him and losing my temper—I'll explain to them that it was a lover's spat. Whatever you want me to say to clear your friend, but I beg of you, Mr. Abernathy, let this part of my past stay buried in the past—at least for now."

Irwin threw his head back and groaned. The ladies watched as he inaudibly debated with himself.

Harper leaned into Cornelia, "Is he okay?"

"Irwin? Oh, he's fine. He does this whenever he's trying to talk himself out of doing something he doesn't want to do."

A few moments passed before Irwin shoved his phone in his pocket. "Okay," he announced, regaining what was left of his composure. "Here's the deal."

Cornelia rubbed her hands in excitement. "Gosh, I love a good caper."

Slack-jawed, Irwin glared solemnly at Cornelia, working up the gumption to continue. "We will go inside, but for no more than ten minutes. Each one of us will be responsible for searching a different part of the store. That way, we can cover more ground quicker and efficiently. Beatrice, since you're the only one who actually knows what it is we're looking for, you take Alastair's desk, cabinets, and shelves. Search any place you think he would normally keep or hide papers."

"Got it." Beatrice, cheeks drained of color, blew her nose in a tissue.

"Harper, I want you to cover from the middle of the store to the far back."

"Middle to far back. I'm on it," she grinned, raring to go.

Irwin shoved his hand into his pocket. "And I'll search the front of the store to the middle."

"And what about me?" demanded Cornelia. Bones mewed. "And him?"

"You two will stay out of harm's way. Matter of fact, I want you both where I can find you in case we have to leave sooner than anticipated," explained Irwin. "That means no meandering about. And Cornelia, this part is not up for debate," he added sternly.

"Fine," she grumbled, remembering that time when she wound up wandering off in the middle of the night, attempting to 'go to the job' because she believed it was thirty years earlier. Luckily, Darren had fallen asleep on her couch that evening after a long bout of movie watching, heard her banging around, presumably in her search for keys, and caught her just before she drove off in Irwin's car. Shaken up, confused, and deathly afraid, Cornelia had finally agreed with them about never leaving her on her own.

Irwin snapped his fingers "Oh. And one more thing. It's still fairly light outside, so we should be able to see well enough without having to turn on any lights. Additionally, remain quiet at all time. That means no talking. That also goes for making any loud noises of any kind. Remember, ladies, we don't want to do anything to draw attention. Am I clear?"

All three women nodded.

Irwin lowered his voice, turning tacitly stern. "Once I open that door, the second we step inside, we are all technically criminals in the eye of the law. If anybody is having second thoughts and wants to back out, now's the time to do it." His speech fell on deaf ears. Beatrice, Cornelia, and Harper all nodded an emphatic no. "All right then, ladies. Follow me." Heart hammering in his throat, Irwin stepped up to the door.

"*Dum-dum-dum-dumm*," hummed Cornelia.

"Shush!" admonished Irwin, turning the key in the lock. As expected, the door opened unimpeded. The group let out a collective sigh. Irwin drew in one long, last cleansing breath for courage. "Let's get going. We've got only ten minutes to do this, so make it count."

All three trailed closely behind Irwin, while Bones, never one to follow the crowd, darted around the four-some, and dashed off in the direction of his favorite lounging spot.

"Here, Cornelia. Take this," murmured Beatrice, handing her the penlight she'd brought along. "I don't want you to fall and hurt yourself."

"Thanks." Cornelia pressed the light off and on. "But won't you need it to see the papers?"

"Don't you worry about that," Beatrice scowled, the color returning to her face. "Trust me, I'll never forget what that damn thing looks like."

CHAPTER 18

Olivia Crane

THE PHONE RANG upstairs in the book shop. "*Abernathy &*
Crane. Olivia speaking. How can I help you?"

"Hello, Olivia? This is Taylor Maldonado. Sorry to call
you at work, but there's been a development. Do you have
a free minute to talk? It's rather important." She glanced
around the packed, bustling bookshop, growing annoyed
that she was unable to locate either Irwin, Harper...or
Cornelia. Even Bones appeared to be MIA.

Shit.

"Um, yes. Sure. Now is fine," she mumbled into the
phone. "I can talk." Olivia signaled to one of the
customers ready to check out. "I can take you here," she
said, pulling the mouthpiece from her face. You, too, sir."

"You're obviously busy right now. Why don't I call back later," offered Taylor.

"No, that's all right," urged Olivia. "I can hear you."

"Well, apparently, miracles do happen, and we might have caught a break."

Olivia held her breath.

"I heard back from the police—a Detective Moore."

Olivia gasped.

"Yes. He mentioned knowing you, too."

Olivia colored.

"Anyway, from what he told me, the coroner's report came back this morning and cleared your husband of any wrongdoing."

Olivia's heart stopped. She stood frozen in place, unable to respond—terrified she hadn't heard correctly.

"Olivia?" Taylor shouted into the phone. "Are you still there?"

"I'm here," she whispered, not wishing others nearby to overhear, "but I'm not sure I understand."

"Simply put, the victim—in this case, Alastair Brooke—died of a heart attack. Plain and simple. Nothing nefarious or disputed. In other words, no murder took place. What your husband described to the police happened exactly the way he said. It all checked out."

"But what about all the blood? Even Darren said there was blood everywhere. And what about all of Alastair's other injuries?"

"Evidently, the coroner ruled those incidental and a result of having a heart attack, and then banging his head on the furniture and collapsing onto a cement floor."

"And they're one-hundred percent positive it was a heart attack, right?" asked Olivia, pulse racing, not ready to get her hopes up too high. "They aren't going to change their minds again and accuse Darren?"

"Tests proved conclusively that Brooke died of natural causes, although strangely enough, Moore did happen to mention that the guy had a ton of laxatives in his system."

"Laxatives?" blurted out, Olivia.

"Yes. Totally bizarre. Not enough to kill him, mind you, but enough to make him wish he was dead."

"No surprise there. Alastair was always full of shit," mumbled Olivia offhandedly, not intending to let such a crude, ill-timed comment slip out.

Taylor didn't take offense and chuckled. "That's certainly one way to look at it."

Olivia turned farther away from any onlookers and spoke lower into the phone. She faced the wall, modulating her words. "Does this mean Darren can come home?" She squeezed her eyes closed, gripping the phone with both hands.

"It appears so. I can't imagine that he won't be released soon, although the Assistant District Attorney—your favorite guy—is trying to push for his own expert to go over the coroner's findings."

"Why?"

"So he can take this to trial. Claims he wants a jury to decide."

"Can he do that?"

"He can, but he won't. I know the Head DA, and she isn't going to waste taxpayer's money suckling Carter's fragile ego. —Hold on a minute."

Olivia heard Taylor cup her mouthpiece but managed to make out people talking. She turned around and caught sight of Christopher handling the register, ringing up a long line of waiting customers. She walked over and squeezed his shoulder in appreciation before stepping off to the far side of the room.

"Sorry about that, Olivia, but I have to go. I'll phone you back as soon as I know anything more, but no worries."

"Thank you, Taylor. Thanks for everything."

"Not a problem. Take care."

Olivia tucked her phone into her pocket. She turned around, smiling at Christopher, her eyes glistening with happy tears.

"Everything okay?" he asked her, handing the last person their purchase.

Olivia nodded. "That was Taylor. She said Darren's been cleared and that she's waiting to hear back about when he will be formally released."

"What! Aww, man, that's wonderful news!" Christopher hugged an overjoyed Olivia. "Where's Harper? She's going to be ecstatic." Christopher twisted his head around. "Matter of fact, where is everybody else? I came downstairs to talk to Irwin but didn't find him. And, aww shit, where the hell is Cornelia?"

"All excellent questions," stammered Olivia, much too ecstatic to be entirely pissed off. She reached into her drawer and punched in a few numbers into a cell phone. "Yup. Exactly what I thought," she seethed, realizing where the GPS located Cornelia. "Chris, can you do me a favor and keep an eye on the shop while I track down our missing three Musketeers?"

"Sure thing," he laughed. "They can't be that far."

"That's exactly what I'm afraid of."

Meanwhile, next door...

HARPER CREPT AROUND, quietly combing through various pieces of furniture. She gently lifted a wood leaf of an antique corner desk and peered inside. Nothing. She scooted around a tall, vintage armoire and opened its doors and drawers. Empty. She bent over and peeled back an antiquated area rug. *Nil.*

Meanwhile, on the other side of the shop, Irwin did much of the same, exhaustively searching everywhere, but producing equally disappointing results.

In the back of the store by the register, Beatrice tore through Alastair's paperwork, sifting through stacks of invoices, catalogs, ripping apart envelopes, and peeking through various drawers and cubbyholes. She searched in, over, behind, and under bookshelves. Nothing.

Cornelia waited as instructed, seated comfortably on the Queen of England's comfy contribution with her trusty sidekick, Bones, relaxing dutifully by her side. He had his husky fur body stretched against the arm of the sofa, nudging and rolling around, finally positioning himself onto his back to expose his belly.

"What gives?" murmured Cornelia, amused. "I thought you hated getting your tummy rubbed."

Bones meowed, then crooked his furred head, nuzzling it playfully into Cornelia's ample upper thigh. She couldn't resist. "You win." She rubbed him first under the chin and then scooched him behind his ears. Bones, thoroughly relishing the massage, rewarded Cornelia with a loud serenade of lengthy vibrating purrs. Basking in the attention and not wanting it to end, Bones smooshed his furry head harder against Cornelia's leg.

"Ah, you like that, do you?"

"How are you doing, Cornelia," whispered Irwin, coming from around the side. He lifted a vase and shook it gently, then peered inside.

Cornelia flipped Irwin a bored thumbs up, then turned her attention back to Bones. "If you climb up on my lap, I can pet your back, you spoiled creature." She tapped her thigh in encouragement. However, Bones failed to oblige. Instead, he opted to roll over on all fours, arching his back high. Then he dipped his head low, kneading his sharp claws naughtily into the sofa's royal blue damask fabric.

"Good thing Alastair's not around to see this," mumbled Cornelia.

Irwin slipped his hands behind a mirror and painting but came up emptyhanded. "Anything, Harper?" asked Irwin.

"Nope. Big fat zippo so far," she answered back softly, careful not to yell. "This place sure is dusty, though."

On all fours, Beatrice slid her hand under a shelf ledge, but only found dust and cobwebs. "Ewww," she grumbled, quietly rising to her feet, looking for something to wipe her hands on. Next, she tackled his desk, sliding files, sifting through drawers, and opening cabinets. Finally, she lifted a blotter and found a relatively sizeable yellow envelope underneath. She slid it out and peeked inside. *More invoices probably,* but she slipped the top sheet out for good measure. "What the hell," she softly whistled, staring in absolute disgust at a detailed list of names, dates, and sums—apparently payments owed or paid. "Why, that lowlife, sonofabitch," she murmured, scanning the list for her name, relieved not to find it.

"Did you find something?" asked Irwin, wanting to get the hell out of there.

Beatrice shook her head. "Not what I was looking for, but holy cow, this," she waved the paper, "is an entire list of people that egotistical prick was blackmailing."

"Are you kidding?" asked Harper, hurrying over to see for herself. "Can I see?"

Beatrice handed her the envelope.

"This is nuts," she said, handing Irwin the envelope to look for himself. "I always disliked that guy."

Irwin read the names and recognized a good deal of them. He handed the envelope back to Beatrice. "Dreadful."

"You can say that again," hissed Beatrice. "I should destroy it before anybody else gets hurt."

"That's the spirit!" shouted Cornelia, stomping her cane.

"Shush!" reminded the group.

"Oops. Sorry."

The group continued in their search until Irwin, always a stickler for rules, snapped his fingers twice in the air to grab everyone's attention. In a stern, loud whisper, "Time's up, everybody," he said, threading his way through the maze of furniture without knocking anything over to where Cornelia sat waiting in the middle of the store. "Beatrice, Harper—stop whatever you're doing. We need to get out of here."

Harper tiptoed toward Cornelia. "I didn't find anything."

"Neither did I," confirmed Irwin. "Beatrice?"

"Nothing except this thing," she said close to tears, waving the incriminatory packet in the air. Beatrice pounded her fists noiselessly against the counter, disheartened. "Damn it. I really thought we'd find it."

"Couldn't we stay and look around a little bit longer Irwin?" pleaded Harper, in support of a distraught Beatrice.

"Sorry, but the last thing any of us needs right now is to get caught trespassing."

"Mr. Abernathy's, right," agreed Beatrice. "Thanks for at least trying, everyone."

Harper seethed. "I can't believe what a creep Alastair was—to blackmail people is some evil shit."

"Devoid of integrity," agreed Irwin.

"Then what are we going to do about it?" asked Harper, pointing to the evidence. "We can't just pretend we don't know what he was up to and do nothing."

"At the moment, I don't have an answer for you, but it's something we can figure out once we're out of here. Harper, help Cornelia while I grab Bones," instructed Irwin, eager to leave.

Harper helped lift Cornelia to her feet.

"I can see why Bones loves that couch," murmured Cornelia. "Come on, Bones."

Bones jerked away.

"I'll get him. Come on, Bones," coaxed Irwin, bending over to pick the lazy mouser up, but as soon as he reached down behind the cat to support his weight, something brushed against the back of his hand. He shoved his hand further in. "What's this?" he murmured, tugging out a small piece of newspaper free.

Beatrice gasped. "You did it! You found it!" She rushed over to snatch it out of Irwin's grasp, but Irwin jerked it away.

"Not so fast," he warned. "Let's get out of here first. Everybody—now."

The foursome hurried through the back of the store, one close behind the other with Cornelia leading the pack, using her cane to tap, tap, tap her way out while shining the penlight on the ground.

Harper stayed close behind Cornelia, making sure she didn't deviate from course, while Beatrice followed her. Irwin and Bones took up the rear. In less than a minute, the group made it safely out. Without delay, Irwin rushed to seal the door shut, locking it securely behind them. As the relieved foursome let out a collective celebratory sigh savoring their success, the basement light flicked on.

"Mom!" gasped Harper, colliding straight into Cornelia.

"Olivia!" yelped Irwin, bumping into Beatrice and practically knocking her over.

"Ruh roh," grumbled Cornelia. "Foiled again."

Bones, the coward, shot out of Irwin's arms and made a mad dash across the basement, swooping under Harper's legs, around Cornelia's cane, and straight past an incensed Olivia, vaulting straight up the stairs to safety.

"I can't believe you guys!" groaned a furious Olivia, her hands planted firmly on her hips. "As if we don't have enough bullshit to contend with, you three—" She stopped midsentence, somewhat taken back to notice Beatrice Aston—*of all people*—standing amongst them. "What is she doing here?" asked Olivia, confused. "You know what, I don't even want to know," she snapped, then changed her mind. "Yes, I do. Why is she here, and what the hell do you all think you're playing at?"

Beatrice stared down at her shoes to avoid making eye

contact, while Cornelia and Harper remained silent, staring ahead, waiting for Irwin to step up to take the hit.

"Well, Irwin? Looks like you're this rag-tag gang's designated spokesperson—*so talk!*" roared Olivia, her nostrils flaring. "Let's hear it, and as God is my witness, Irwin Abernathy, you had better have a good explanation for this," she snarled.

All eyes were on him, waiting with bated breath to hear what implausible excuse he'd use to explain this total mess.

Olivia tapped her foot, "I'm waiting."

In true Abernathy fashion, Irwin arched his back unnaturally straight, leaving his long, lanky arms dangling by his side; the news clipping still gripped in his fist. "Ahem. It all began with this." He lifted and waved the pilfered paper high up in the air like a white flag of surrender. "However, due to the current and most unfortunate proximity of Brooke's store, it may be wiser to postpone this delicate discussion until we head upstairs. This explanation, I'm afraid, is going to take a while."

"MORE TEA, BEATRICE?" asked Olivia, walking around the table with the tea kettle, making the rounds.

Cornelia leaned into Beatrice. "You might as well say yes. All this woman does is shove tea down people's throats."

"Thank you once again," said Olivia, used to Cornelia's grievances.

Beatrice smiled and held out her cup. "Yes, please. It's delicious."

Olivia finished pouring, then topped off Irwin's cup

before her own. She returned to her seat, calmer and ready to hear the rest of their convoluted story.

"So, let me get this straight," she started. "Even though Alastair's dead and Darren's already in jail, you four decided, you know what? What the heck! Let's see what other trouble we can cause to complete the looming triangle of doom."

"Well said," crooned Cornelia, sipping at her overly sweet, hot tea.

"I'll answer that," interrupted Beatrice, softly. "They did it to help me."

Olivia turned her full attention to Beatrice. "To help you with what, exactly?"

Beatrice took one more sip before speaking. "A while back, I had foolishly asked Alastair to sell an old armoire for me. I figured in his line of business he'd fetch a pretty penny for it. At least enough to help me cover this winter's oil bill. However, I had stupidly forgotten about hiding an incriminating news clipping in the back of the armoire about some legal trouble I had gotten into years ago. When Alastair found it, he tried to use it to pressure me into marrying him. He even had the nerve to tell me that Fate had given him this second chance."

"*Ewww*," drawled Olivia, crinkling her nose in disdain. "He blackmailed you?"

"Yes. He certainly did. Apparently, besides pawning off old, worthless furniture on unsuspecting tourists, blackmail was his thing." Beatrice slid the envelope containing the names and dates of Alastair's other victims toward Olivia for her perusal. "I found this. Quite the collection."

"How awful," agreed Olivia, taking a moment to scan the list of names. "This is revolting. Did you see this, Irwin?"

"I have. Disgusting."

"Evil," said Cornelia.

"I recognize a few names," shuddered Olivia, quick to slide the paper back inside, sealing the envelope closed. "How awful."

"It really was," agreed Beatrice. "When I met up with him that afternoon, my intention had purely been to get the clipping back and destroy it once and for all. Something I should have done years ago, but when I got there, Alastair adamantly refused. He wouldn't give it up and even threatened to out me in front of the entire Pocono community—most especially, to my job. I guess that's when I panicked and picked up that hideous statue to throw at him. I honestly didn't mean for any of this to happen," she sighed.

The room grew still.

"I want to apologize to you, Olivia, and to you, too, Harper. I never meant this craziness to affect your family, and certainly not get Darren in trouble. After we're finished talking, I'll phone the police and turn myself in. I'll do everything in my power to make sure your husband isn't to blame for any of this mess."

Olivia crossed her arms. She leaned back in her chair, staring down at the envelope.

Beatrice faltered, eying Irwin. "Thank you for helping me, Mr. Abernathy. All of you," she said, smiling at Harper and Cornelia. "At least if I have to go to prison for the rest of my life, I won't have to go with my entire reputation in tatters."

"Beatrice, if you wouldn't mind." Olivia held out her hand.

Irwin looked at Beatrice who shrugged her approval.

"Go ahead," she said.

Irwin handed the paper to Olivia.

"Thanks." Olivia read silently to herself while the others in the room waited. When she finished, she rose from her chair, strode over to the stove, and turned on the burner. Holding the paper by its opposite corner, she tipped it to its side and lit it in flames. Once alight, she tossed it in the sink to continue to burn, turning the water on full blast until it crumbled and drained away into nothingness. Then Olivia returned to the table, tore open the envelope, removed the contents inside, and did the same exact thing. "Good riddance," she muttered, with false bravado.

Beatrice sat stunned.

Olivia washed and dried her hands and turned toward Beatrice. "Years ago, I, too, had made a bunch of stupid decisions in my life, and when I say stupid, I mean over the top irresponsible. I wound up hurting a lot of people. People I loved and who loved and cared about me. At one point, I came close to losing my family because of it," she explained, standing solemnly behind her daughter, hands on Harper's shoulders. "But I was given a second chance, although to be honest, I probably didn't deserve it at the time. But even with that second chance, I still floundered. I had problems...big problems, and found it difficult to pull my act together. There were still too many issues I hadn't been able to navigate or solve. In many ways, I couldn't let go of the past. I think I held onto it to punish myself, or as a reminder, much in the same way you did by refusing to destroy the news clipping when you could have. As a result, I became anxious...nervous all the time...and closed off. I lied to cover my tracks and repeatedly broke the trust of my family. Physically depressed and unable to sleep, I turned inward, and at one point, I contemplated giving up."

Harper reached up and laid her hand over her mother's in gentle support.

Beatrice nodded in understanding.

"Then, I met these two." Olivia jutted her chin in Irwin and Cornelia's direction, "and my entire life changed. I no longer had to struggle by myself. In a way, I was given a third chance."

Harper reached across the table and handed a sniffling Beatrice an unused napkin.

"Being truthful with us and coming clean was the start of your first chance, Beatrice," explained Olivia. "The second began when the papers burnt up. From this point moving forward, you must stop being tethered to a past you no longer need to pay for. It's done and over with. It's time to move on, and by destroying the list—hopefully for Alastair's other victims as well."

"Here, here!" shouted Cornelia, waving her empty teacup in the air.

"And now, this is your third chance." Olivia sat down opposite Beatrice. She reached across the table and extended her hands, palms facing up.

Unsteady, and close to crying, Beatrice reached over and held Olivia's hands.

Olivia spoke softly. "I received a call today while you lot were busy fleecing Alastair's."

"From who?" asked Harper in a small panicky voice.

"Taylor. She's my husband's attorney," explained Olivia. "She told me that Darren's been cleared of all the charges and he's coming home."

The room broke out in cheers, all except for Olivia, who smiled tenderly at Beatrice, never once letting go of the woman's quivering hands. "She also told me that the coroner's report showed that Alastair died of a heart attack. Nothing more." The room grew still.

Beatrice's entire body trembled. "I-I, don't understand."

"If I may?" interjected Irwin.

"Please," nodded Olivia, her eyes boring into Beatrice's face.

"I think what Olivia is trying to explain, Ms. Aston, is that from this point moving forward, nobody—including the police—needs to know anything more about what Alastair tried to do to you."

Wide-eyed, Beatrice's jaw dropped. She glanced around the room at all their faces staring at them in total disbelief. "Are you saying?"

"Yes, indeed." Cornelia slapped Beatrice on the back. "That's precisely what he means, my dear. Consider this Hail Mary your third and final chance. So, don't go screwing it up now."

"Oh, my God!" Beatrice leaped to her feet, not sure who to thank first.

While mother and daughter hugged and sobbed, Beatrice embraced a stiff, miserably uncomfortable Irwin, who, unlike everyone else, chose to remain rooted in his seat. He sat rigidly straight with his lanky arms pressed flat against his gangly body. "Thank you, Mr. Abernathy," she cried. "For everything." She pecked him on the cheek.

Irwin flushed.

Beatrice then smooched Cornelia's cheek, hugged and kissed Harper, and afterward ran right over to Olivia, hugging and squeezing her hard. "Thank you, thank you," she whimpered, sobbing into Olivia's shoulders. "I never meant to hurt you or your husband..."

"I know."

"I swear, I wouldn't have let him go to prison..."

"I believe you," comforted Olivia, rubbing her back.

"I was so scared..."

"I understand." Olivia hugged her back.

"How can I ever repay you for everything?" wept Beatrice.

Olivia pressed her forehead to Beatrice's and whispered, "Just be happy."

Clink, clink, clink.

"Ladies and gentlemen," began Cornelia, clanking her teaspoon against her teacup. "I have something I'd like to say."

The elated room quieted.

Cornelia rose from her chair. She leaned on her cane, ready to pontificate like a seasoned statesman. "'I have understood in this case that the scales of justice cannot always be evenly weighed. And I must learn, for once to live with the imbalance. There are no killers here. Only people who deserve a chance to heal.'"

"Wow, that was freakin' profound," remarked Harper into Irwin's ear. "Is that a quote from one of her books?"

"Not this time," explained Irwin. "Those are Hercule Poirot's words."

"Who?"

"Hercule Poirot, one of the world's greatest fictional detectives and brainchild of author extraordinaire, Agatha Christie—Cornelia's *shero*."

CHAPTER 19

Darren

"HONEY! I'M HOME," shouted Darren stepping through the bookshop's front door, followed shortly by Irwin and Olivia not far behind.

"Dad," shouted Harper, triumphantly flinging her arms around his neck. "You're free!" Although Darren had only been gone for a few nights, Harper recognized a drastic change. His generally serene, gentle smile had been replaced by a distant, reserved expression. Something she'd never seen in him before.

Olivia flung her coat on a nearby chair. "Like Taylor said, they had to let him go since your father's alibi checked out. Thankfully, there was enough corroborative evidence proving it wasn't him, even without having to mention you know who."

Darren heard the last part but refrained from asking.

"Are you on bail?" asked Harper.

"No bail," explained Irwin. "However, Detective Moore personally warned him to stay out of trouble."

"There goes the neighborhood," goaded Cornelia.

Darren turned his attention elsewhere. "Listen, guys, I hate to be a party pooper and all, but how about we finish this discussion over dinner? I'm in desperate need of a shower and a nap," he said, looking entirely worse for the wear. Darren didn't bother to wait for an answer before trotting upstairs. Olivia rushed to follow him.

Darren gripped onto the railing, dragging his lethargic legs up each step painfully slow, deliberately, as if at any second, something else would happen to make all this disappear again. He couldn't bear to relinquish this newly acquired taste of freedom again, only to watch it snatched away, becoming nothing but a taunting, unreachable memory.

Olivia noticed and pressed him forward. "Come on, slowpoke. Put a move on it."

Darren huffed. "Going as fast as I can, Liv."

Once upstairs, she massaged his back. "Why don't I make you something to eat now? You must be starving. I'll get it ready for you while you're in the shower."

"I'm honestly too tired to eat, Liv. Those idiots I got locked up with had me up practically all night."

"More of a reason to eat." Olivia closed the door separating the shop from the living quarters upstairs.

Downstairs, Harper made sure her father was out of earshot before turning to Irwin. "What about the statue? The fingerprints?"

"The autopsy showed that while Darren's fingerprints were on the statue, it never actually made physical contact with Alastair. Somehow, they were able to figure out that the blood splatter on it came afterward."

"Wow. Science sure is amazing," interjected Cornelia. "I bet it also indicated the difference between how long Alastair was dead versus when he was reported dead. How cool is that?"

"Another tidbit from one of your mystery books?" asked Harper.

"Nope. Television," One of those crime stopper shows."

"I suppose..." muttered Harper, not entirely impressed. "Hey, Irwin? Where's Christopher?"

"Christopher drove Taylor back to her office. He said he'll be back shortly." Irwin hung his coat on the peg. "How's everything been here? It looks pretty quiet."

"Now it is, but we were super busy this morning," said Harper, working hard to ignore the surge of jealousy nipping at her heels. She straightened out a pile of books ready to tip over. "Oh! Remember the author that's supposed to come next Friday for the signing?"

"Who?"

"The guy who wrote that book on extraterrestrial beings taking over the banking system."

"Coll?"

"Yeah, him."

"What about him?"

"He canceled. Something about a kidney stone."

"And this too shall pass," Cornelia chuckled from her chair.

Irwin exhaled. "Is there anything else I need to know?"

Upstairs...

DARREN STOOD under the hot water, letting it beat along the top of his aching shoulder blades. If washing away the stench of captivity could only be so easy. After living years behind bars, the fear of returning—being sent back—but this time for a crime he didn't commit, had scared him way more than he felt comfortable admitting to anyone.

Arrested. The only good thing that had come out of this whole insane situation; knowing that Olivia still loved him. But loving him and being *in love* were two different animals, and not necessarily interchangeable. Somehow, Darren had to make her fall hard in love with him. But how? After all that had transpired over the years, that would prove to be a tall order, and perhaps one which Darren would never pull off. Still, he had to try.

Darren finished washing and stepped out of the shower, only to be surrounded by the welcoming aromas of homecooked food wafting through the air. His weak limbs barely moved on their own, yet his empty stomach continued to chorus for Olivia's cooking.

For the last few months, they had gone from discussing the mundane to actually conversing about more rooted, more relevant topics. Not only parenting Harper and helping her achieve her aspirations but theirs...together as well.

Darren perched himself on the edge of the bathroom sink, He leaned in to examine his short, cropped hair, and the beginnings of a beard and mustache. Only the slightest hint of gray had begun to peek through, lending him a rather distinguished appearance to what Olivia referred to as his 'perpetually confused face.'

Olivia.

Beautiful, still out of reach, Olivia. His former lover, the mother of his only child, and inarguably, his best friend. The one person Darren had loved the hardest and hurt the deepest. She was also the woman who he had abandoned years ago to embark on a life of crime and drugs. Olivia, who, when he needed a place to stay after doing his time, had opened her home and welcomed him in, essentially saving him from surefire disaster.

Asking for yet another chance to be a part of her inner sanctum would take considerable time and dedication on his part, but even then, there was no guarantee that he hadn't already blown his shot. He had only himself to blame for that.

The late afternoon's waning sun flooded the kitchen with a warm, soft glow. A plate of food waited for him at the kitchen table, adding to the ambiance.

This is where I need to be...

Despite exhaustion, Olivia moved about the kitchen. He couldn't stop watching her long, curvaceous body or her natural gracefulness and vigor. Darren had always admired this woman's strength, coveted her beauty, and now, more than anything, craved her love and respect.

So beautiful. Damn it, Liv, he thought through covert glances. *You don't know how much I wanted to be home with you.*

Lifting his fork half-way to his mouth, Darren debated on whether or not to tell her about his stay in the jail. About all the crazy dreams and yearnings. Part of him wanted to share everything, much like he had back in the day when they were lovers. The other, wiser, more considerate less asshole part of him, promised to keep it to himself.

Why dump more of a burden on her? Lord knows, she'd seen more than her fair share; left to raise our child alone while I did time in a 10x13-foot cement cell.

Darren started to speak, but Olivia beat him to the punch. "Okay. Dishes are done, the kitchen's clean, and you're fed." She dried her hands on a dishtowel. "If it's all right with you, I think I'll try to squeeze in a nap before my shift. Irwin wants to keep the shop open later as we get closer to Christmas Eve."

Darren wanted to beg her not to leave him. To sit and rest and allow him to take care of her for once, but instead, he merely nodded.

"I have to admit; this staying open late thing is killing me. I mean, it's the holiday season, so of course, we're extra busy. I get that, and money-wise, we're doing great. Harper said we hit our projected numbers within the first two weeks of December, whatever that means."

"I can cover your shift if you want me to," offered Darren, despite his own body feeling like a Mack truck had run over it.

"Thanks, but you look ready to keel over yourself."

"A little tired, but I don't mind." Years ago, Darren would have never offered to help anyone. Embarrassingly, not even Olivia. Back then, he had only cared about himself; his needs, his wants, his addiction...doing whatever he needed to do to satisfy his unrelenting and demanding drug habit.

Olivia peered down and rewarded Darren's proffered selflessness with a warm, ingratiating smile.

Damn, you're gorgeous, Liv.

Olivia stretched her arms and back. "Gosh, I'm stiff."

Darren swept his eyes covertly across her lovely face, down her long, gorgeous neck...

"Besides, the shop's been crazy these past few nights, and I don't want to leave Harper with that ancient register of ours. It's been a real nightmare lately."

"I'll take a look at it."

"Thanks. There's no rush. I've got the hang of it. It's Harper who's struggling."

Darren finished his food, pushed his dish away and leaned back in his chair, exhausted but content. "Delicious as usual. Thank you."

"You're very welcome." Olivia reached to clear his plate, but Darren stopped her.

"I got it. You've done more than enough."

Olivia stood behind Darren and massaged his shoulders, sending an urgent, hungry tremor shooting throughout his body. "Well, you looked like a man in serious need of homecooked sustenance."

She should only know...

"Poor Harper," mulled Olivia. "I don't think she has gotten much rest. She's been taking the couch for the past few nights and letting Cornelia use her bedroom."

"Take my word for it, the couch sucks."

"Noted," laughed Olivia. "After what happened with you, we decided to keep Cornelia close."

"What about Irwin? He's usually particular about keeping Cornelia at her house."

"Our Irwin hasn't been himself much either these days, even for Mr. Grumpy. Harper and I thought he needed some time for himself."

Darren did know. He'd watched his friend hurt, not only throughout the holidays but practically every other day as well. The loss of Gilly, then her daughter, Dakota, had caused Irwin more sadness than one already lonely person should have to endure. Then again, Darren had to admire Irwin's endless love—and devotion. The kind that only comes around once in a lifetime. The kind he wanted to have again with Liv...

"She's had enough to contend with recently."

"Who?" Darren's concentration had failed him.

"Harper! Keep up," teased Olivia. "After all, this is supposed to be her winter break, and all the kid's been doing is work, work, and more work." Olivia opened the pantry closet and hung her apron on the hook. "Anyhow, now that Christopher's back, that should change."

"What do you mean?" Darren faltered. "What's Christopher being back here have to do with anything concerning my daughter?"

Olivia laughed. "Really?"

Darren stared at the woman he loved, downright perplexed. "What am I missing here?"

"You poor, poor, lost, pathetic soul." Olivia pulled out a chair and plopped down. She studied Darren's face, only to break out laughing even harder. "Men."

Darren winced, his eyes jutting side to side, not entirely sure where this conversation was headed. "And what's that supposed to mean?"

"You, Irwin, even Christopher. Thickheaded, I swear. I seriously don't know how the three of you function in the real world."

Darren had to agree. "If this past week was any indica-tion—poorly."

"No truer words were ever spoken," Olivia rubbed her tired eyes.

"Back to Christopher."

Footsteps stopped. Darren and Olivia glanced up.

"Did I hear my name?"

Darren jumped out of his seat. "Hey man, good to see you," he said, giving his young friend a bear hug and a friendly slap on the back. "I had wanted to do that at the station today, but you know—"

Christopher laughed. "No problem. Time and place, right?"

"Right," agreed Darren. "And never that place again."

"Agreed!" The two guys laughed.

"Hungry?" asked Olivia, already grabbing a plate.

"No, I'm good. I grabbed a coffee and a muffin with Taylor. The least I could do was treat her to lunch."

"Is that what you call it?" said Olivia, only slightly amused.

"Listen, I need to know what I owe her?" asked Darren.

Christopher slid out a chair. "I'm one step ahead of you and asked her the same thing this morning, and she said nothing. If this goes any further, which she highly doubts, we'll have to revisit her fees, but for now, she said to tell you this one's on the house."

Both Olivia and Darren shook their heads in protest.

Christopher threw his hands up. "Believe me, Taylor's not usually this altruistic. She'll charge you if you're called back in—and believe me, she doesn't come cheap—so take the gift and run with it while you can."

"What're the chances of that happening?" asked Olivia, worry etched across her weary face. "I mean about them bringing Darren back in?"

"For now, who knows? But it would sure help a ton if Cornelia remembered more. Any chance of that happening?"

The room fell silent. Olivia kept her expression neutral.

"Nevertheless, please tell Taylor I really appreciate her showing up for me," said Darren.

"Yeah, about that," said Christopher. "I invited her to the party."

"Party?" shouted Olivia and Darren. "What party?"

Christopher glanced between the two. "Oops," he groaned, hands in front of his chest in surrender. "Maybe I wasn't supposed to say anything, but I wouldn't worry. It's not for a few days, yet."

"Harper again," grumbled Olivia.

Christopher smiled. "You didn't hear it from me."

"No worries, son," Darren laughed. "We got your back," he said, knowing full well how pushy his daughter got once an idea got lodged into that stubborn head of hers.

"Phew." Christopher swiped his forehead in mock relief. "Actually, Darren, there was something else I wanted to talk to you about, but maybe now isn't the best time to discuss it. I mean, with everything else that's going on."

"Is something wrong?" inquired Darren, already fearing the worse.

"No, not at all, but I kind of need to run something by you."

"How about tomorrow? I'm ready to fall on my face." Darren rose gradually from his seat, moving as if his legs had weights attached to them. "I think Olivia's not far behind me."

"That works for me," agreed Christopher. "But if it's all right with you, I'd like to keep this conversation between us for now."

Darren glanced at Olivia. "I think we can handle that. Liv?"

"Works for me," replied Olivia, playing innocent and already in the know.

"I'll catch you later, then," said Christopher, heading toward his apartment.

Olivia rose sluggishly to her feet and groaned. "Every part of my body hurts."

Darren rushed to her side. "Tired, huh?" he asked, offering her a helping hand.

"Completely shattered. You?"

"The same."

"Good. Follow me," she winked.

Darren grinned ear-to-ear. He didn't have to be told twice.

CHAPTER 20

Cornelia Parish

OVER THE NEXT FEW DAYS, life at the bookshop started to settle down. Despite the harrowing past few days, routine inevitably kicked in, and everyone picked up where they had left off, all except for one member of the *Abernathy Bookshop Gang*.

"—exactly how I instructed three years ago," whispered Cornelia into the phone. She left the water running full blast in the bathroom sink to drown out her voice. "Yes, of course, Rodney. I understand...No, it has to be tomorrow while I can still remember what the hell I'm talking about...Yes, I'm sure, it's time...No, I can get there myself, but thank you...of course not—Yes, yes, I know,

Rodney...driving without a license is illegal. Stop fussing. I promise to get somebody to take me..."

Harper

"*Pssssт. Psssst.* HARPER?" whispered Cornelia, "Hey, Harper, you awake?" she asked, poking Harper in the arm.

"Oh, God, not again," she grumbled, tugging the warm blanket around her head to block out the intrusion. "Go away, Cornelia. I'm not breaking into any more stores."

Cornelia used her thumb to part-open one of Harper's eyes.

"Why are you all dressed up?" Harper mumbled, squinting. "Oh, no!" Harper bolted straight up, her head twisting left and right. "Did I forget about one of your appointments?" Still half asleep, she jumped out of bed, groping on the floor for a tossed pair of jeans.

"Harper."

"How late are we?" she asked, hopping on one foot to pull her jeans on over her pajama pants.

"Harper!" Cornelia yelled, somewhat amused. "We're not late, but I do have an appointment. Please get dressed without killing yourself."

Fifteen minutes later, a showered, fully dressed but petulant Harper emerged. She schlepped into Cornelia's kitchen and grabbed an energy bar from the pantry. "Want one?"

"I'd rather die," grumbled Cornelia. "I don't know how you eat those things."

"Bite, chew, swallow. In that order." Harper tossed the wrapper. "Have you eaten? I can make you scrambled eggs and toast, or we can stop by your favorite donut shop and grab something. It's up to you."

"I'm not hungry."

Harper stopped mid-chew. "*You're not hungry*—as in you already ate, or you're not hungry as in you feel sick?"

"Neither. Not hungry."

Now Harper was really confused. "Where are we going, by the way, and what time do we have to be there?" She checked her phone. "Weird...I don't have an appointment in my calendar. Are you sure you have one, Cornelia?"

"New doctor. New place. I have the address, and we need to leave now." She handed Harper a slip of paper with only an address on it.

Harper skimmed the information, shrugged, and typed it into her phone's GPS to get the directions. The address came up along with the name of the place. "Heart Home Living Center? This can't be right." She glanced at the paper again. "No, that's the address." Harper looked up at Cornelia, standing there like an effigy, waiting. "Are you sure you have the right information?"

"It's the correct information."

Harper, uncharacteristically slow on the take, failed to put the pieces together. "Strange place for a doctor's office. I'll go next door to get the car keys from Irwin."

Cornelia extended her hand and jiggled a set of keys. "He gave me his second set last night."

Harper frowned, becoming irritated. "What do you mean he *gave you* the other set? Since when does he—" She stopped herself. "Okay, Cornelia...what's going on? Because none of this is adding up, and I'm not awake enough yet to figure it out." Then Harper noticed a large packed suitcase in the hall. "Why is that there?" Harper, starting to hyperventilate, began putting the missing pieces of Cornelia's subterfuge together. "No, no, no, no...," she whimpered.

"It's time, kiddo."

Harper wrapped her arms around her body and rocked. "You can't do this, Cornelia. Not now. Not after everything," she pleaded. "Wait for a few months or better yet, maybe next year would work." She couldn't stop babbling. "I'm going to get Irwin."

"No!" roared Cornelia, startling Harper. "You will do no such thing. This is my decision, Harper. My life. My disease. I have spoken to Irwin and the rest of you for months, and for months you all keep telling me what I need. Now I am telling you what I need, and I will go— with you or without you." Cornelia spun on her heels and marched toward the suitcase, keys in hand.

"Stop! You can't drive anymore."

"Watch me."

"You don't have a license."

Cornelia snorted and turned. "Really, Harper? Is that all you got?" She shook her head disappointed and kept walking.

"Stop...*please*."

Cornelia turned around slowly to face Harper with stubborn determination inscribed all over her face.

Harper had lost the battle. "I'll take you." Her words came out flat, garbled, and choked behind tears. "I'll take you."

CORNELIA TOOK A SINGLE SUITCASE. Nothing more. In that one solitary case, a few outfits, all purposely interchangeable. Cornelia had selected and packed them the day after her doctor confirmed her diagnosis.

"Are you sure, Dr. Tate? Tests can be wrong." Cornelia had asked him, already knowing the answer even before the words left her mouth.

"I'm afraid, so, Cornelia, my old friend. I'm deeply sorry," confirmed Dr. Tate. "This isn't the kind of news I wanted to deliver to one of my favorite patients."

"That makes two of us."

WHAT CORNELIA DIDN'T bother to pack were any personal items. No photos, no books. No trinkets, no baubles. Besides her wedding band, she had left all her jewelry, including the heart-shaped necklace, behind in a velvet box. Besides clothing, footwear, a bathrobe, and some toiletries, there was nothing else personal, except for her favorite ink pen—a gift from Irwin to commemorate Cornelia's first published novel. That, she had decided, was something she still needed to take along for the last leg of her journey.

Harper shuffled to the hall and picked up Cornelia's suitcase, surprised to find it wasn't heavy. "Is this all you're taking?"

"It's all I need."

"There's hardly anything in here," she shook the suitcase for emphasis. "Don't you want to take anything else?" Harper strained to keep her voice steady against the pressure of wanting to breakdown.

"What else do I need? What else will I remember I need?"

"What about your books? Your photo albums...or I know, your wedding photo—did you at least pack that?"

Cornelia shook her head. "It's time to go."

Harper didn't move. Instead, she extended her arm and wiggled her fingers. Cornelia obliged and handed her the second pair of keys.

"Out of curiosity, how did you get ahold of these?" asked Harper, lifting the suitcase.

"I snatched them from Irwin's utility drawer while he was in the bathroom."

"Of course, you did." Harper grinned. Once outside, she tossed the suitcase in the trunk.

"Shush," reminded Cornelia. "We're on our last caper together."

"Oh? Are we now," grumbled Harper.

"We sure are, doll! Let's go out with a bang."

Harper wasn't too sure about all that, but she was determined to do whatever it took to make her friend—*her closest thing to a grandmother*—happy—no matter what.

FIFTEEN MINUTES LATER, they were pulling into the long, winding driveway of an impressive tall brick building.

Harper let out a long, suffering breath. "I'll let you out at the front, and I'll go park the car."

"No. I'll walk with you."

Harper shrugged. "You're the boss." She drove slowly past the entrance to park the car. "I just want you to know, while you're safe and comfortable, tucked away in this place, Irwin is going to murder me."

"He'll be fine."

"But I'll be dead." Harper turned off the ignition. She glanced over at Cornelia trying to hold it together, tough it out, but in truth, she looked as tense and uneasy as Harper did. "Give me the word, and we can turn around and drive home, Cornelia."

"I'm slipping away, doll. As much as I'd like to pretend otherwise, my body has rights over me, and she's telling me she's tired. But we had a good run. Did a ton of stuff together and met so many fabulous people." She reached over and gently squeezed Harper's hand. "I even got to fall in love a few times and be loved back. Not too shabby."

"There's still more time...places to go, people to meet, shops to break into..."

Cornelia smiled. "Not for me. My life of crime is over." A few more cars pulled into the parking lot. "Trust me, I hate this as much as you do. I don't like slipping away like this and certainly not in front of you or the others—not if I can help it."

"We don't care about any of that stuff. We only want you to be safe and happy."

"I know, Love, but there's no way you can care for me twenty-four hours a day, seven days a week. For right now, I'm more here in the head than not, but it's getting harder and harder for me to hold it together." Cornelia paused. "You know what I'm saying is true. You and the others have done your darndest over these years to keep me safe and happy, and I love you all for it, more than I can ever express, but now it's time for someone else to step in."

Harper understood. She hated what she was hearing, but she understood.

"Don't fight me on this, Harper. Please. I need to do this. I need to be in control and make my own decisions while I still can." Cornelia sighed. "Plus, I want you to remember me the way I was. Not like this. Not like what I am turning into. This isn't the real me."

The two women sat in silence, each lost in their thoughts.

Harper sighed. "Irwin is going to lose it big time when I tell him."

"He can be a big doofus sometimes, but he'll eventually come to terms with my decision, even if he hates to admit that I did the right thing. Once Irwin calms down, he'll realize that this is best for everyone concerned—including him."

"I don't know, Cornelia. You've seen how he's been since Gilly, then Dakota, and now…"

"—me. I know. It's going to be a rough patch for a bit, but I am confident that with your love and patience, he'll soldier on. Do me a favor."

Don't cry… Don't cry… Harper nodded.

"Tell him not to bring me any of those sappy flowers of his every week. I want the good stuff. The gossip. The chinwag, the chatter, the news. Tell him I want to know everything, like old times… he'll know what I mean."

"Oh, Cornelia…" Harper sputtered, close to defeat. "Irwin's not going to be able to go on without you. You've been his best friend for decades, his rock. You got him through everything he's had to face. To be honest, you've helped make him human."

"He has you now."

"It's not the same thing."

"It doesn't have to be." Cornelia stiffened her shoulders, gathering her resolve. "Time to go."

The two friends ambled into the imposing building and went to the front desk.

"Good morning," said the handsome, chipper young man at reception. "How can I help you?"

"I'll leave that up to you, cutie. I'm open to

suggestions," jested Cornelia, causing Harper standing behind her to blush with embarrassment.

Cornelia leaned over the desk. "Is she turning red yet?" she asked mischievously.

"Bright," confirmed the young man, whose name tag read, *Michael*.

"Good. Mission accomplished. Michael, I am your next internee, ready to check in."

Michael laughed. "Name, please?"

"Cornelia Parish. I'm supposed to ask to speak to—"

"Cornelia," resonated the sweet voice coming from the person briskly walking towards them from the side. "I'm Joanne Burberry, your personal health coordinator," she said, extending her hand. "Your attorney, Mr. Davenport, phoned and told me to expect you."

"Attorney?" hissed Harper from behind. "Since when do you have an attorney?"

"Good old, Rodney." Cornelia gave Harper a slight shrug. "I'll tell you later."

"Oh, Lord..." Harper shook her head, wondering what else Cornelia had failed to mention.

"I can take that from you," offered Joanne to Harper, indicating the suitcase. "Cornelia has a busy day ahead, checking in and getting settled, but we welcome friends and encourage the family to visit as often as they like."

Harper nodded, reluctantly handing over the suitcase.

"Okay, doll, time for you to get going." Cornelia wore a big, fake smile. "You better get the car back before Irwin notices it's missing," she whispered behind her hand.

"The car?" Harper's eyes grew wide. "Don't you think he's going to notice that *you're missing*?" retorted Harper, beyond astounded.

"Good point."

Harper leaned down, hugged Cornelia tight without hurting her. "I don't want to leave you here," she whispered into her friend's ear.

Cornelia lightly pushed Harper back. "You're not leaving me here against my will. Now go. Please."

"I love you, Cornelia."

"I love you too, Harper. Take care of my Irwin for me. I know he can be a bit of a pill, but he's one of the best human beings I have ever known."

The two friends hugged again. "I'll come to visit you so much, you'll get sick of me," sobbed Harper.

The dam finally broke, releasing a torrent of shared tears between the two women.

"Listen, I need you to know something," said Cornelia, sniffling. "When the day comes when I can no longer recognize you, please don't be hurt or think it somehow means that I didn't really love you, because I am telling you here and now, that's a bald-faced lie. It's this wretched disease talking, not me. Remember today and me telling you how much I have loved you since the day we first met. In so many ways, you are my grandchild...my free spirit... my future warrior of the pen. Go out into the world and make me proud. Do all the things you've dreamt about, and then some. And while you're at it, drag that handsome young fella along with you also." Cornelia paused and frowned.

Cornelia struggled to conjure up his name.

"Christopher," Harper offered in a choked, heartbroken whisper.

"Damn it, I knew that," winked Cornelia, lips quivering.

But they both understood she didn't.

CHAPTER 21

Irwin

Surrounded by dense woods, nestled on a hill stood the Senior Living Center overlooking the Appalachian Mountains. On any other day, Irwin probably would have described the cluster of brick buildings as charming, but as his car approached along the winding road and the butterflies in his stomach churned, 'charming' was the least of his first impressions.

He checked the instructions, making sure to park close enough to the largest, central building where he had been informed he'd have to first sign in.

The staff was friendly, competent, and experienced with reluctant visitors. As he waited for the elevator to take him to the Rose Wing located on the second floor,

Irwin studied the brochure bragging of the kitchenettes, spacious living rooms, and a supposedly 'spectacular view of the mountainous landscape.'

Room 112.

Irwin didn't know what to expect, so he knocked softly at first. When that failed to elicit a response, he rapped the door three more times until a familiar voice, albeit less friendly than usual, greeted him.

"It's not locked."

Irwin turned the knob and opened the door slowly. Instead of going inside, he chose to remain planted in the doorway. She sat on a cushioned chair facing a huge outside window with her back toward him. Neither spoke until finally, Irwin broke the ice. "I don't understand why," he said stiffly, his shoulders slumped in a loss.

A moment went by before she answered.

"Because you wouldn't."

"But I wanted to take care of you," he said, failing to mask the quiver in his voice. "I would have watched over you. Made sure your days were filled with anything and everything you ever wanted."

Cornelia spun around. Face contorted, she slammed her tiny, veined fist on the armrest. "Don't you think I already know that?" she yelled, her small body strained with irritation. "Shit, Irwin, don't make this any harder than it has to be. Go home."

Irwin didn't budge. Tears of hurt streamed down from his red-rimmed eyes.

"Didn't you hear me? Leave." Cornelia's hands twitched and quivered as she spoke. "Go find somebody else to talk to, listen to you nitpick and grumble."

"But I want you."

Cornelia shook her head. "Well, I'm afraid you can't

always get what you want, my friend. Hasn't life taught you at least that much yet?" she snapped. A painful moment passed before her rage began to subside. "It's hard to explain how lonely and isolating this disease is. I used to love being busy, working on projects, hobbies, puzzles... and now...now I can barely remember how to do the simplest of tasks. Simply put, I need more than you can give."

"Cornelia—"

"No, Irwin. This you can't fix. I'm dying. Maybe not today or this minute, but more and more each day." She paused and leaned back in her chair. "No use beating around the bush. My disease has progressed. My motor skills are shot to shit. It's like an Olympian feat for me just to tie my shoes or buckle a belt. Who knows the kind of trouble I can get into with a pair of scissors or worse, a nail clipper! You know it—you've seen it."

"You're fine."

"Yes, for now. For today, but dementia is a hungry, relentless beast and soon enough, I'll require twenty-four hour supportive care. I refuse to saddle you or the others with that."

"We love you. We could have made it work."

"I know you would have tried, but at what cost? Harper didn't accept a sizable scholarship from a university in New York on my account. No, Irwin. I refuse. I'm not having it. I want to live here...not with you and the others, all waiting around to watch me die."

Irwin gulped.

"Ah, I see. You didn't know about that, did you? Well, don't be hurt. Neither did I until I found the letter she hid when she let me use her bedroom last week." Cornelia stared ahead, fixated on getting it all out. "And what about

Christopher? Did you know he's ready to drop out of law school for the same reason? And then there's our Olivia... you know that poor thing doesn't handle stress well. She practically has a massive anxiety attack every time I pull one of my stupid stunts. And Darren? He's got no chance in hell's bells of getting back into that woman's bed with me always screwing things up." Cornelia bowed her head. "And finally, there's you. My dearest and precious friend. The closest person to me in the entire world. Is it so terrible that I want you to remember me the way I was, the way we were when we were together? Is it so unfair for me to want to decide at least a part of my fate?" Cornelia clasped her hands on her lap. "Besides, you old fool, you've been through enough loss. I'm not going to let you do this to yourself. Now, go away and let me be."

"What will you do here? In this place?"

"Oh, I don't know. Write. Maybe transcribe my stories to someone. I can still do a bit of that. Sort of, but with my memory, I intend on sticking to short stories," she said wistfully. "I'll do that much until...I can't."

Irwin took a tentative step inside.

"Don't."

"Please, Cornelia. Let me take you home."

"No, Irwin. This is my home now."

"This will never be your home," he roared. "Home is with us—with me."

"Go home, Irwin...just go."

Irwin didn't mean to sob or lose his temper. On the entire trip over, he'd practiced in his head how best to handle today, but no matter what he did, he couldn't control his heart from breaking, nor make the defeat stop. "I...I can't do this without you," he pleaded.

Cornelia turned entirely around facing the window,

once more giving Irwin nothing but her back. "Oh, but darlin', you must."

BEFORE TAKING HIS LEAVE, Irwin stopped at reception to speak to Cornelia's healthcare coordinator. Within minutes, a pleasant enough looking woman dressed in a casual pantsuit came out to greet him, her slightly greying, blond bob swinging as she walked.

"Joanne Burberry, Cornelia's personal health coordinator, but please, call me Joanne. We're not very formal here," she said kindly, reaching out to shake Irwin's hand. "I understand you're Cornelia's friend?"

Irwin nodded. "Irwin Abernathy."

"Wonderful. I was hoping we'd get a chance to chat. We can sit in my office, or if you'd rather walk and talk, I can give you the official tour."

"I think I'd prefer your office if you don't mind."

"Not at all." Joanne spread her arms wide and gestured for him to follow. "Please, this way."

The office decor looked as lowkey and pleasant as it's occupant. "Take a seat." She moved a chair beside him instead of sitting at her desk. "What can I help you with today?"

Irwin removed his hat and sat down. "I'm not sure where to begin. This—Cornelia's decision to come here came as quite a shock. I'm afraid I'm still processing it all."

"I understand," she nodded. "What I can tell you is this, our residents are all extremely important to us. We want them to be comfortable, happy, content—and protected, which is why we work so hard to offer a secure and peaceful environment here at Heart Home Center.

Our goal is to make their stay as pleasant and as comfortable as home."

"Cornelia has a home," Irwin retorted, eyes wide with incredulity. "With me."

Joanna smiled. "Yes. Cornelia told me about you, and about Olivia, Darren, Harper, and Christopher. You are all enormously important to her, but especially you."

Irwin twisted his cap in his hands. "Then why come here? I mean, it's quite obviously a nice enough place, but Cornelia has us."

"I'm the last person who has to tell you how highly independent Cornelia is—or how stubborn," Joanne said soothingly. "When she initially contacted us two years ago, she made her reasons for coming here quite clear—her love for you and the others being paramount."

"Two years ago?" Irwin shook his head, stunned. "I had no idea..."

Joanne pivoted her chair and leaned in closer to a stiff-backed Irwin. "Cornelia understands what she is ultimately facing...the rapid mental decline of dementia, and the potential danger she poses to her loved ones. She's a proud woman, Mr. Abernathy, and this is a terribly challenging situation to face."

Irwin interrupted. "I thought that's what we were doing, keeping her safe. We had each been taking turns watching her, and she was never left alone. We even had a GPS thing made for her to wear in case she wandered off."

"Ah, yes, the infamous heart-shaped necklace. She's told me all about it."

Irwin tugged at his shirt collar. "I didn't realize she knew about that," he muttered, uncrossing his legs, looking away.

"As I said, Cornelia is a proud person. Highly intuitive

and obviously deeply loved. But the reality of this disease is complicated. As you are already aware, Cornelia, for the most part, is fairly cognitive, with moderate cognitive decline, and some added signs of increased health complications. Technically, with constant supervision, she could probably still live at home for a while."

"That's what I said—"

"Yes, I understand that, but that's not what she wants, Mr. Abernathy. Believe me, there are situations involving memory loss and confusion which can become extremely difficult and taxing for caregivers and their families. Cornelia's memory loss and confusion in the earlier stages are mild compared to what lies ahead."

"She sounds fine to me."

"And yet she tells me that she is having more and more difficulty recalling names, events, and at times, processing what you and the others are talking about. Which is why, before her symptoms progress, and while she is aware enough to make certain decisions, she has decided to come here where we can work with her and take the strain off of her family and friends' shoulders. As a personal care home, we have various specially trained staff who will watch over Cornelia closely to make sure value is placed on her most cherished memories. This includes creating a specific care plan to meet her medical requirements and proficiencies."

Irwin rubbed his forehead, not sure what else to add.

"I want you and the others to rest assured, Cornelia will have all the personal attention, compassionate care, and conveniences one would and should expect."

Irwin nodded.

"Mr. Abernathy, like I told Harper earlier, we strongly encourage family and friends to visit. Please feel free to come as often as you like. I know Cornelia would love that."

"Miss Burberry—*Joanne*. I don't mean to be disrespectful, but how the hell do you know what Cornelia would love?"

"Mr. Abernathy, this is painful, and I know, not what you expected to happen. The shock must be terribly difficult. If it makes you feel any better, I think I can share something with you without breaking Cornelia's patient confidentiality. It will show you that this isn't what she ultimately wished to happen either—in her words, not mine."

"I see." Head bent, Irwin rubbed the back of his neck.

"Cornelia loves you very much, Mr. Abernathy, which is why—" Joanne stood and skirted around her desk. She unlocked the bottom drawer and selected a manila folder. "She asked me to give you this."

Inside the folder, a sealed letter with Irwin's name scripted elegantly across the envelope.

To my dearest, most cherished friend, Irwin...

IRWIN'S FEAR of abandonment had again overwhelmed him. As a child, his parents had left him in the care of his grandmother. As a young man, people in his life tended to come and go, but never stay. In his middle years, Irwin met the love of his life, and for a tiny morsel of time—he was happy, fulfilled, and content—only to have the promise of their life together viciously ripped away. And now, as Irwin sat in his parked car outside of Cornelia's 'new home' —he gazed ahead at everything and nothing. Her delivered letter to him read; the tear-stained pages left strewn across his lap.

As her friend, he had no choice but to witness the longest friendship of his life deliberately trickle into oblivion. To watch helplessly as all their shared, cherished memories faded and crumbled into dust...a haunting casualty of the next impending storm. The cruel biting realization that he had no power to stop it all but destroyed him.

While shallow breaths threatened to consume, Irwin did something entirely unfamiliar—this time facing his uncertainties by consciously changing the conversation looping unrestrained in his head, blindsiding him with loss and desertion.

Irwin took ten deep, full cleansing breaths. In his ornery, most familiar cantankerous fashion, he commanded the sharp pain in his stomach to stop and desist. He consciously instructed his body to loosen the heavy stiffness emanating from his shoulders, while guiding his quaking limbs to stop shaking—all while confronting the overpowering fear-filled inner voice commandeering his mind.

I will face you.
You will not win this time.
My love is stronger than fear.

IRWIN MUMBLED this mantra until his breathing steadied, and his aged hands stopped trembling. Pushing the key into the ignition, he made his short journey back home. A whole lot more shattered, still very much afraid, somewhat more determined, but wretchedly alone.

The next day...

SHE DOESN'T WANT to see me." Irwin cleared his dishes from the kitchen table. "That much is clear." He sponged off the counter and rinsed the dishrag under hot water.

"Of course, she does," insisted Harper. "What are you talking about? You're her best friend."

"You weren't there. She turned her back on me."

"No, Irwin, Cornelia turned her back on her old life, but never on you." Harper reached over and covered his hand with hers, squeezing gently. "Listen, she might not be here physically with us anymore, and for that matter, not always mentally around either, but she'll always and forever be in our hearts."

"Engaged in greeting card claptrap now, are we?"

"Wow..." Harper winced. "Okay. Let me explain this to you in a way even your old negative ass can understand. Agreed, I haven't known Cornelia as long or as well as you. The two of you have shared a friendship together that my *claptrap* will never do justice to, but damn it, Irwin, I do know this—that stored somewhere in the far from reach recesses of Cornelia's heart are words. Millions of them, which she can no longer retrieve on demand. Her whole life has been based on the exchange of ideas, philosophies, and opinions. It's been the way she chose to express herself."

"And?"

"And that's where you come in."

"Me?"

"Yes, you."

"Oh, I don't think so."

"Bullshit. Cornelia needs you more than ever now."

"I highly doubt that, Harper. Lest we forget, she now resides in an adult living center replete with round-the-clock care."

"So freakin' what?" Harper crossed her arms and frowned. "Oh. I get it—your feelings are in a bunch because how dare Cornelia not want you to be the one to wipe her ass and change her diapers? Give me a break, Irwin."

Irwin turned away, duly chastised. "I don't know what to do to help her."

"Fair enough. So, do what you do best."

"Complain?"

"—put the words back into her world."

Irwin chucked the rag in the sink. "And by that, I assume you mean read to her?"

"That's precisely what I mean."

Irwin circled the kitchen, his hands drooped by his side. "Have you not been listening, Harper? The Cornelia you and I knew is disappearing—almost gone. She can barely remember from one moment to the next as is."

Harper stomped in front of Irwin and blocked his way, poking him hard in the chest. "So what? If I remember correctly, when we first met, you were reading to Gilly's daughter, Dakota, in a hospital for like what, how many years? And-she-was-in-a-freakin'-*coma!*"

Irwin and Harper stared each other down. In retreat, Irwin rubbed his strained, tired eyes.

Not one to be placated, Harper marched across the room and dragged a box labeled *Photo Albums & Frames* across Irwin's kitchen floor toward his back door.

Irwin watched, riveted. He couldn't help but reflect back to when they had first met. Back then, Harper had been such a confused teenage girl, spending an inordinate amount of time in the library, sitting in a chair and staring at him for hours—most of the time laughing at him, and leaving impertinent, snarky little notes stuck inside various library books for him to find. This is the same girl who had once run away to hide in the library's woman's bathroom all because she refused to face the burdens of the world. And now, standing before him was a self-assured, strong young woman—perfectly comfortable to meet him face-to-face, demanding he step up and face his fears.

"All well and good, but what about you?" he blurted out, not sure if he was ready to hear her answer. The thought of losing one more person in his life felt too much to bear. "Now that Cornelia's no longer living here, will you accept that scholarship to attend school in New York?" He didn't realize how hard he was holding his breath.

"How did you—" Harper wagged a finger. "Ah, she told you, didn't she?"

"Cornelia found it by mistake."

"Sure. She was being nosey, and you and I both know it," laughed Harper. "Whatever. I'm still not ready to commit to that...but please, not a word to Mom or Dad—but *especially Mom*. You know how she gets."

"My lips are sealed." Irwin exhaled, grateful for the temporary reprieve.

Harper slipped on her coat. "Look, I'm leaving in a few minutes. Are you coming or not?"

Irwin hesitated.

You will not win this time. My love is stronger than fear.

"I'll get my coat."

Harper didn't have to be told twice. "I'm driving."

"Dear God," Irwin grumbled, tossing her his keys, then snapped his fingers. "Give me a minute. I'll meet you in the car."

"You got it." Harper lifted the box of photos to take with her, while Irwin headed into his study.

"Where are you? ...Where did you go?" he muttered while searching up, down, across, below, and above. "Ah—found you."

Moments later, Irwin slid into the passenger seat and locked the door.

"About time."

Irwin flipped the paperback face down on his lap before buckling in. "You may proceed," he said, clutching the overhead handle in a death grip.

"Oh, sheesh, Irwin. Do you always have to look so petrified? I do know how to drive, you know."

"That remains to be seen."

Harper started the engine. "So..."

"So?"

"So, I see you've selected a book."

"No one can accuse you of not being observant."

Harper twisted her neck to check for any oncoming traffic before slowly backing out of Irwin's driveway. "I'm dying to know which one you picked."

Irwin begrudgingly held it up. "*The Case of the Bulging Muscle*," he said, enunciating the title.

"Hold up!" Harper hard-pressed the brake before ever leaving the driveway. "Let me get this straight," she snickered, slapping the steering wheel in fits of laughter. "You're-you're-going to read *that book* to her?"

"Clearly."

"Aloud?"

"No," Irwin harrumphed, rolling his eyes. "—in sign language."

"Oh man..." Harper snorted, hugging herself. "This is going to be *totally* epic."

Beatrice

"WHAT'S YOUR NAME AGAIN?" Cornelia sat propped up in a chair with a handmade throw blanket wrapped snugly around her small frame. Over the past few weeks, her appetite had drastically diminished, as well as her weight.

"Beatrice."

"Ah. Beatrice," Cornelia repeated, staring as if she didn't believe her. "Have we met before?"

Beatrice nodded. "We've bumped into each other on occasion," she answered, smiling.

"Hmmm." Cornelia tilted her head, staring.

"Is there something wrong?"

"You sure don't look like a Beatrice to me," Cornelia mumbled, her gaze slightly blank.

Beatrice swallowed, fumbling at a loss of words. "Well, I'm afraid that's the name I was given."

Cornelia used her tiny fingers to collect lint off her lap blanket. When she glanced up, she grinned. The two women sat in silence until Cornelia spoke again. "Names are funny, aren't they? Our first official titles and introduction into the world. Slapped on us by good-intentioned parents before our true personalities have even had a chance to reveal themselves."

"That's true," Beatrice nodded, stunned by the verbosity of Cornelia's statement. "But what would we be called in the interim? Baby? It? Him? Her? Those no-names are kind of cold and heartless."

"I suppose," Cornelia agreed, "but some people are handed the short end of the stick."

"What do you mean?"

"I mean they are given stupid names. Sometimes ridiculous names, or names that don't live up to their, I don't know what to call it...spirit potential, maybe?"

"I don't know either, Cornelia, but I think over time, most people eventually morph into the essence of their given name."

"Yes, perhaps most do. But I think that's because people make themselves fit in. They accept whatever's handed to them because they never want to make waves or speak out of turn. 'Be a good girl, Cornelia. Do as you're told.' 'Don't talk like that, Cornelia. It's not lady-like' she hissed, staring off into the distance, in a blank, aloof stare.

"It's not easy, this world," murmured Beatrice, taken back by Cornelia's unexpected outburst.

"I agree, but why merely exist when you can choose to live?" Cornelia stopped fussing with the lint and stared straight into Beatrice's face. "For example, you're obviously not a Beatrice."

Beatrice blinked. "What do you mean by that?" she asked, too bemused to be offended. In truth, Beatrice had always disliked her name, wishing her parents had given her something lighter, brighter...less damn *suitable*.

"I think I should give you a nickname if we're going to

be hanging out together like this. Something that fits you better," announced Cornelia, not really asking.

Beatrice squirmed in her seat, not at all pleased. She dreaded the probability of being saddled with yet one more atrocious moniker. Throughout the span of her life, she had her fill of demeaning nicknames, many of which relegated her to a painful past. Beatrice suspected Cornelia's pick would do the same; another curt reminder of her all-too-many shortcomings. A name like—

"Arabella," declared Cornelia.

"I'm sorry," Beatrice's head snapped to attention. "What did you say?"

"Arabella. It means, 'yielding to prayer,' but the 'Bella' part means 'beautiful.' Don't bother asking me how I remembered that."

Arabella? Beatrice flushed, shocked to the point that she had to clasp her jaw in utter disbelief. "You think I'm beautiful?"

"Don't be ridiculous. Of course, you are, but not only because you're pretty on the outside, you had nothing to do with that, the roll of the DNA dice and all, but because you're bright." Cornelia sized her up and gave Beatrice a once-over. "I get the feeling you are smart, tough... resilient. I like smart, tough women—always have."

Beatrice's lower lip quivered.

Cornelia leaned forward, eyes bored into hers. "You also have the most striking green eyes, when you're not busy camouflaging them behind those dreadful eyeglasses. Where'd you get those things, anyway? They should be banned."

Beatrice removed her bifocals to inspect them.

Cornelia's right. They are dreadful.

"Do yourself a favor," advised Cornelia. "Swap out

those God awful glasses for a stylish, sporty looking pair—
or better yet, be bold. Try contact lenses. You're young.
You're lovely. Shine, for heaven's sakes." Cornelia leaned in
and tugged the hem of Beatrice's blouse to inspect it. "And
while you're at it, stop dressing like such a damn
chameleon. Live a little. Maybe try out a new fancy hairdo
or wear something different—preferably colorful instead of
this drab—I honestly don't even know what color to call
this hausfrau getup you got going on here."

Beatrice leaned back in her chair, dumbfounded.
Barreled over by Cornelia's take-no-prisoners, fiery dispo-
sition. She paused momentarily before permitting the feel
of this new, strange, but welcomed label to wash over her.

"Well? Are we reading today or not?" carped Cornelia,
her eyes starting to glaze over, looking as if her clarity of
thought was minutes away from fading again.

Beatrice wriggled in her seat, but this time perched a
bit taller. She arched her back, lifted the book Cornelia
chose close to her face, and voice strong, began to read.
"'*Slumped over her office desk, head pounding from
exhaustion, Nour wanted nothing more than to kick off
her shoes, close her eyes, and curl up into a ball of nothingness; escape from the insanity determined to squeeze
the breath out of her,*'" whispered Beatrice, her voice raspy
and strained.

"Louder, Arabella," barked Cornelia, leaning back in
her recliner with her short little legs elevated, and her
small hands crossed over her chest. "No whispering
permitted," she admonished, eyes closed. "This ain't my
funeral, yet."

Epilogue

At the cemetery...

"What a month, and it's far from over," grumbled Irwin, standing beside Gilly's snow-covered headstone. "It started off with Harper harassing me to decorate the shop for the holidays, which I assumed would happen, but honestly, every single solitary holiday known to mankind? Total overkill." Irwin cleared his throat.

"Have I ever mentioned Alastair Brooke to you? Owns the antique store next to mine...I know I must have ... Anyway, he decided to once again go on one of his harassment tours, sending me more of his longwinded threatening letters and list of complaints. Apparently, his personality DNA helix did not recognize the concept of holiday cheer." Irwin rubbed his hands. "I say *failed* as in the past tense since he's dead. Literally, not figuratively." Irwin stepped on the crunchy, frozen snow on the other side of Gilly's headstone. "Oh," he said, clapping his leather gloved hands together. "I'm not entirely sure how this works, where you are currently stationed, but please take whatever steps necessary to remain as far away from Alastair Brooke as possible. Don't bother wasting any of your heavenly effort on that pugnacious ingrate. The man's incorrigible...nothing but a vile blackmailer." Gloves cupped around his mouth, Irwin bowed his head and puffed a few times in an attempt to coax feeling back into his frozen fingertips.

"Alastair died from a common, run-of-the-mill, clogged artery heart attack. Nothing more sensational. Just the irascible man's time to go—despite his almost getting clobbered to death by a naked mermaid statue." Irwin cocked an eyebrow, "I beg to differ," he said, shaking his head emphatically. "I am not unempathetic, Gilly. What you fail to understand is this: Besides being a neighbor from the darkest depths of Satan's seventh level of hell, it turns out old Alastair had somewhat the flair for attaining people's private, highly sensitive, and most assuredly embarrassing information. Then he used whatever he uncovered to extort his victims. As it turns out, this time, he picked the wrong mark when he targeted Beatrice Aston—now dubbed by yours truly as the *allusive mermaid assailant*. However, turns out she wasn't Alastair's only target, but let us save that convoluted story for another, considerably warmer day."

The wind howled, whipping Irwin in the face with his scarf. Small snowflakes flitted, swooped, and danced in the air. Irwin rushed to brush off the top of Gilly's headstone while he continued to lament. "It's been a harder than usual month without you. Lonely...I thought by now it would get easier—the 'time healed all prognosis'" He crinkled his nose. "Another vapid lie." A strong wind blew, picking snow up from the ground, further cutting visibility.

"Olivia? I'd say she's doing better...far happier recently. Funny enough, she and Darren have been working overtime to convince the rest of us, but especially Harper, that nothing is going on between them. You should see the act they've been putting on for our collective benefit. Quite the campy performance... pretending to be merely friends and cooperative co-parents." Irwin scoffed. "Hard to pull off when one is always giddy in the presence of the other, and forever dropping smoochy hints and transparent layered innuendos. All rather sloppy if you ask me, but it keeps Harper highly amused and hopeful. Then again," Irwin whispered loudly, "we both know it doesn't take much to keep her entertained." Irwin glanced over his shoulder to make sure he wasn't being overheard. "It's kind of ironic how Harper now wants her parents back together again. A complete one-eighty from three years ago when I had to practically separate her and Darren by way of a border wall."

"Lame joke, unfunny man," sniggered Harper, trampling across the snow covered grass in her tall snow boots after returning from visiting her grandmother's grave. "I see you're talking about me again, huh?"

"Gilly, our delinquent Harper has returned."

"Hey, Gilly," she waved. "While I'm here, let me tell you about your lover boy."

Irwin grumbled something inaudible. "Don't you have anyplace else to be?"

Harper exaggerated twisting her head around and shrugged. "Like where?"

"I don't know." Irwin stretched his neck and pointed. "Look, Christopher's over there. Go and annoy him."

Off to the side, Christopher stood at his mother's grave. Irwin and Harper watched as his hands moved enthusiastically, as if in the middle of describing something important.

"I don't know...," she groaned, her head slightly tilted. "I mean, he looks sort of busy. I wouldn't want to interrupt him."

Irwin snorted. "But imposing yourself on me is perfectly acceptable."

"Okay, fine." Harper *tsked*, rolling her eyes. "I get the hint. Gilly, it's been nice seeing you for all of fifteen seconds. I'll be back for our girl chat as soon as Mr. Grumpy over here isn't around to kill the mood."

Harper thrust her mitten covered hands into her coat pockets and stomped her way over to a bench, trudging through the snow to wait. Not a moment later, Christopher glanced up, coaxing Harper over to join him. Even from a distance, Irwin detected the longing in Christopher's face, watching how his eyes followed Harper approaching him. Irwin smiled watching Christopher as he drew Harper in close as if making a formal introduction. Even from afar, Irwin could see the young man proudly grinning ear-to-ear when Harper, not only didn't put up a fight but melted into his embrace. "Now that's a man in love. No doubt about it." Irwin stared forlornly. "I remember wearing the same dopey grin plastered across my face whenever you were nearby." Irwin swatted the latest snowflakes lovingly off the top of Gilly's headstone and cleared his throat, again. "I still do." A single, almost frozen tear welled in the corner of his eye.

"Now, here's something I think you will find entertaining." Irwin clasped his gloved hands behind his back and rocked from foot to foot. "It appears our Christopher had a friend from law school who moved into our neck of the woods last year to set up shop—a beautiful female friend if one is partial to that type, which I, for the record, am not. Nevertheless, when Harper found out, she had a royal meltdown...utterly consumed by jealousy. Christopher, initially blindsided by the sudden outburst, handled Harper's eruption as poorly as expected," Irwin chuckled. "Needless to say, there were times over these past few weeks I felt for sure we were close to having another death on our hands."

A sharp, bitter cold gust of air blew past. Irwin adjusted his coat collar higher around his chilled face, his cheeks pink and numb. Hands wedged deep in pockets, he stomped his feet against the iced earth, hopping back and forth to feel warmer. "I'm not sure if you ever had occasion to cross paths with the elusive Beatrice Aston. I'd describe her as reasonably intriguing, in a snooty, supercilious, surly sort of way." Irwin blew hot breath into his gloved hands but quickly gave up, thrusting them back into his coat pockets. "She works for our township, however, in what capacity, I'm not entirely certain. Office assistant, perhaps? We've dealt with one another sporadically over the years if something related to the municipality and the shop arose, however, nothing social. Matter of fact, up to now, I rarely, if ever saw the woman. Then Alastair dies, and she's in and out of my book shop twice a day buying calendars and cookbooks." Irwin shivered. A bitter gust of frigid air blew, whipping Irwin's scarf clear across his face. "I mention her only because she has recently taken up reading to our Cornelia, which is another reason why I thought to—"

"Irwin!" signaled Christopher, his bundled body waving in the distance. "We're freezing! We'll wait for you in the car." Christopher wrapped a proprietary arm affectionately around Harper's shoulders, propelling her forward.

Irwin nodded and half-waved. "Where's Olivia?" he shouted back, having to raise his voice against an oncoming strong gale of wind.

"She's still over there talking to grandma," shouted Harper, hugging herself and bouncing to keep warm. "We passed her on the way. I'll let her know you're still here, but don't take too long."

Irwin dismiss-waved her away. "I liked it better when I didn't have to contend with all this confounded foot traffic." Irwin instantly bowed his head, regretful. "I'm sorry. I shouldn't complain. They mean well enough." A stronger flurry of snowflakes, transported by a gale of wind, fluttered and fell. "It's certainly brutal out here. I'll give them that much," he mouthed softly.

"Hurry up, Irwin," yelled Harper one last time. "The snow's really starting to come down heavy. We need to leave while we can."

"Yes, fine. Just a few more minutes," he yelled back, giving the thumbs up. Irwin deep breathed, mentally preparing to deliver the bad news.

"I have something else to tell you, Gilly. Something I've dreaded, which is why I have saved it for last." He raised his face up to the darkened, foreboding sky. Tiny snowflakes landed on his lashes. "Ah. How appropriate." A thick, white, sheet of ominous clouds moved swiftly across the horizon, filling the entire sky, giving off a foggy effect. "The weathermen said to expect a blizzard, but who knows? They aren't exactly known for their accuracy." He tugged his cap down tighter around his pink, cold ears. "I despise the winter with a passion, but thankfully the pending storm nixed Harper's plan for a holiday party."

Irwin drew in a deep, icy breath. His eyes widened, watching in fascination as his breath crystalized mid-air.

"Okay. Here it goes. This concerns Cornelia. Remember our last visit when I told you her symptoms were worsening? How she was constantly yelling, the increase in irritable mood swings, her forgetting our names—mine included? On top of that, she's been interjecting her book characters into every conversation and scaring a few of our customers away with her tall tales. Frankly, I found it amusing, at least until the confrontation with Mrs. Solano, our local busybody. Don't laugh, but Cornelia threatened to put a hex on her if she dared criticize one of our local authors again. Of course, Olivia jumped in and saved the day, plying the incensed Mrs. Solano with a handful of free bookmarks, a pen that reads 'Happy Ramadan' etched on the side—which I assume the exasperating woman will never appreciate—and a snack bag bursting with broken candy canes."

Irwin shivered, unable to feel his toes.

"Anyhow, Cornelia had been periodically bringing up the topic of selling her house for some time now. And I, in my infinite wisdom—*note the sarcasm*—didn't take her seriously. Stubborn woman...had it in her head all along to move into one of those adult living facilities whether I agreed or not, *and* she did it right under my nose—without warning anybody. Except for Harper, who swears on a stack of any books brought to her that Cornelia coerced her into taking her there before anybody knew any better, which knowing Cornelia, I believe."

Irwin stomped his feet on the hard, frozen ground. "Can you imagine the shock?" he grumbled, getting worked up all over again. "This happened last Wednesday, our only late day. I arrive to find the shop packed with perplexed customers milling about, some too afraid to approach Olivia standing by the register, muttering incoherently and slamming customers' books on the counter.

"Meanwhile, Darren, barely useful as is, bumbled around the shop like a lost puppy, fussing over anything to keep clear out of Olivia's way. Eventually, I found Christopher in the backroom, ineffectively consoling a distraught, guilt-ridden Harper. Even Bones, that insufferable cat, went into hiding. I found the furry reprobate bunched up under Cornelia's chair, utterly listless. We have repeatedly tried to ply him with food, but he refuses to eat. When I ask you, has *that* greedy mongrel ever turned down a free meal?" Irwin sighed. "Don't worry, I'll bring the rascal to the veterinarian before he wastes completely away."

Off in the distance, a familiar car horn sounded, followed by a succession of aggressive high beams flashing on and off. Irwin rolled his eyes, refusing to concede to Harper's juvenile attempt to rush him.

"Where was I? Ah, yes," he continued, not missing a beat, "Of course, once I could be coherently filled in on what happened, I hightailed it over to that place, demanding in no uncertain terms that they allow me to take Cornelia home, but when I got there, the obstinate woman refused to budge. In fact, Cornelia turned her back on me. Wouldn't even discuss it." Irwin frowned. "Then she ordered me to leave." He paused. "I failed her. Much like I failed you and Dakota."

"Excuse me," interrupted the furious voice directly behind Irwin. "What a load of hogwash. You never failed Gilly or Dakota—or *Cornelia*, for that matter, and don't you *ever*—*EVER* say such a stupid thing again, Irwin Abernathy!" snapped Olivia, attempting to pinch him through his coat.

"Ha-ha! Foiled again," Irwin sputtered like an insolent child, twisting sideways, gripping his arm protectively.

"Hi, Gilly. It's me, Olivia. Sorry to barge in like that, but don't believe a single word this ridiculous man is telling you. He didn't fail anyone, especially Cornelia."

"Yes. I did."

"No, you did not, and I'm not going to let you do this, Irwin," argued Olivia, pointing a finger in his face. "You've..." she choked up. "—you've been the best damn thing that ever happened to me...to all of us—and I can pretty much guarantee, if Gilly and Dakota could, they'd be all up in your face yelling at you, too!"

Irwin pursed his lips, not ready to concede. "She should have told me."

"*She did tell you*, but you weren't listening. None of us were. *Ugh*..." Olivia stomped her way in front of Irwin to face him down, straight on. "You were there for Cornelia for as long as she needed you to be, but now she has different needs, complicated medical concerns that you can't possibly deal with, and you know it. Her choice to leave wasn't to hurt you, but to face this last leg of her journey *her way*—not yours, not mine, not anybody's. *Hers.* Cornelia wanted the ability—no, scratch that—*the dignity* to call the shots about how her last days will play out, and that's okay." Olivia's voice cracked. She took hold of Irwin's shoulders and stared into her friend's red-rimmed, tear-filled eyes. "You are a dear friend, Mr. Irwin Abernathy, and the closest thing I have ever had to a father. I'll be damned if I let you go on blaming yourself over this," she sniffled, finding it difficult to blink back her tears. "This is life, Irwin. It's messy. It's complicated. Sometimes, it's even beyond painful, but like it or not, we only get one shot to get this shit right before it's all over...before it's time to go. You did everything humanly possible to keep Cornelia safe and happy, but most of all, cherished."

Irwin's shoulders slumped in defeat. "She still should have told me," he said, his jaw jutted defiantly forward.

"Irwin, to be blunt about it, Cornelia wanted to decide how and where she wanted to die; away from all of our know-it-all opinions and judgments—but especially yours. Not because she doesn't love us, but because she does. More than anything else, she wanted us to remember her as the dynamic, talented, hilarious, brilliant, meddling woman we all love—and not this dilapidated version."

Unflinching, Irwin glared deep into Olivia's eyes. "How do you know this?"

"Because Cornelia told me. The night before she left." Olivia placed her finger over Irwin's lips. "And before you start getting all bent out of shape—she swore me to secrecy. Told me that if I *dared* say anything to you or anybody else, she'd rise from the dead and haunt me for the rest of my breathing days. Her words, not mine. Matter of fact, she actually promised to come back as a ghost and barge in on me and Darren...you know, when we're doing it. She even threatened to shrill-laugh until he shriveled up. I couldn't risk it."

Irwin snorted, the next best thing he had to an *almost-laugh*.

"Listen, Irwin...our Cornelia lived a full life surrounded by people crazy-in-love with her. But now her body has different plans. As hard as it is, we have to respect that." Olivia used her coat sleeve to dry his wet, tear-streaked face, then pecked Irwin softly on the cheek. "Now, pull your act together and let's get the hell out of here before this blizzard hits. I can hardly feel my toes as is." Olivia threaded her arm tenderly through Irwin's. "Gilly, I'm taking your man home now, but no worries—I'm sure he'll be back next week to whine and complain to you further. Let's go, Irwin."

Without a drop of fight left, Irwin merely shrugged. "You see what I have to put up with, Gilly?"

As if in response, the grey, gloomy skies above split open, liberating the expected promise of snow in a blustery torrent. Large, crystalized, icy flakes fell from the heavens and beyond, attaching to the frozen earth, and coating every surface.

Olivia protectively embraced her devoted friend's arm. "She knows, Irwin," Olivia whispered, her cheek resting on his snow-coated shoulder. "She knows."

NOT THE END.

Not even close...

Turn the page for a sneak peek of

UNLIKELY FRIENDS
Book One

by Sahar Abdulaziz

UNLIKELY FRIENDS

No matter how old you are, it's never too late to heal.

SAHAR ABDULAZIZ

CHAPTER 1

Irwin

IRWIN ABERNATHY, barely able to conceal the venom oozing out of every pore on his craggy old face, cringed at the slightly hungover, college-aged female with smeared day-old mascara caked beneath her drooping eyelids, making her look like a rabid raccoon.

"I think this belongs to you," he said, dangling with two fingers the powdery orange Cheeto he had found lodged between the pages of her returned library book.

"Huh? Ha! Right..." She reached over the reception desk to reclaim it, then popped it into her mouth.

"Ohmygawd, ewww," Irwin gagged, struggling to control his retching reflex. He took three rapid panting breaths

until the feeling subsided. "You have a late fee," he griped, his eyes watery but detached. "You owe a dollar-ten."

"Do I?" The young woman fumbled through her pockets, digging for change, but only managed to collect a combination of pennies, dimes, nickels, a single quarter, and one tortoiseshell button to dump onto the desk. "Hold up," she said, waving a crooked finger with a nail covered in chipped black polish in the air. "I have more; just give me one-hot-second."

Irwin glanced over the woman's shoulder at the long line forming behind her and ever so slightly bit his bottom lip. "No, take your time. Really," he said, eyes rolling to the ceiling. "I have all day."

If the young woman heard him, he couldn't say, and although irritated by her total lack of social decorum, Irwin couldn't help but be riveted, mesmerized by how easily she plunged her arm into her soft canvas bag, only to belt out a few colorful expletives when she pulled out everything but her wallet.

"Ma'am, if you could step to the side for a moment while I help the next person..."

"Damn it. I know it's in here somewhere," the woman mumbled, completely ignoring Irwin's request, depositing a pen without a cap, a twisted, smooshed granola bar, and a tampon, thankfully still in its original wrapper, onto the desk. "One more second, I swear." She shook her bag and stuck almost her entire face inside. "Come to mama," she said, voice muffled. Irwin's brow furrowed, but even he leaned closer in suspense.

"Ah-ha! Got it," she crowed triumphantly and gave a cute curtsey to the sarcastic slow clapping taking place behind her and a wide smile to Irwin, who could only stare back dumbfounded. Then she whipped a twenty-dollar bill from her purse and waved it in the air. "I'll need change."

Irwin's nostrils flared.

A twenty-dollar bill? What do I look like—a pole dancer?

Irwin plucked a single dime from the discarded change pile and slid the remainder of the money and junk back towards her. Then he plucked the twenty from between her two-finger grasp and held it up to the light, hoping against hope that it turned out to be a fake so he could have her arrested and dragged out of the library by her forelock, banished for life. But alas, the bill appeared legit.

"Here," he said, handing her the change. "And here's your receipt...or perhaps a future bookmark."

The young woman snorted at Irwin's wisecrack and flashed him an acerbic smile. "*Ciao*," she called over her shoulder, saluting him with the receipt as she pranced out of the building through the automatic doors, appearing not to have a care in the world. Irwin watched in total fascination as her hobo bag swayed in lockstep with her every swish and shimmy. Just one more colorful character to add to the book he never actually intended to write.

"Next," Irwin bellowed, glancing at the clock behind him and wishing he could be in his bed reading instead of here, waiting on Neanderthals and social misfits.

"Excuse me," interrupted a well-dressed man, pushing past the next person waiting on line. "Where's the restroom?" he asked Irwin as the young child whose hand he held tight—presumably his son—used his free small hand to squeeze his crotch through his pants, evidently to prevent an accident.

Irwin pointed. "Down the hall, to your right."

"Thanks," said the father, dragging his kid forward by the arm. When the kid glanced back and caught Irwin staring, the little monster returned the favor by sticking his tongue out.

"Next!"

Two adolescent boys reeking like unwashed armpits, their baby sister, and their mother barreled noisily forward. Irwin made a mental note to breathe through his mouth until they left...and possibly for a few minutes after.

"You three, put your books up here!" ordered their stressed mother, who then proceeded to dump her load with a loud thump on the desk, leaving them stacked high and precariously unbalanced.

Free of books, her boys moved to the side to wait, much to Irwin's olfactory relief, but the little girl had other plans and clutched her book tightly to her chest, refusing to acquiesce.

"Come on, Becky, give me your book," coaxed her mother, but the child, with a flair for the dramatic, could not be deterred and started to wail, easily hitting an operatic pitch.

As a matter of record, Irwin disliked children, specifically children who used loud noises to torture others. And although he appreciated this little runt's adoration for the written word, as a professed bibliophile himself, he did not welcome her predilection for being a screeching, bombastic shrew.

"Becky!" admonished the mother, attempting to tug the book free from the child's death-grip but having little success. "Give...me...the...book."

"No!" yelled the tenacious child, her brow stubbornly creased and lips in a tight pout.

"You better stop this right now! Give me the book."

"No!"

"Listen, just give me the book for two seconds. I'll give

it right back to you as soon as the nice man scans it."

"NO!" screamed Becky, twisting her tiny body away from her mother, who strained to retain her grip.

"Enough," hollered Becky's mother, snatching the cover and pulling it toward her.

"Ma'am, don't pull on the cover. It might—" The cover tore in half. "—rip."

Pint-size Becky, her half of the cover still clenched in her tiny, grubby fingers, lost her balance and tumbled backward onto her bum.

"Oh no! I'm so sorry," screamed the mother, reaching down to help her child. "I'll pay for the book," she said to Irwin. "Now see what you've done!" she yelled at Becky, now sprawled out spread eagle on the floor, kicking and screaming. Meanwhile, her two malodourous brothers giggled off to the side, thoroughly enthralled by the spectacle.

"Grab your sister!" their mother snapped at the two hyenas. "I'm sorry," she said to Irwin. "I really am. I don't know what's gotten into her lately. What do I owe you?"

Irwin, whose heart broke—not for the child, but for the damaged book—was half-tempted to call the lady a liar after witnessing this same bratty child on more than one occasion behave like the spoiled, unruly little tyrant she was. But unemployment held little attraction for the aging librarian, who was close to retirement, so he begrudgingly remained silent. He rung up the woman and wisely kept most of his more colorful snide observations to himself.

Choosing to become a librarian had been more of a calling than a career choice for Irwin, who proudly acknowledged a sizable familial lineage to a host of renowned readers and book hoarders. One of his great uncles, his grandmother's brother, had at one time owned his own publishing company. It had been a reasonably prosperous business until Uncle Mortimer, charged with extortion and racketeering, was sent to prison where he languished and died. Irwin's grandmother, Ethel Chamberlin Abernathy, never believed the stories surrounding her brother's guilt and proclaimed to anyone willing to listen that she had no doubt he had been framed. However, as much as Irwin adored his grandmother, the blind loyalty she held for her nefarious sibling was wasted, especially after Irwin conducted a Google search of his own. Not only did his uncle extort, gamble, and racketeer his way into vast amounts of wealth and prestige, but at the time of his masterminding, Mortimer had involved himself in some highly shady deals, some of which turned out fatal. Nevertheless, Irwin, unwilling to see her hurt, refused to reveal to his grandmother what he had discovered. Instead, he let her go on believing her imaginary accounts until the day she perished, steadfastly safeguarding the secrets of Ethel Chamberlin Abernathy—the one decent person in his miserable, wretched life who had not only raised and loved him but protected him from himself.

***

By early evening, Irwin felt ready to call it a day. That was until he spotted a young woman, probably no older than fifteen or sixteen, sitting alone on his favorite cushioned seat by the computer station. He noticed she wore reading glasses but no makeup. Each of her long fingers boasted a silver ring, and a stack of leather bands obscured her thin wrists, some laden with beads or charms. Irwin couldn't imagine how heavy they made her arms.

Long, dangling feather earrings hung from her ears while her chestnut brown hair, piled high upon her head, mimicked what the library's style magazines refer to as the "messy bun."

Messy was right.

Irwin was curious as to how the girl had sewn her unquestionably homemade jean skirt, with fitted bands of yellow calico fabric in the middle, which he thought complimented her white peasant blouse nicely. But it was the work boots that really set the stage for him, like something straight out of the 60s. A hippie-dippy special.

Unfazed, the girl glared back at him, making Irwin wince.

Busted!

She'd caught him prying. Embarrassed, Irwin looked away. As a consummate people-watcher, he abhorred being outed—and certainly not by a child.

Second time today. I must be getting rusty.

"Irwin," called Roger Ledbetter, one of the library staff and, in general, a human hemorrhoid. "Janice wants you to either cover for Regan in the children's room or go back to the circulation desk. She said it was your choice."

"I'd rather get a lobotomy than be stuck in the children's room," Irwin replied flatly, not joking.

"Front desk it is. Roger that."

Idiot.

By seven-forty-five, the library speakers began making announcements that the library would be closing in fifteen minutes.

Thank God.

Irwin was exhausted and ready to go home to a steaming bowl of soup, a couple of water crackers with slices of cheese, and a hot cup of tea, perhaps even a hot bath instead of his typical quick shower. And then off to bed. Glorious bed, where he could finally finish his new cozy murder mystery uninterrupted.

"I'm heading upstairs to make sure everyone's gone," called Janice Stroop, the head librarian and resident know-it-all. "Irwin, can you handle the adult section?"

Irwin, can you handle the adult section?

Irwin merely nodded.

Such an irritating woman.

He started from the back row, collecting forgotten jackets and hats, returning books to their proper place, and pushing in chairs, all while mumbling, grumbling, and complaining in his head until he glanced up and noticed the young hippie girl grinning at him.

What's so funny? "We're closing in five minutes," he barked.

"I heard."

"That means you have to leave."

"Evidently."

"So? Hop to it. Shake a leg." Irwin snapped his fingers. "What are you waiting for? A personal invitation?"

"I'll leave," she said, "soon-ish," and went right back to reading her book.

The nerve.

Irwin continued his appointed rounds, but just a tad bit grumpier, knowing there was nothing he could do but wait the little waif out.

Ten minutes later, he returned, anxious to kick the insolent girl to the curb, but by the time he arrived, she was long gone, the book she had been reading left face down on the chair.

Everyone thinks I'm their maid.

He lifted the book and turned it over. "*All the Light We*

Cannot See by Anthony Doerr."

Now, why would someone her age be reading this?

He was quite impressed by her selection: a *New York Times* bestseller about a French girl and a German boy whose paths collided during WWII and the occupation of France.

Maybe for school.

As he turned to walk away, a piece of paper fell out of the book and fluttered to the floor. Irwin picked it up.

It read: "See you tomorrow, Mr. Grumpy."

Why that little...

"Irwin, let's go already," yelled Janice, shaking her keychain in the air, ready to flip off the lights. "I want to lock up and get home sometime tonight."

Irwin slipped the note into his pocket and returned the book to the shelf.

"Tonight, Irwin," called Janice, tapping her foot by the front door.

Irwin sprinted to his locker, grabbed his coat, his hat and keys, and tripped on one of the book carts along the way, stubbing his toe.

Argh!

Irwin brushed past Janice, out the door, limping to his car.

"Good night, Irwin."

"Good night, Janice," he replied, but in his head—where he held most of his truest and most revealing conversations—he thought otherwise.

What's the chance I'll die in my sleep and never have to come back to this place again?

Janice locked the door. "See you tomorrow, bright and early."

God, if you're up there, feel free to kill me now.

WOULD YOU LIKE TO KEEP READING?

Get your own paperback or ebook version at
Amazon or Barnes and Noble

Unlikely Friends by Sahar Abdulaziz

OTHER BOOKS
BY THE AUTHOR ~ SAHAR ABDULAZIZ

Satire/Humor
Unlikely Friends [Book 1]

Thriller/Psychological Suspense

As One Door Closes

The Broken Half

Secrets That Find Us

Tight Rope

Expendable

The Gatekeepers Notebook
2020 Release

Non-Fiction/Health
But You LOOK Just Fine

Children's Book
The Dino Flu

ACKNOWLEDGMENTS

I never anticipated writing another story about Irwin Abernathy and the crew. *Unlikely Friends* [Book 1] had initially been written as a one-and-done, or so I thought. But book characters are a funny lot. Sometimes, if you're incredibly fortunate, they'll refuse to leave you alone. Case in point: *Devoted Friends*.

There are many people I would like to thank—incredible friends and talented colleagues who have been immensely supportive, encouraging, and reassuring. Starting with my brilliant editor, J.C. Wing, who thankfully keeps me from committing indiscriminate comma crimes, em dash blunders, and other random grammar and punctuation offenses. Most of all, I wish to thank JC for loving my characters as much as I do; making sure I write their stories in the most engaging and authentic manner possible.

Thank you to *Wind Lark Publishing* for a beautiful interior design and *Deranged Doctor Designs*—my creative and gifted cover designers for another fantabulous book cover.

A BIG thank you *to The Lady Writers of the Poconos*—

Susan Moore Jordan, Kelly Jensen, Belinda Nevill Gordon, Catherine Schratt, Evelyn Infante, and Mary Ann Moore. Besides the fact that you ladies are super talented, I can't imagine writing anything without your sound advice, inspiring insight, warm smiles, and friendship.

I would also like to thank my amazing [brave] early readers who kindly wade through my early messes, and somehow, still love me: Harriet Van Houten, Diane Bukoski, and Jen Bradley.

Thank you to fellow Pocono Liar, lawyer, former Constitutional Law professor, author, and friend, Michael Ventrella. I genuinely appreciate your generous insight and knowledge.

Lastly, thank you to my family for your enthusiasm, your encouragement, the delicious pizza, sneaking me chocolate, drowning me with tea, and dragging me away from the computer kicking and screaming whenever necessary. Most of all, thank you for your love. I love you all. Indubitably.

ABOUT THE AUTHOR

When Sahar Abdulaziz isn't busy plotting a stabbing, a garroting, or a murder —all on paper of course—she's busy writing about her crew of highly-entertaining, quirky, unpredictable book characters. Some have been lovely, bighearted, gentle souls, merely temporarily lost and in search of answers. Others have been more on the eccentric side, unconventional, writing their own rules—determined to live their best life to the fullest. A few...*okay, more than a few*, have been devious, duplicitous, and dangerous—undeniably not the kind of personalities one would want to cross paths with in a dark alley or locked in some seedy hotel room.

Sahar is the author of nine novels—including *Expendable, Tight Rope, Unlikely Friends,* and her latest release, *The Gatekeeper's Notebook*. Most of her work is realistic fiction: psychological thrillers/suspense, and satire. As in real life, many of her characters find themselves facing complicated life challenges. However, despite whatever life-trajectory her invisible idiosyncratic friends ultimately take, Sahar is determined to tell their stories. Eager to put pen to paper to share their compelling accounts, no matter how hilarious, convoluted, or torturous their adventures become.

Rep'd by Djarabi Kitabs Publishing and Limitless Publishing.

Facebook:

https://www.facebook.com/AuthorSaharAbdulaziz

Twitter:

https://twitter.com/Sahar_Author

Website:

https://www.saharraziz.com

Instagram:

https://www.instagram.com/saharraziz/

Blog:

https://www.saharraziz.com/